THE
IMAZIɣEN
DRUID

RAVEK HUNTER

First Edition, September 2018

Copyright © 2018 Ravek Hunter Literary LLC

All rights reserved.

ISBN: 978-1-948782-13-5 (paperback),
ISBN: 978-1-948782-08-1 (eBook)

www.WorldsOfAtlantis.com

For Mrs. Wife,
who gave me two incredible boys
that I hope will be proud to read their father's work one day.

<u>Fantasy Novels by Ravek Hunter</u>

Red Wizard of Atlantis

The Fallen

Saving Eridu

The Imaziyen Druid

Shadows of Lyonesse

Beasts of Courth

Ys (Coming 2022)

If you enjoy reading books by this author, please remember to leave a review at your favorite bookseller!

To learn more about the backstory, mythology, and character development in these stories or to view world maps visit us at:

https://www.WorldsOfAtlantis.com!

<u>Children of Atlas</u>

It was from the stars they came, out of the vast darkness of the Primeval Cosmos, plunging from the sky in a great wingless beast consumed by smoke and fire. It fell with a thunderous crash upon the earth plowing a long black rift across the open plain before it came to rest in a final shudder of sparks and lightning. The smoking shell of the massive creature lay shattered, yet from its broken maw came hundreds of odd-looking figures that crawled through the acrid haze and stumbled disoriented onto the lush green grass of a new world.

The Sylvan watched the arrival of the newcomers from the quiet repose of the forest. They scrutinized these strange bi-pedal aliens with blue-tinted skin and elongated heads and large almond-shaped eyes that had come uninvited to their tranquil isle, until now isolate and protected from intrusion by the vast expanse of the Primal Sea. They observed how the slender forms worked as a collective to remove the shiny scales of their battered host piece by piece to make shelters, how they buried their dead, how they mourned their passing.

When that was done, they brought red glowing crystals that shown bright even in daylight from the metallic frame of the silver beast's remains. The crystals they handled with great care and reverence, depositing them in caverns deep in the earth near an inlet on the coast. It was there too, that they began to build with stones.

These were a people with no hope of return or rescue, determined to survive and resolute in their struggle to make a place for themselves. A permanent place that would bring irrevocable change the Isle. To the land, to nature, to a way of life that had existed since time began.

Still the Sylvan watched.

The prophesies spoke of events such as these that would herald the beginning of the Fourth Age, the Age of the Golden Aspen, the Age when the winds from the north would bring an icy chill even in the summertime. And end the elves isolation from the rest of the world forever.

In time the Sylvan learned that the unusual blue-tinted people called themselves the followers of Atlas, the one who had risen among them and offered up hope for a new future. They would name the spine of the island in his honor and build a shining city on the sea that would become known as Atlantis.

And they thrived.

Recorded in the Fourth Age of the Golden Aspen by Watcher CrellianRafkarSil of Avalon

Freedom is Imaziẏen

Freedom is the gift of life from the Spirits

It flows through me as it did my ancestors

And the nature that is everywhere and around me

I feel it in the long green grasses of the Ibhr Rrbi between my toes

The beating of my heart in the still quiet

It is the rush of the wind through my hair

When I run; the exhilaration that fills me

The taste of rain on my tongue

And the smell of the earth.

Freedom is Imaziyen

Elder Shaman Frinya of the Imaziyen
from the "Song of Freedom"

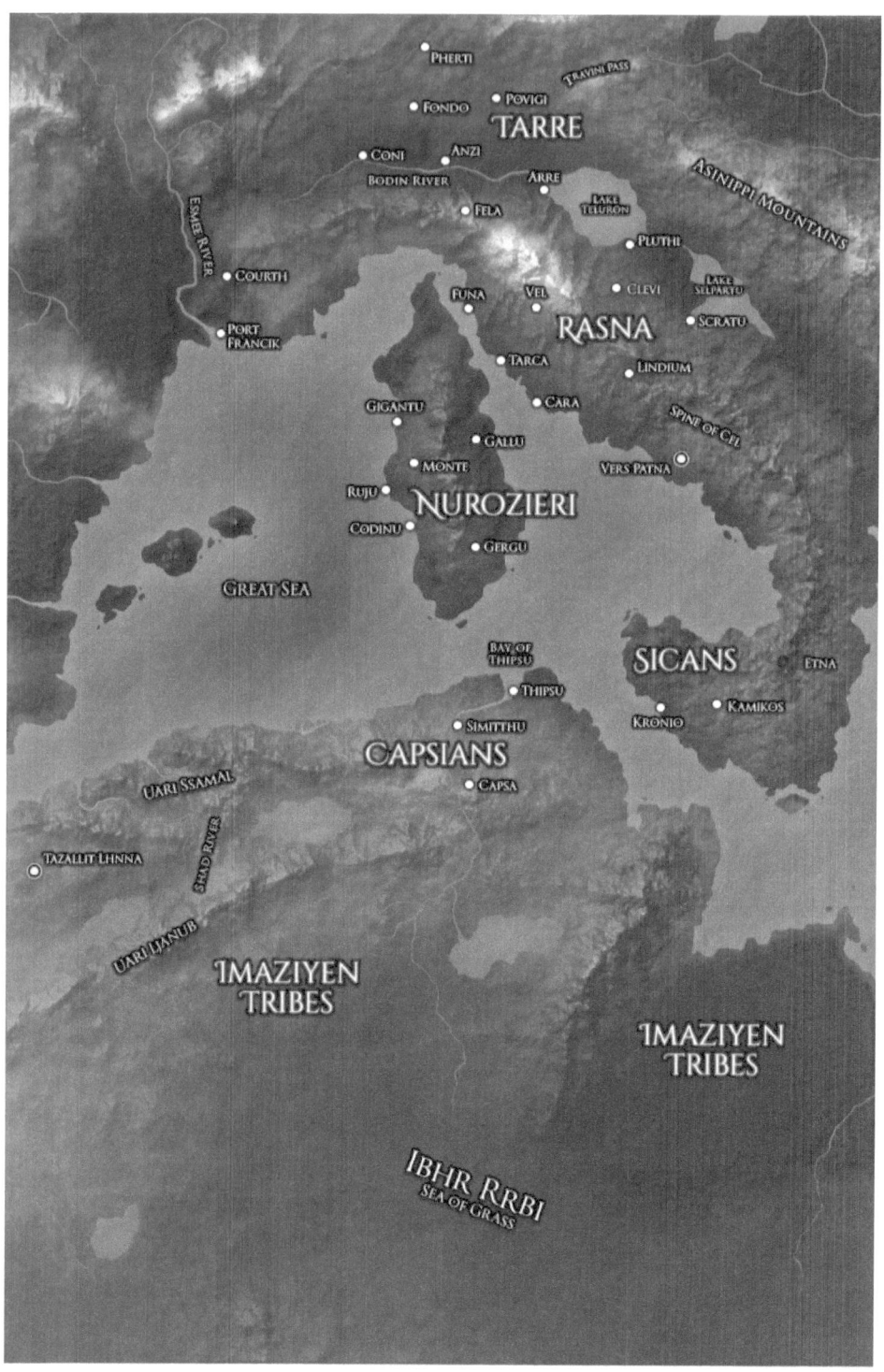

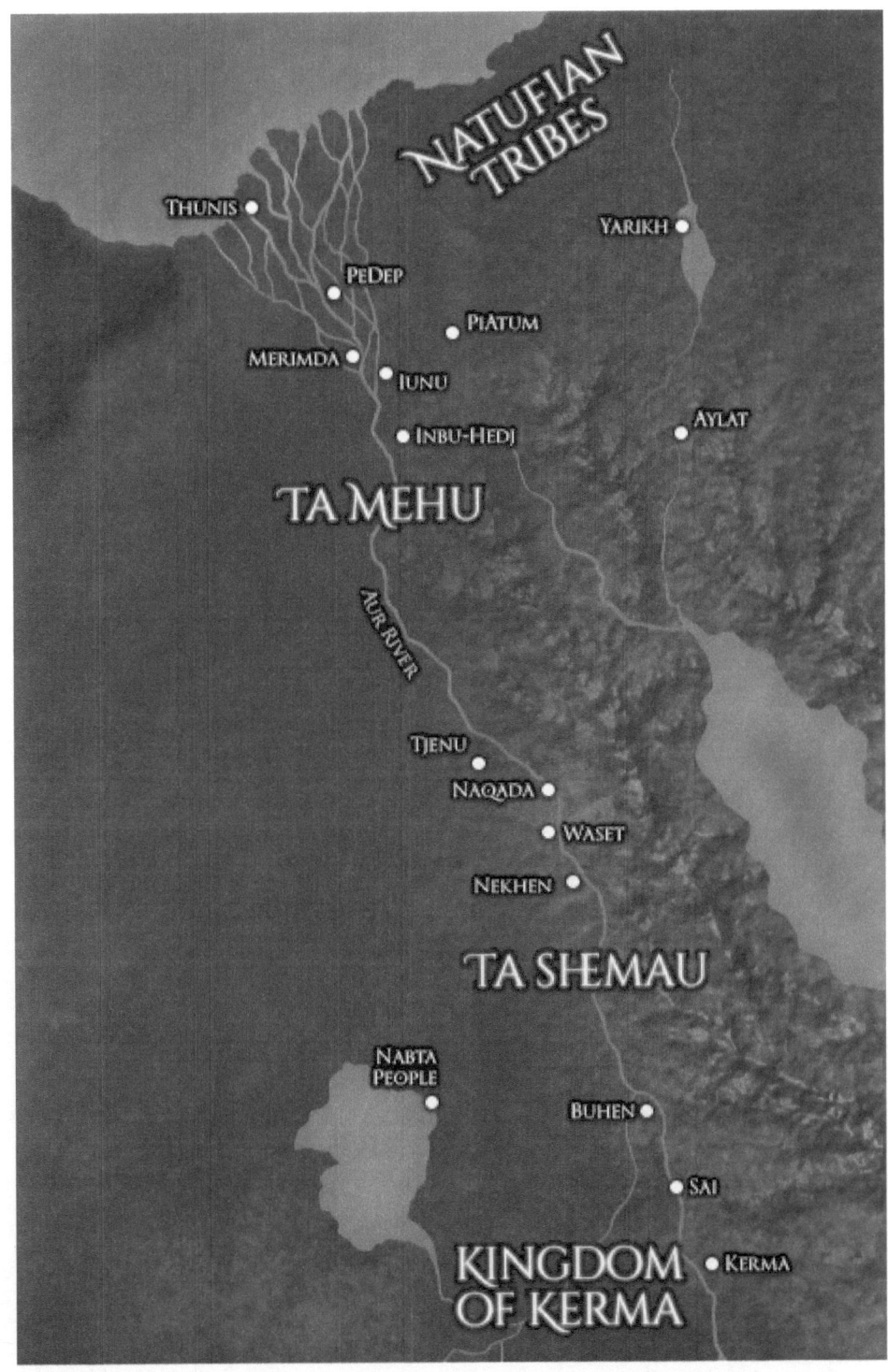

Table of Contents

Chapter 1

The Mammoth

There are two things in my existence that I cherish above all others. The first is love, which I have often found fleeting and disappointing. The second is freedom. Until I walked among the people that call themselves Imaziyen I do not truly believe that I understood what that meant. To the Imaziyen freedom is everything. Because of their wisdom, I now feel the wind and taste the rain and my heart is content.

—*Wodanaz the Wanderer*

Sylvan Year (SY) 5476

Khulani sat bareback atop his brown bay, surveying the unending expanse of the low, rolling hills over green savanna that stretched to the horizon in every direction. A cool breeze gently stroked his face like the soft linens his mother used to wear. The memory brought with it a slight pang in the pit of his stomach. He missed her. It would have been easy for him to let melancholy take him down the path of those sad memories, even so many years later, but not today. He had wild hare to hunt. The shamans of his village wanted wild hares for stew as the evening meal, and Khulani would not fail in his duty.

He glanced to his left and inspected his Hunt Pack. Ten young men—boys, really—sat in silence on their own blacks or bays, searching the tall grasses for any sign of movement that might give away the location of the elusive hares. Of course, Khulani already knew exactly how many hares there were nearby and where they were, but he preferred to keep that information to himself for now and let his boys work. He had a special connection with animals that not even the shamans could explain, a gift or endowment from the gods, as they referred to it. Khulani could feel the energy of the animals around him, know their feelings, and interpret their disposition toward him and others. It was a great advantage when hunting, as they were now, and his Hunt Pack knew it. However, they also accepted that they needed to stay sharp and focused without depending on him to do their work for them. So he waited and watched with them.

Khulani admired how magnificent his men looked on their mounts, almost as if cast with a mold. Each had the lean build of a runner, the dark ebony skin of one who spent his life outdoors, and short black hair cut thin enough to see the shape of the skull beneath. Each of them wore a cape of his own making—from the skin of a hartebeest, saber cat, or mountain wolf—that fluttered idly over his bare shoulders and back, and they wore leather leggings with sturdy leather boots lovingly fabricated by their mothers. Khulani's own cape was from the hide of a great lion, and he decorated it with clusters of feathers that he hung from the cape's loose ends. He always had a propensity for feathers. He didn't know why. They made him feel calm and content somehow, like the choker he wore around his neck adorned with beads, shells and more feathers—a gift from his father. His men displayed their own jewelry with charms carved from bone and ivory. They were mostly trophies from memorable hunts. This was his Hunt Pack, and he was their Hunt Master, and they were a fine-looking group indeed.

"The rain is coming," the man next to him said quietly.

Khulani looked up at the dark clouds moving swiftly overhead. "Not today, Rebiku. They will come tomorrow."

"Too bad," Rebiku replied. "I wanted a bath."

Trying hard not to laugh out loud, Khulani glanced over to see his friend's broad smiling face daring him to do so. "Rebiku, you will be a man soon and will have to learn to bathe more often than when it rains. Otherwise you will never find a wife!"

Somehow, Rebiku's smile broadened even more. Khulani's friend was known for his big, toothy smile and implacable sense of humor that often manifested itself in surprising ways. "Then I will marry a goat!"

The others chuckled quietly at that.

Khulani rolled his eyes. "Your mother would . . ."

His reply was interrupted by a terrifying cry of pain carried on the wind. It came from the north, just beyond a rise in the terrain. Khulani was sure it was an animal, but he was too far away to sense what it was. As quickly as his thigh muscles twitched at the flanks of his bay, a thought went out to his mount, spurring it into forward motion, and his Pack quickly followed.

Khulani had a special relationship with his horse, as did every Imaziyen warrior, but the fact that he could share its thoughts and know its condition intimately made the relationship symbiotic. He called his mount Wind Dancer for his impressive speed and agility that few other horses in his tribe could match. Wind Dancer proved it again today by swiftly cresting the grassy hill before any of the others—and there they stopped.

In the shallow valley below, a desperate scene was unfolding. A female mammoth, only recently delivered of a baby calf and in a much-weakened state, was enraged and frantically fending off a pack of five jackals. She was positioned protectively over the calf, which was lying on the ground covered in fluid and blood, struggling to stand. Despite her courageous efforts, the jackals had nearly brought the fight to an end. The calf's ears, trunk, and tail were shredded from attempts by the jackals to drag the baby away from its defiant mother, she herself bleeding from a hundred wounds all over her long-haired hide and losing blood quickly. She could have given up the calf and saved herself; instead she fought to protect it. Khulani could feel her exhaustion and how quickly she was running out of energy to keep up the defense. The mammoth staggered to turn in one direction or another in an effort to face a jackal only to be hit from the opposite direction by another. Yet, to her credit, there were two dead jackals at her feet and one severely crippled and urgently crawling away from the deadly animal.

Most Imaziyen would not have interfered with the life-and-death struggle they witnessed. This was a display of nature in its ugliest, raw form, and it should have been up to the spirits to intervene if they wanted a different outcome. Khulani was no typical Imaziyen. He could feel the desperation, fear, pain, and sadness from the new mother as well as the single-minded ferocity of the jackals.

Khulani dug his heals into his mount, and Wind Dancer sprang forward at a fast gallop, with the Pack following close behind. This was not the first time they intervened with an event in nature, and so far, the spirits had never punished them for it. Still a distance away, the great mammoth finally collapsed, and three of the jackals pounced to finish her off. The remaining jackals ran in toward the calf to drag it away from its mother's kicks and rolls—her attempt to right herself again. It was not to be.

In full gallop, Khulani loosed his arrows, and they found their targets without fail. Something inside him always asserted itself when he was in a state of heightened action, giving him clarity and focus beyond what others considered normal. Even when his arrows seemed to stray far from their mark, he could somehow will them to take the right course. It was almost as if he were releasing a part of himself—something inside him that he didn't realize he was restraining until he needed it.

The jackals, in a wild frenzy, did not recognize their fate until the Imaziyen were upon them, and all five were pin-cushioned with arrows before Khulani and his pack stopped their mounts next to the fallen mammoths. The calf was severely injured but still alive. The mother was in much worse shape. She had lost too much blood and suffered wounds that would not heal in time to save her. She lay on her side taking rapid, labored breaths, fearful of the men who sat on their horses nearby. Khulani could sense it all, and he motioned to the others to back away while only he approached on foot.

Drawing closer, he willed feelings of safety and comfort upon the mother to calm her. The mammoth's breathing slowed, and she relaxed. It would not be long now. Khulani walked to the fallen calf and helped it to stand. It would live if he could get it back to the village quickly enough. Slowly, he helped it to its mother's side. The calf was very weak. It had to find its strength, and Khulani sensed that the mother knew what she needed to do. Barely did she have the strength to shift so that the calf could suckle for the first time in its short life. The milk and the comfort of her long trunk lying gently over her baby's side would be the mammoth's final act of maternal instinct. Khulani felt it all, and for the first time he experienced a new emotion from an animal that he did not know they could conceptualize: gratitude. The emotions were overwhelming. He had never sensed a connection with an animal so powerfully before. Something had changed. And then she died. He felt the mammoth's spirit leave her body to join the others among the stars. The hunters looked on in silence as Khulani wept.

Khulani was not ashamed, nor did he regret his display of raw emotion when he could not save an animal he thought died unnecessarily. It wasn't the first time his Hunt Pack had witnessed the spectacle of his sentiments and likely not the last. They sat quietly with legs crossed in the shorter grass and waited respectfully. Not one of them would move until he was back with them again. They would wait until they starved, such was their devotion to him.

Grief was always the hardest emotion to deal with, and he almost considered it a curse that he felt it so acutely. He could hunt a hare or a hartebeest and feel no remorse at all. Perhaps he knew that the spirits had already chosen the life that would be sacrificed for his tribe's nutriment and survival. Khulani wanted to believe that was the case. He could at least rationalize his feelings if it were true.

No. It was not a curse. It was a gift—a beautiful gift that was born in him because of his mother. She was once a powerful shaman highly respected in their tribe. The spirits returned her to the gods a few years ago when she fell into a deep ravine foraging for herbs in the mountains. By the time she was found by the other shamans traveling with her, she was too far gone to be helped. It was a hard thing for a young child to deal with. From when he was very young, his mother taught him to embrace his gift and learn to use it. She had also just begun to teach him the ways of the Imaziɣen and the importance of reverence to the nature spirits. He missed her deeply.

The young mammoth stirred from suckling his dead mother's milk. Although badly injured, he had energy coursing through his body and he stood on his own. This one had a strong spirit inside of him, thought Khulani, and he knew he had to get the little beast back to the tribe if the mammoth was going to live to see another sunrise.

"Rebiku!" Khulani called out to his friend. "Prepare a litter for the calf. I will take him to Frinya."

Rebiku was not only Khulani's friend; he was also his second in authority of the Hunt Pack. They were the same age and had been close friends since the day they were old enough to walk. Rebiku could easily have led his own Hunt Pack, was even offered one by the elders, but he always said that the place where he was happiest was by Khulani's side. He knew better than anyone the emotional toll that Khulani's gift took on him. They spoke about it many times when they were alone together.

"Are you well, my friend?" Rebiku asked.

"I am. Some animals have a stronger sense of themselves than others, and some seem to feel emotion that is almost as real as our own, beyond just instinct. I have never felt it stronger than I did just now." Khulani always felt better when he spoke about it.

"Then let us help you bring the calf back to the village and feed it well. It will grow large like its mother, and you will be comforted by that." Rebiku smiled, and Khulani couldn't help but smile back at his friend. His friend understood, even better than his own father could.

With the help of his comrades, Khulani built a sturdy frame and then carefully secured the calf on the litter, attaching it low to reed-woven ropes he strapped to his mount. To keep the mammoth calm, he reached into its mind and encouraged it to sleep. An animal of its size would quickly demolish the litter if it panicked or struggled.

"Take the meat from the mother and send Gaya and Yani to hunt the hare in the long grass. The shamans cannot be too upset with my interference if they have a belly full of stew." Khulani mounted. He was not worried about his sturdy bay. It was fifteen hands high with a beautifully arched neck, pronounced withers, a thick body, and thin legs. Imaziyen horses had tremendous stamina for long hunts and exceptional agility to chase down prey. Khulani might have to stop to rest Wind Dancer a dozen times before he reached the village, but he sensed his mount was up to the task.

Rebiku laughed and patted Khulani's shoulder. "Be well, brother. I will see you when we return." Then he walked over to where the Hunt Pack stood next to their horses and relayed Khulani's orders.

Khulani departed without so much as a glance back. He didn't want to see any part of the mother mammoth butchered. The emotions of her departure were still fresh in his mind. He could only take comfort in the knowledge that by the time he reached the village his feelings would be nothing more than a vague memory. Later, he would happily consume the meat along with the rest of the tribe. It was strange the way the spirits worked.

He thought a lot about the spirits. They were the essence of nature—the wind, rain, animals, grass, mountains, rivers, and even rocks were represented by their own spirit. Keeping the spirits happy with respect and prayers affected the tribe in their everyday lives. If the spirits were happy, then the tribe would prosper as well.

Their gods, Tafukt the Sun and Ayur the Moon, required more attention, especially from the shamans to whom they supposedly granted powers of magic. His tribe assembled on a regular basis to honor their gods with rituals and ceremonies as well as the occasional sacrifice of a gnu or hartebeest during the solstices and full moons. Khulani assumed that the deities were pleased with the Imaziyen and continued to bless his tribe with a good life on the savannas and the places where his people roamed. He hoped it would always be so.

The terrain transitioned to flat grassland the closer he came to his village. A strong gust of wind whipped over the tall green grass, bending it forcefully toward the southeast. Khulani shifted on the thick cloth strapped to Wind Dancer's flanks and glanced behind him. He would have to build a sturdy shelter for the calf he dragged behind him on the heavy litter, now that the poor animal had no mother to hide under. The mammoth was still sleeping, despite the bumpy ride, and Khulani could feel its contentment.

It was strange that he was the only one in his village who had his unusual gift. Yes, his mother was a shaman, and she could use magic granted by the gods. Except that the shamans didn't understand it either. Not really. They *did* understand that his gift involved a very specialized nature magic, not like the magic they could weave to control nature, but more passive, without requiring effort or concentration. It was simply a part of who he was.

His special gift made him different from the other boys growing up in his tribe. Fortunately, his ability did not cause fear or contempt from his peers, rather, they accepted his differences and respected him. That was the nature of Imaziyen culture: accepting others' strengths and weaknesses and leaving it to the spirits to judge. So much of their lives was dependent upon nature that they revered it in every form and abhorred any disruption that might affect the balance and anger their gods or any of the nature spirits who served them.

In the distance, Khulani could make out the smoke from cooking fires. He would be in his village by late afternoon. He knew that his arrival with the mammoth in tow would turn a few heads, but no one would say anything about it. They had seen him drag in all manner of beasts since he was a child. He wished he could hurry and get there more quickly—he knew the calf was not out of danger yet. He had only stopped the bleeding and worried that infection would set in if the wounds were not cleaned properly soon. But moving any faster would also endanger his charge, so he continued at a steady pace.

Khulani distracted his mind with thoughts about the Gathering at Tazallit lhnna, City of Peace, that he would be attending for the first time this year. He would not be alone, as several boys and girls who were coming of age would be attending for the first time, including Rebiku. There would be a special ceremony at the Gathering where he and the others would be honored as warriors, shamans, men, and women for the first time. He was nervous about that part, since there would be no guarantee that he or Rebiku would be selected as warriors or even recognized as adults. If he did have that fortune, then he would have the right to marry, own property, and vote at council meetings. That was all a few weeks away yet, and until then he would be considered a boy no matter his accomplishments.

Approaching the outskirts of his village, Khulani came upon several boys only a few years younger than he who were taking turns wrestling in a circle of flattened grass. They were naked except for snug loincloths, and when they saw Khulani with his unusual cargo, they all ran over and excitedly pummeled him with questions. Khulani laughed at the cacophony of eager voices, "Boys, boys! Quiet now, you will wake my new friend!"

"What are you doing with it, Khulani?" one of the older boys asked. He was clearly the alpha male of this group. "Will you cook it tonight for the shamans?"

Khulani frowned at the boy. "You know better than that, Narouz. I will look after him for a while until he is ready to return to the others."

"I just wanted meat tonight," the boy replied, abashed.

"You will have meat, but not from this one. Rebiku is bringing enough for the entire village."

Narouz's expression brightened considerably. "That is good news, Khulani! May I pet your friend?"

Khulani feigned indecision and then smiled. "Yes, you can. Be gentle. He was almost food for the jackals today."

Narouz stepped to the mammoth calf and carefully laid his hand upon its thick fur. The place where he touched flickered with a sudden twitch, and he jerked his hand back quickly. The other boys laughed, then quieted immediately when Narouz cast a dark look in their direction. Then he laid his hand on the animal again. "He feels warm and wet."

"He likes your touch," Khulani assured him.

Narouz looked confused. "You said he was asleep . . ."

"He is, and he takes comfort from a friendly hand."

Narouz nodded, and the other boys impatiently ran over and gently stroked the calf.

Khulani studied Narouz carefully. *The boy is learning his role well,* he thought. If Narouz wanted to lead the tribe one day, like his father the Amgar, he was well on his way.

After allowing the boys to spend a few more moments with the calf, Khulani sent them away and continued into the village to seek out the healing shaman he knew would understand his need.

"What have you brought me this time?" Frinya asked when Khulani walked into her hut.

"I have brought a mammoth calf. Frinya, it needs your help."

Frinya was one of the shamans who could heal and was considered an elder of the tribe. She was pretty for her age, as old as his mother would have been if she still lived. Her long silver hair fell over ebony shoulders, and her light gray eyes conveyed a mystical appearance. She wore a silk and raffia dress the length of her lean body and stacks of metal jewelry on her arms and ankles. The jewelry chimed lightly against each other when she moved.

Frinya followed Khulani to the litter holding the mammoth calf. She knelt next to the quiet animal and put one hand on its head and another on its chest. She closed her eyes to concentrate on the spells Khulani knew—by the slight movement of her lips and the feel of static electricity in the air—she must be casting. He sat down on the other side of the calf and waited. With every minute that passed, he could sense the calf's condition improving, and with the improvement came relief.

A long while later, Frinya opened her eyes, and Khulani was startled to realize he was staring directly into them from the other side of the calf. "He will live," she said. "Now let him rest. You can release him to me now."

Khulani was always unsettled when she told him that. She knew as well as he that he held and strengthened the life force of the injured animals he brought to her, never giving it an effort beside his will to do it. He had to make a conscious effort to release his hold on the animal and felt a little weakness afterward.

"Now go," she said. "I will send word in the morning about his condition." She stroked the mammoth gingerly with the backs and palms of her hands, like a mother with an infant child. It surprised him a little to see her act this way since she had never raised children of her own. Shamans almost never did.

Khulani rose and carefully untied the litter from his horse, trying not to disturb the sleeping calf.

"Thank you, Frinya." Khulani bent and kissed her on her forehead before he turned to leave. Frinya simply nodded in reply.

The village was situated on the grassy savanna at the midpoint of the Shad River between the mountain ranges Uari Ssamal to the north and Uari Ljanub to the south. The tribe settled here several years ago and expected to stay only a few more seasons before following herd migration trends to a new home on the Ibhr Rrbi—Sea of Grass. Khulani walked his horse along the wide dirt paths arranged in rough streets and past the uneven rows of simple grass and reed huts his people lived in. Most huts were only one- or two-room dwellings, while a few were larger and more elaborate, with as many as a dozen rooms. Huts were built to accommodate the size of a family rather than one's station within the tribe. As he led his horse home, the scents of cooking stew, baking bread, and roasting vegetables was making him hungry. There were several large open huts without walls where the communal cooking took place in ovens, open fires, and grills situated around the village. He could also smell the fragrance of wood drying in kilns just outside the cooking huts, wood that would fuel the cooking in a few weeks.

Khulani had not walked far when he heard a commotion at the eastern edge of the village, near where he was. At first, he thought maybe an aurochs had escaped its pen, causing trouble, until he heard the lilting wail from a woman, and then another, and another. A chill ran up his spine. Something terrible had happened. Tying his horse's simple bone-and-leather bridle to a nearby post, he joined the flow of his people running toward the disturbance. In his haste he neglected to bring the bow and leather quiver that were strapped to his horse, so he pulled his long, curved dagger in case there was danger. Other tribesmen ran next to him carrying spears, axes, or bows, and he knew that he was in good company. Imaziyen men were trained with weapons from the time they could walk. Any one of them was equally proficient on foot or on horseback with the weapons they carried.

When he arrived at the edge of the village, he was greeted by the sight of his tribe's people surrounding the remains of four bodies on the ground. The women were still making a ruckus, and he found it hard to hear what was being said, but by the look of the deceased men, it was clear they had all been ravaged by a beast with fearsome claws. Khulani recognized the men as members of a Hunt Pack led by a man named Bochus—he was not among the dead. Just then the crowd went silent, even the wailing women, and they parted to allow the Amgar, chief of the tribe, pass through.

"Where is Bochus?" the Amgar demanded. He was a commanding figure a little more heavily muscled than the younger men and tall.

A man a few years older than Khulani rose from the edge of the crowd and stepped forward. "I am here, Amgar."

"What has happened?"

Bochus bowed his head in shame before he replied. "We were attacked by a long-tooth in the Ibhr Rrbi. It killed these men and wounded others before we could drive it off."

The Amgar briefly showed alarm before his stern visage returned. "The Ibhr Rrbi? You were not in the mountains?"

"No, Amgar." The man appeared sincere. "The long-tooth attacked my Hunt Pack in the open savanna in the daylight. I cannot explain why."

"These men are your responsibility, Bochus," the Amgar spoke in a quiet, almost consoling voice. "See to their families and proper burial. I will consult the elders about this tragedy." The Amgar did not wait for a response. He turned and walked away with purpose.

Khulani was stunned. Why would a long-tooth attack an armed Hunt Pack in full daylight? And why was the beast in the Ibhr Rrbi to begin with? Certainly, the long-tooth was a fearsome lion nearly the size of his horse, with fangs the length of his dagger, but they never left the mountains. Never! And they would never attack an armed group of men, especially during the day. They only hunted at night. It didn't make sense. He waited for the families of the dead to arrive and claim their sons and husbands. When they were done, Khulani approached Bochus.

"Honored Bochus," Khulani began.

Clearly upset, Bochus turned on him in anger. "I am not honored today, Khulani! I have failed my Hunt Pack, and they will probably not follow me again."

Khulani knelt before the leader of the Hunt Pack in a show of respect. "It was not your fault, Bochus. Something is not right with the long-tooth. Think about it, Bochus! What you said about it doesn't make sense!" Khulani stood and took Bochus's arm in his hands. "Remember my gift."

Bochus turned to Khulani, tears welling in his eyes. "You are right, young leader. The long-tooth was not itself. It has a taste for the flesh of man, and it will kill here next."

"Why do you think so, Bochus?"

"Because the only reason it left any of us alive was so it could follow us back to the village with our injured and dead."

Chapter 2

The Long-tooth

Khulani arrived at the two-room hut he shared with his father. His mind was absorbed with thoughts about what Bochus had told him of the long-toothed lion. It didn't seem possible for an animal to have complex strategic thought beyond the immediacy of the hunt. He conceded to himself that he had never been in the vicinity of a long-tooth, but they were said to have no greater capability than that of any mountain lion. Except, of course, for their greater size and strength. Perhaps they possessed greater intellect as well. Almost instinctively he removed the straps from Wind Dancer before rubbing the horse down and washing himself clean of blood and dust.

Inside, his father was sitting on mats on the floor eating stew from a wooden bowl with a wooden spoon. He smiled broadly when Khulani entered. "Greetings, son, are the shamans pleased with your rabbits?" His father was speaking the old tongue, a language that emphasized clicking consonants in the dialect that only the elders and a few others spoke to keep the language alive. The elders passed it down to their children, as his family had done for generations. Now his father taught him. It was the first language of the Imaziɣen when all the tribes were one. After the tribe split into many, a thousand years ago or more, the northern tribes lost the clicking consonants over time. The tribes that went south might well still use them, but they had moved so far that there was little contact with them anymore. His father considered it important to their heritage and honored their ancestors by speaking the old tongue at home.

"Rebiku is fetching the rabbits with the Hunt Pack," he spoke back with clicks. "I found an injured mammoth calf that needed attention."

Khulani's father barked a laugh. "You will be a compassionate man, my son. I hope that never changes in you. But I am sure the shamans will have different opinions."

"The shamans are who they are, and I am who I am." Khulani didn't care much what the shamans thought. The scent of the hot food made his stomach rumble. He filled his bowl with stew from the pot on the hearth and joined his father on the floor.

"This year will be your first at the Gathering. The Elder Shamans will be supporting your claim for rights. Keep peace with them, son," his father cautioned.

Khulani sensed his father's concern. "I will always give the shamans the respect they deserve. More importantly, you should know that Bochus had some trouble today." Khulani told his father everything that happened earlier with the Hunt Master and the Amgar, and what Bochus told him afterward.

His father sat quietly in thought for a while before he spoke. "The Amgar will be calling the Elder Council tonight. I will tell him of Bochus's words if he doesn't already know." Without standing, he tossed his bowl into a nearby basket to be washed later. "I have seen the long-tooth only one time in my life—long ago when I was leading my Hunt Pack near the Uari Ssamal. We were chasing a small group of hartebeest that we separated from the herd and cornered in a steep ravine. Before we had a chance to do anything, a long-tooth sprang upon them from a hidden spot on the incline. It killed the largest of the hartebeest instantly and disappeared with its prize within seconds." His father chuckled. "We were nearly trampled by the rest of the hartebeests desperately trying to flee."

Khulani had never heard this story from his father before. "Was there anything unusual about the long-tooth that you noticed?"

"Only that it was very big." His father shrugged. "They are cunning predators that ambush their prey from concealment and have no trouble navigating the rocky terrain of the mountains. I have never heard of one in the Ibhr Rrbi."

Shifting to lie on his side with one arm propping up his body, his father fixed him with a stern gaze. "Bochus is not one to exaggerate. His tales are always boring because he does not embellish. I believe him when he says something is unusual about this long-tooth."

Khulani's father was a great warrior with a seat on the Elder Council and a trusted advisor to the Amgar. Over the years, he had seen everything that crawled, slithered, and flew across the Sea of Grass they called the Ibhr Rrbi. What troubled Khulani was the steady certainty in his father's eyes that something was especially wrong about this rogue long-tooth. He had the look of a warrior preparing not for a hunt, but for a battle.

Just then Rebiku popped his head into the hut, and Khulani's father eagerly waved him in. "Sit, Rebiku, and share a bowl of stew with us." His father spoke in the tribal language, since Rebiku was not proficient with the old tongue.

"Thank you, Elder Boa, I am famished," Rebiku replied respectfully. "Khulani, Yani and Gaya found eleven big rabbits today. The shamans are very happy!"

Rebiku's big smile was infectious, and Khulani laughed. "Did you have to skin them as well, or will the shamans eat them whole tonight?"

Rebiku yelped a quick laugh, then hesitated, glancing at Khulani's father, before realizing he was quietly laughing as well. Boa was an elder of the tribe, but he had a more relaxed view of things, and Khulani knew he did not mind the small jokes the younger men spoke about the more conservative elders, especially the shamans.

As he had with his father, Khulani told Rebiku about Bochus and the long-tooth while he ate his stew. His friend took it all in stride. He never cared to speculate much about things, preferring to deal with realities of the moment.

"We should hunt it." At first Khulani thought Rebiku was telling one of his usual jokes, but his smile was genuine.

"Didn't you hear what I was saying?" Khulani chided. "It killed four of Bochus's warriors, Rebiku, and he said that it could have killed them all if it wanted to. Bochus and his Hunt Pack are seasoned warriors with a decade of experience."

Rebiku's infectious smile was relentless. "And we are the best."

Khulani wanted to roll his eyes, Rebiku was the bravest and most foolish Imaziyen he knew. "We are the best at hunting hare for the shamans' stew and hartebeest on the open grassland. What makes you think we would fare any better than Bochus?"

"We have you." Somehow Rebiku's smile expanded even farther on his face.

Quiet during the entire exchange, Khulani's father spoke up. "I know your spirit, my son. It is the same as your mother's. Your gift will be pulling you in unexpected directions the rest of your life. Whatever you do, take care to do it well."

"I will, Father." Khulani turned to face his friend. "Very well, if the long-tooth is sighted near the village, then we will find it and kill it."

The next morning there was no news from any of the sentries regarding the long-tooth. Khulani suspected that maybe it followed Bochus's Hunt Pack for only a short while before returning to the mountains. At least that's what he hoped. It was not unusual for an animal to leave its natural territory to find food or mate, but it would always return to where it came from unless it was driven out by a more powerful predator. The odd thing was that, except for humans, the long-tooth was at the top of the food chain.

Khulani barely finished his breakfast of flatbread and berries when Frinya arrived at his home leading the mammoth calf. To his pleasant surprise, the calf was stable on its feet and nibbling at any green plants it could find. Feelings of content and calm came to him from the mammoth, a combination that he knew equated to happiness in nearly every animal. Frinya had done her job well.

"He is doing much better, if not fully healed yet. That may take several more weeks," Frinya said as she handed Khulani a large waterskin. "This is a special mixture of magic-imbued goat and sheep milk that will allow him to regain his strength faster. I will bring more tomorrow. Make sure he stays out of the weather."

"Of course, Frinya. I will build a shelter right away. Is there anything I can do for you?" Khulani asked.

"Yes. Next time have Rebiku bring me a fatter rabbit." She turned and walked back down the path to her hut. Khulani was not sure if she was joking or not, so he made a mental note to tell Rebiku later.

After a short reunion with his calf, Khulani set to work building a shelter for his new charge. From the moment of the mammoth's rescue, he could feel a deep bond forming between the two of them. It was not the first bond he shared with an animal. Just the previous year there was a wolf that lost its mate, and for months it followed Khulani everywhere. The people in his village were afraid of the animal and ran away when they saw it. Some of the warriors even wanted to kill it. Finally, the Elder

Shamans forbade him to bring the wolf into the village at all as it was causing so much distress. Khulani was forced to sleep outside the village for several weeks until he could convince the wolf to return to its own pack. He was sad to see the wolf go, but he also knew that the longer the wolf stayed with him, the harder it would be for it to survive on its own. Fortunately, the mammoth calf was not likely to eat anyone.

By late afternoon, Khulani completed the large shelter for the animal and hoped he wouldn't have to make a larger one later. Once the calf was healthy again, he would do his best to encourage it to return to the herd. Until then, it would be up to him to keep the still-nursing calf properly fed. Frinya advised him to feed the calf half of the large skin of milk that evening and the rest in the morning. He hoped Frinya didn't stop bringing the milk every day; otherwise he would have to find another mammoth for the calf to suckle.

The hut he built for the calf stood near his own and not far from a growth of plants safe for it to eat. He would not pen the mammoth in or tie it down—if it decided to roam for plants, then it was free to do so. Hopefully, no one would complain if it pulled up their gardens.

So far, there was no news regarding the long-tooth, at least not from any of the tribespeople who stopped briefly to watch him building the mammoth's shelter. Since he was free for the evening, he decided to walk to the center of the village, which they called the Meeting Place. It was really nothing more than a wide, open area that served as a common area to find friends, play games, hear the latest gossip, or trade for trinkets with the occasional Capsian merchant. Today, like almost any day, the Amgar and the Elder Council were at the Meeting Place, and his father among them, mingling with the tribespeople. Khulani was glad to see that there was laughter and light conversation echoing around the clearing. It was a good indication that all was well with the tribe, despite the sadness that still prevailed due to the recent deaths of Bochus's warriors.

Although Khulani was not yet considered a man, he was respected by the tribespeople as if he were one already. *Mostly due to the gift I am blessed with,* thought Khulani. It wouldn't be long before he and Rebiku would visit Tazallit lhnna, where they expected to be officially announced. When that happened, the respect would have been earned, and he could walk with his head high as a fully accepted adult warrior of his people. Until then, he would not dishonor his father by walking in shoes that were not his own. Others his age, with different talents, had tried. In the end, their own ego brought shame upon them and their family. He and his father had lost enough already.

He spied Bochus standing with one of his warriors nearby. Bochus noticed Khulani at the same time and motioned him over. Khulani quickly walked over to stand with them. "Greetings, Bochus. How are you today?"

"I have fewer tears than yesterday." Indeed, Bochus's eyes were red, and he looked tired. Khulani understood—the men in his Hunt Pack were as close to him as brothers, perhaps closer.

"My heart is heavy for you and our brothers." Khulani made a slight nod and placed a hand over his own chest as a show of respect.

Bochus and the other warrior with him returned the gesture, then the Hunt Master placed a hand on Khulani's shoulder and leaned in close. "I want to speak further with you about the long-tooth. You have a unique insight into the behavior of animals that might be useful if we are faced with its aggression again."

The warrior with Bochus smiled knowingly at Khulani and walked away. He must have already known what his Hunt Master was thinking.

"I will always help as best I can." Khulani kept his gaze steady on Bochus. If it wavered, Bochus would think him unsteady, immature, and unable to deal with the serious nature of their discussion. Khulani did not know Bochus well, but he knew well enough the character of this well-respected Hunt Master. "For you, Bochus, for the Amgar, and for our people." Khulani thumped Bochus's chest for emphasis.

Bochus smiled. "I believe you are ready for Tazallit lhnna, son of Boa, and you are ready to face the long-tooth if need be."

Bochus was about to say something more when a young boy, about nine years old, ran into the Meeting Place speaking loudly and too fast for Khulani to understand. A woman near the boy understood enough that she became exited as well and began to scream, "Uhu! Uhu! Uhu!" The boy continued to shout, and he was crying, gesturing with a stick he carried to somewhere outside the village. Immediately the Amgar and the elders descended upon him, asking questions and trying to calm him at the same time. Bochus looked at Khulani with wide eyes, afraid of what the boy might be saying.

Finally the Amgar straightened and gestured for a few of the tribespeople to take the hysterical boy and the woman away. Then he called, "The shepherds are missing! Bochus! Ouzmir! Bogud! Zila! Call your warriors and find the boys!"

Khulani was shocked. Never had he lived in a time of warfare or strife. Never had the Amgar called the four most experienced Hunt Masters together with their warriors into frenzied action. Bochus did not hesitate, nor did any of the others in the Meeting Place. The Hunt Masters called for their warriors and sent men running wildly through the village to send out the word.

In only minutes, the four Hunt Packs were gathered together in the Meeting Place, over one hundred of the tribe's best warriors bristling with spears and carrying long curved blades at their sides. The Amgar faced them. He, too, was prepared for battle and ready to lead them to whatever fate the spirits had in store for them. Khulani found it all very impressive, and he desperately wanted to go with them. He knew that his gift would help them find the beast.

A hand settled on his shoulder from behind, nearly causing him to jump. "I know you want to go, Khulani. Be patient. Soon you will have as much right to die as a warrior as any of them." It was his father.

"Yes, Father." Khulani nodded, but it didn't dampen his desire in the slightest.

"Khulani!" Rebiku ran up next to him. "What has happened? Are we under attack?"

Khulani glanced at his friend. It was odd to see a worried, serious expression on his face. "I don't know. The shepherds are missing, and the Amgar is taking *four* of the best Hunt Packs out to find them."

"Is it the long-tooth?" Rebiku's voice shook a little as he said it.

"No one has said, but I believe everyone is thinking that."

The Amgar led the warriors out of the Meeting Place toward the edge of the village where their horses were waiting. The warriors ran together swiftly and in silence. There were no cheers or best wishes. That was not like the Imaziyen. Celebration would only come if they returned with the shepherds. Alive. Khulani worried for what those brave warriors would find in the Ibhr Rrbi and how many would be joining the spirits before the day was through.

Chapter 3

Stalked

Khulani sat upon his horse next to Rebiku, staring out into the Ibhr Rrbi wondering about what must be happening with the Amgar and the warriors he led to find the shepherds. The Amgar's last command before departing was for everyone to stay within the village and for the remaining Hunt Packs to be vigilant and patrol the perimeter. To Khulani's relief, that order included his Hunt Pack, and they were not forced to endure the shame of hiding with children.

His men were spread out behind him, riding parallel to each other in a long line sweeping through the tall grass. They rode bareback or on thick fabric strapped to the horse's flanks, and they controlled the movements of their mounts with halter and bridle with a bit made of bone or ivory. Their task was to keep watch on the northeastern approaches to the village and report anything unusual they detected to the Elder Council. It was the exact opposite direction of where the shepherds went missing and the least likely to lead to any trouble.

Khulani was frustrated by the assignment, knowing that he could be more useful elsewhere. He reminded himself that the Gathering was only a few weeks away, and soon he would be counted a warrior as much as any of the other men and women.

"Do you sense anything?" Rebiku kept his voice low, as if he might be heard by the long-tooth or whatever they were watching for.

"Nothing more than usual." Khulani pointed over to his right. "A couple of hare over there, the hartebeest that you can see, and a few birds."

Rebiku laughed. "Well at least the day is nice and there is no rain."

The sky was clear, with only a few puffy white clouds sliding by lazily in front of the soon-to-be-setting sun. Khulani grunted. "It will rain again tonight." He could feel the rains coming, just over the horizon.

Rebiku just shook his head, smiling. "You should put down that spear and be a weather shaman like your mother."

Khulani smiled at that, and they rode on in silence. His thoughts always tended to turn to his family in the quiet of the savannas. His father was a great warrior in his youth and now held the revered position of an elder on the tribal council. From an early age, Khulani's father taught him to hunt and fight. He taught him the art of tribal politics and negotiation. Most importantly, he taught him how to compromise and take positions that were best for the tribe rather than for himself. Khulani was being molded into a leader as his father and father's father were before him. Already he was the proud Hunt Master of a Pack of warrior-hunters made up of boys around his age. His Hunt Pack was the most successful in the tribe, even more so than the older warriors' Hunt Packs. Mostly due to his special gift, he supposed, but the tribe was proud of him, and despite his success at such a young age, very few held any jealousy.

Even so, Khulani had little interest in tribal politics or becoming a leader. His mother told him before she died that his path would be through his gift. That's where he would find his destiny, his passion and fulfilment. She also warned him that he was to serve a greater purpose, but his memories were very vague, and he was too young then to understand much of what she told him about that. He never told his father of his mother's visions, since they happened just before her accident, and afterward he kept it to himself to avoid losing the time he and his father spent together. Besides, it didn't hurt to understand the important lessons his father passed on to him about leadership and negotiations.

Khulani abruptly realized that something had changed in the environment around him. They were headed for an area where the grass was taller and the brush cover was more abundant. He held up his hand to halt the Hunt Pack. No one said a word, not even Rebiku. Every one of them knew what Khulani was about.

He gazed across the savanna, but his senses were turned inward. Where were the animals? There was never a time when he could detect nothing. Not even a rat or snake. It was as if they entered a zone of death, similar to the mammoth boneyard, except even in that place there were vermin. Khulani heightened his senses and focused on finding *something,* anything alive that could give meaning to what he was feeling.

Then it was there.

A cold streak of lighting ran up Khulani's spine. He couldn't see it, but he knew it was nearby, close enough to strike. Pure evil, darkness, and despair washed over him—and a singular need to kill. This was an animal, Khulani was certain, and it was alive, but the spirit of the animal was not in it, leaving him unsure about what it was. Whatever it was, the beast was dangerous and set to kill them all.

Khulani made a quick motion with his hand, and the others quickly drew their long-curved daggers or readied spears. Instantly the creature's attention was on him. He could feel the weight of it. And he sensed something else . . . hatred. That was an emotion he never felt from an animal. Somehow, he knew that it could feel him as much as he felt it, and the hate that he could detect from it was laced with doubt.

Then it was gone.

Khulani released a long breath that he didn't realize he was holding.

"What is it?" Rebiku finally whispered.

"I don't know, but it is gone now." Khulani felt himself shaking with fear or nervousness, maybe a little of both. He looked toward the west where the sun was close to the horizon. Tafukt was soon to take his rest, leaving the darkness to Ayur. "We have to get back to the village and warn the elders. This thing is intelligent, and I worry for the safety of our people this night."

~~~

"Yes, Father, I am sure it was an animal." Khulani stood in front of the Elder Council, recounting what he experienced on the Ibhr Rrbi.

"And you say it had no spirit, so you could not know what it was?" Elder Boa had the first right of questioning because Khulani was his son.

"Yes, Father."

Iken, another of the elders spoke up. "Who else saw this beast?"

Khulani shrugged. "No one, not even I. The beast was hidden from our eyes somewhere in the tallest grass. I could only sense it."

"Could you have been mistaken?" Elder Iken countered. "Maybe the excitement of these days has made you anxious?"

Elder Boa interrupted Khulani's reply. "You know my son's gift, Iken." He turned to the rest of the elders. "My son has not been declared at Tazallit lhnna, but we will not disparage his honor by questioning the truth of his words."

The elders murmured, and most nodded in agreement. Elder Iken also nodded. "Then tell us, Khulani, what does your gift tell us about this threat to our people?"

Khulani nervously cleared his throat. "It was very hard to understand this one's intent because of its overwhelming need to kill. I believe it circled around to the east side of the village, away from the shepherds and the mountains. No doubt it did not think we would expect it from that direction."

Almost as one, the elders gasped.

"What are you saying, Khulani?" his father asked in almost a whisper.

"It will come to the village tonight."

All at once the nine elders began speaking rapidly to each other, almost frantic. His father motioned for him to leave, and Khulani couldn't have been happier to comply.

Rebiku stood outside the hut, waiting for him with a worried expression on his face. "Are you well, brother?"

Before Khulani could speak, the Amgar came riding down the street at a fast gait with Bochus a step behind him. When he saw Khulani standing outside of the elders' hut, he quickly dismounted and walked up to him.

"Something else has happened." It wasn't exactly a question.

"Yes, Amgar." Khulani replied and prepared to answer further.

With only a nod, the Amgar pulled aside the hartebeest-skin flap and walked into the elders' hut. Khulani could hear the elders quiet at his entrance.

Bochus, already dismounted, was standing nearby. "What happened?"

Khulani related his story once more before he asked, "Did you find the shepherds?"

Bochus nodded sadly. "We found what was left of two of them. We know nothing of the others. Your story explains why we were not attacked. If this thing is as clever as you suspect, then our people will live in fear until we can hunt it down."

He placed a hand on Khulani's shoulder and nodded to Rebiku, then he followed the Amgar into the elders' hut.

It was already dark, and Ayur graced the night sky high and full. Elderly men and women shuffled along the streets and avenues formed by the lines of huts, lighting torches throughout the village. A village of over three thousand, Khulani thought to himself. How could they protect them all? There were not enough warriors to surround the entire village without wide gaps, and he would only know the beast was near when it was close enough to strike. He hoped the Amgar could come up with a plan fast. Every moment that went by was a moment of his tribe's vulnerability.

"What should we do now? Wait?" Rebiku's eyes were wide, and the slight waver in his voice revealed his nerves.

Khulani pondered a moment. "Gather the Hunt Pack and meet me in the Meeting Place. We will start a patrol while the Amgar and the elders decide what is best."

"Where will you go?"

"I need to put the mammoth calf in his hut and feed him. Now go, quickly. I will meet you soon."

Rebiku nodded and darted away at almost a sprint, while Khulani turned in the opposite direction and set off at nearly the same pace. It was only a moment before his hut was in sight in the distance at the southern edge of the village. There was light shining through cracks between the edge of the doorway and the door flap, which he found odd since he knew his father was not home and would not have left the hearth unattended. Still more alarming was the absence of the mammoth calf's silhouette, which he would have expected to be lingering near his hut after dark. Worried now, Khulani picked up his stride.

Nearly there, he could hear what he thought was the sound of singing, low and gentle, coming from his hut. He slowed to listen more carefully. It was a lullaby that was commonly sung to babies, and it was coming from the adjoining hut he built for the mammoth. Cautiously, he walked into the darkened room. The mammoth was there, and so was Frinya. She was holding a waterskin high to feed the calf while she sang the soft tune. The shaman's back was to the door, so she did not see him walk in. Khulani stood quietly, listening to the song. It reminded him of his mother and caused pain in his chest, as would often happen when he missed her.

The room was dimly lit by a stone that Frinya must have caused to glow. No doubt the mammoth would have been frightened by the flame from a torch. The lighting and the song conjured images from his childhood, and for a moment Khulani thought he might be overwhelmed by emotion. By the time Frinya finished her song, the mammoth had drained the last of the milk from the waterskin and stood content. Khulani, still captured by the nostalgic chorus, had to wipe a few tears from his face.

"Greetings, Khulani," Frinya said without turning.

"How did you know I was here?"

She turned, and Khulani was struck by her painted features. White dots surrounded her eyes and formed a line down her nose. On her right cheek, the symbol of a sun god Tafukt was drawn in red clay, while on her left cheek, the symbol of the moon goddess Ayur was depicted. There were many other symbols on her face and neck that Khulani did not understand. The look was striking against her black skin and long, silvery white hair. "How do you know the animals are near?"

Khulani's was so surprised by her appearance that he disregarded his former question. "Frinya, why are you painted tonight? Is there a ritual that I have forgotten?"

"No, Khulani. I have had visions about this evening. You need to prepare your—"

A man shouted something from outside the hut. Startled, Khulani bolted out to see what was happening, with Frinya following close behind.

"The Amgar commands everyone to the Meeting Place! There is danger. You must go now!" He was one of the Amgar's warriors, and after shouting the message once more, he ran to the next street. In the distance, Khulani could hear more shouts from similar messengers.

"The Amgar must have decided the best way to protect everyone is to bring them together into a small area and surround them with warriors. It is a good plan." Khulani watched families from nearby huts rushing to follow the Amgar's orders.

Frinya didn't look convinced. "It is a good plan for one night or two, but not for many nights. The beast will have to be hunted down quickly if we are to have any peace."

Khulani suddenly realized he had a problem. "What do I do about the calf, Frinya? I can't leave him here."

"There will be no room for an animal of this size in the Meeting Place with all the tribe gathered there." Frinya's eyes sparkled oddly in the light of the full moon. "Go, Khulani, I will stay with the calf and keep him quiet and calm."

"I can't leave you here alone, Frinya!" Khulani felt his panic rising. "What if the long-tooth or whatever I encountered in the Ibhr Rrbi finds you?"

"If that is the will of the spirits, then that's how it will be." Frinya smiled broadly, revealing several gaps between her teeth. "I am not without protections."

"Even your protections may not be enough! This thing is not an animal anymore. It has no spirit. Leave the calf and come with me." Khulani protested.

Frinya's eyes grew dull, and her expression transformed into a look of someone accepting their fate. Khulani had only seen that look in warriors who thought they were about to die. "My obligation to nature demands that I stay," she said. "And your obligation is to this tribe. The survival of our people may someday hang on your ability to protect them." She took Khulani's hand. "I am an old lady, Khulani. My time has passed. No longer can I affect the fate of the tribe, but you can."

"Frinya . . ." Tears streamed down Khulani's face, and he didn't know why. Something inside told him that he would never see Frinya alive again if he abandoned her now.

The shaman's eyes flamed with the fire of anger, and she slapped the hand she was holding. "I am not asking, Khulani! Go!"

Khulani ran. He ran as if his life depended on it. The streets were empty. Everyone had fled to the Meeting Place as commanded, and no one lingered in their homes. It was as if the people just vanished, leaving behind everything. He was glad of it. No one would hear his sobs as he ran.

Chapter 4

Loss

Khulani was running like he'd never run before, until he tripped. Something in the dirt-packed street caught his foot, sending him tumbling and then sprawling across a mud puddle. He looked around, feeling embarrassed, but there was no one to witness his humiliation. It began to rain. Khulani sat up and put his arms across his knees. "Maybe the rain will take some of the mud off of me," he muttered to himself.

He considered what he was doing. Frinya was once his mother's closest friend and was practically a mother to him after she died. How could he forgive himself if something happened to her? She was alone, in the dark, with a mammoth calf for company. Maybe she would be just fine and he would return in the morning to find her feeding the calf.

Something was not right.

She was too insistent, protecting him, as if she knew something. *She knew something.* It was her visions! She *was* protecting him, even if it meant her own life. Khulani could not let her die this way.

Jumping up from the puddle, Khulani reversed his course and ran as fast as his legs would carry him back toward his hut. He was only two streets away and didn't have far to go. Rounding the last corner, he stopped dead. He sensed the beast was near again. Somewhere up ahead, close to his hut. Then he was alarmed to see Frinya walk out of the mammoth calf's hut and stop in the middle of the street, facing away from him. There were no huts beyond his own, only the open grasslands. What did she see?

There was movement in the darkness. It looked like it might be a horse, except that it moved differently. The only illumination was the moonlight, and it was hard to see any detail. The massive creature approach Frinya slowly. Even from a distance, Khulani could see two large, forward-facing green eyes that glowed not from the reflection of the moonlight, but from within. Frinya was chanting, but she did not move to avoid it. Not a muscle. The creature came closer to her, hesitantly, as if uncertain about this frail little woman unafraid to face it.

It stalked into the light as it circled Frinya, and Khulani could see the massive head with two long, protruding fangs, dirty-yellow fur, and paws the size of his chest. It was no horse, although it was as *big* as a horse. Indeed, it was the long-tooth they feared. Khulani could sense the pure evil that pervaded its essence and the absolute intent to kill that drove it.

Recovering from his brief shock, Khulani started to run again. He didn't have his spear, so he pulled his long dagger while he ran. He had to get to Frinya before—

It pounced.

Frinya thrust her arms toward the long-tooth, engulfing it in erratic webs of electricity. She was a second too late; it already had her. Long, daggerlike claws ripped into the flesh of her thin frame, pulling her closer even as the long-tooth roared from the pain of the electricity. Its body writhed with pain, yet it did not release her.

Khulani was almost there. He could still save her. He gripped his dagger tight and prepared to jump on its back. Frinya was screaming, and the lighting faltered, coming only in brief fits. Almost there, just two more steps. The long-tooth stood on its hind legs and held Frinya in its claws close to its body, looking down on her. Blue sparks continued to dance across the creature's huge frame, causing its muscles to twitch here and there while Frinya struggled with what little strength she had left.

Khulani jumped.

Frinya's screams abruptly cut off, replaced by the sickening crunch of her skull crushed in the long-tooth's powerful jaws. Blind rage flooded through Khulani. When he landed, he drove his dagger deep between the shoulder blades of the massive cat. Frinya's body crashed to the ground as the long-tooth spun its bulk around with such force that Khulani was thrown five paces away onto the ground.

Quickly he recovered to face the advancing long-tooth, the dagger still lodged in its back. It was moving slowly again, and Khulani was unsure if it was because of the dagger or because it was preparing to pounce on him. He desperately looked around for a weapon, something to keep the cat at bay.

Nothing.

The long-tooth was gravely injured. Khulani could sense the pain of the dagger that had pierced a lung, causing difficulty breathing. Nonetheless, the evil that pervaded its mind with the need to kill spurred it forward as if there were no injury at all. Khulani would have to do something, or he would be the next to lie in a heap beside Frinya.

Poor Frinya.

He focused on the long-tooth, willing it to stop. Nothing happened. Khulani redoubled his efforts. He tried to reach the animal that was once inside it. There was nothing left of its presence. He kept searching. It was like thrusting his arm in a lake expecting to catch a fish. He remembered how he moved a stone once. It was a small stone, and it moved only a short distance. Still, power moved through him that day. He needed that power again.

Khulani extended his arms toward the beast, willing the energy to flow through him. He felt it there, begging to be released. He just didn't know how to release it. Beyond desperate and nearly within the grasp of those deadly claws, Khulani closed his eyes and stopped struggling with himself. He felt a trickle of the energy leave him and then a sudden gush. There was the sound of twisting branches and vines, and abruptly the long-tooth roared with anger.

Daring to open his eyes, Khulani was astonished at what he saw. Only a pace away, the long-tooth was wrapped in thick branches that had sprouted out of the dirt road from nowhere. For a moment he felt relief. He would retrieve a spear from his hut and finish the beast off.

The long-tooth struggled violently against its ensnarement, crushing and breaking branches with each fit of movement. If Khulani didn't hurry, the cat would escape in seconds. He had no time to retrieve a spear. Instead, he concentrated on releasing more energy. He focused again, but this time there was nothing inside of him. All the energy was gone. His eyes snapped open to see the long-tooth nearly out of its branchy prison.

Two eagles abruptly caught his attention. Almost identical, their brown feathers were highlighted by luminous blue streaks along the edges and tips, a unique feature Khulani had never seen in another of their breed. Why were they flying at night? The pair just arrived and hovered nearby as if to watch the conclusion of this bloody spectacle. Then, impossibly, they transformed into two figures clad in long brown-hooded robes with lengths of multicolored beads and feathers trailing from the heavy fabric in various places. Their hoods were up, concealing their features, but their size and shape gave them away as a man and a woman. Together they extended their arms, energy crackling between fingers adorned with multiple metal bands that flashed gold and silver in the pale light of the moon. The branches, still barely clinging to the limbs of the struggling long-tooth, burst into blue flame, consuming the big cat altogether.

Khulani stumbled back from the intense heat, far hotter than any flame he could produce, and watched the long-tooth scream and twist in the unnatural fire. It lasted only seconds, and soon the charred remains of fur and bone were all that was left, leaving the scent of burned flesh hanging heavy in the air. It was over, or so he thought, when something like a shadow rose from the smoldering corpse, coalescing into a writhing ball of the blackest black, filling Khulani's heart with such fear that he never felt before in his life.

"Buadhach," Khulani heard the soft, steady voice of the female say, "are you ready?"

The larger male figure nodded. "I will merge my power with yours now, Grian."

The two strangers extended their arms again toward the black orb. Khulani subconsciously felt a strange tingling sensation in the back of his mind, different, but not too dissimilar from the feeling he experienced when he was communing with animals. With fascination he watched the orb struggling against some unseen force, as if it were being constricted into a smaller space. The raw fear emanating from it slowly faded with each constriction until the black orb was no larger than a light globe. Without hesitation, the hooded man walked over and plucked it out of the air, studied it carefully for a moment, and then walked back and handed it to the female.

"Is it safe?" the one she called Buadhach asked.

The woman shrugged. "For now." She handed the black orb back to Buadhach. "Give it to the brothers Fergus and Finn. Tell then to take it to Caomh the Enlightened with all haste."

"Yes, Grian." The man immediately transformed into an eagle once more.

"And Buadhach, tell them absolutely no delays."

Maybe it was Khulani's imagination, but he could swear the eagle nodded before it flew swiftly away to the north. Stunned by everything he was witnessing, he watched it fly until it disappeared into the darkness of the night. When he turned to look back to see if the woman was still there, he was further stunned to find her only a pace away, staring into his eyes as if she could see straight into his soul. He didn't have the power to look away. She was younger than he expected, perhaps only a few years older than he, and she had long red hair that framed her pale skin and bright green eyes. Her face was decorated with blue tattoos of symbols completely foreign to him. How could he not hear her approach?

"You are tired and you need to sleep." Her words were soothing, and she spoke them as if she commanded rather than suggested.

He *was* tired. His legs felt unsteady. Maybe she wouldn't mind if he sat down for just a moment to gather his strength. The pretty woman was moving her hands in a strange pattern, and her delicate features held an expression of sorrow. Was it for him? His vision blurred. Khulani wanted to speak, to say something. He was just so tired. Exhausted and completely overcome by the entire experience, he collapsed, letting the blessed, comforting darkness take him.

~~~

"Khulani, my son, wake up." His father's voice was quiet, calming and strong. Khulani wanted to wrap the sound around him and sleep on. He felt safe.

Fingers on his shoulder shook him gently. "Wake, son. You must eat and drink, or you will die." There was urgency in that voice, although he felt neither hungry nor thirsty. Perhaps a little later.

"We must wake him now, Elder Boa." It was the woman he recognized as the Elder Shaman Tafrara speaking. She was one of the tribal healers. "If you would allow me to take a more aggressive approach?"

"Do it, then," his father agreed.

Soft, kind hands were placed lightly atop his bare chest. Her touch was warm and soothing. Then there was a slight tingling before energy shot through his body, producing such pain that he sat up rigidly, screaming with a hoarse voice. When the pain ended, he looked around wildly at those gathered near him. All the faces were a blur.

"He is awake now," Tafrara stated coolly.

Khulani's father suddenly filled his vision. "Are you well, son?"

Still numb from the abrupt awakening, Khulani didn't really know how he felt, except that his throat was parched and dry and his stomach growled like a caged beast.

"Water," he croaked.

Almost instantly a waterskin was shoved in his face, and with his father's help he drank deeply from it. After he nearly drained the entire skin, he took a deep breath and looked with clarity at the people in the room. To his surprise, the entire Elder Council, along with the Elder Shamans and the Amgar himself, stared back at him.

Tafrara still stood next to him. She placed a hand on his head, and he flinched, expecting the worst. A mischievous smile appeared on the shaman's crooked face. "Be still, boy, no need to get jumpy." Then she put her ear to his back and thumped his chest before stepping away to face the Amgar. "He will be fine. You may speak to him now."

Without hesitation, the Amgar stepped up beside Khulani and placed a heavy hand on his shoulder. "I am happy that you have come back to us. You are too young to die as a warrior without ever experiencing the joy of being one."

"Where is Frinya?"

His father laid a hand on his other shoulder. "Her body has been returned to the earth and her soul is with the spirits."

"So soon?" The pain in his heart was back, and it saddened him that he was not a part of her burial ritual.

"It has been seven days, my son."

He couldn't believe it. Seven days?

The Amgar cleared his voice, drawing Khulani's attention. "When we found you, Frinya was dead, there were the burned remains of a giant long-tooth, and you were unconscious and nearly lost to us as well." He glanced over at Khulani's father briefly. "We must know what happened."

Khulani was tired and hungry and wanted nothing more than to be left alone to grieve for Frinya. And yet he knew that he must get through this in order to have the peace he so desired. Over the next hour he told them everything and answered what questions they put to him. The only part he left out was his spontaneous use of magic that ensnared the long-tooth before the strangers arrived. He would speak to his father about that when they two were alone. As it turned out, the elders were most curious about the strange hooded people who saved him in the end.

"They must be Druids," Tafrara stated flatly. "What color was their skin?"

"I only saw the face of the woman," replied Khulani. "She had hair the color of fire and pale skin under a painted face."

"They were likely Druids from Eriu—far to the north and across the Great Sea." She looked around the room at the other elders. "No Imaziyen has ever been to their land."

"Then the mystery is why they were here and why they decided not to stay for us to honor them." The Amgar was clearly disappointed that he missed the opportunity to meet them. The Druids were revered as the closest humans to nature on earth, with the ability to commune with the nature spirits. To have one, let alone two, in his village would have brought the Amgar great honor among the other tribes.

Tafrara patted the Amgar's arm on her way out of the hut. "The Druids are a reclusive sort. I'm sure there will be enough of them at Tazallit lhnna for you to impress."

The Amgar glared at her back until she disappeared through the flap door. Even he knew better than to get into a battle of wits with an Elder Shaman. Khulani cast a quick smile at his father, who winked back at him. They both knew that the Amgar and Tafrara were lovers.

~~~

"Tafrara did not understand your injury." Khulani's father paced the space of their hut. "The story you gave left us wanting. It sounded as if you froze in the face of danger. But I know that cannot be true!"

Khulani sat on his mat watching his father. "It is not true, Father. There is more to it. Much more."

Stopping in midstride, Khulani's father visibly calmed and sat on a mat next to his son. "What more is there?"

"When I was very young, mother showed me how to move a stone with my will alone." Khulani nearly choked up at the memory of it. "She told me it was just the beginning, but then she died, and there were no more lessons. I used the same trick to save myself from the long-tooth, but I think I tried to control too much of it and it nearly burned me to a cinder from the inside."

Khulani's father sighed. "I never wanted this for you, my son. Your mother's gift seems to have manifested itself fully in you now."

"So you knew about this talent?"

"I knew about it within your mother, not that it transferred to you as well. Your mother experienced something similar once. She said that drawing the power so quickly and without proper training could burn a body out. It sounds much like what happened to you."

Khulani shivered at the thought. "What now, then? How do we explain to the elders that I am not a coward who falls over at the sniff of danger?"

His father shook his head. "It is not for the elders to decide now."

"What do you mean?" Khulani was confused and a little angry. "The Gathering at Tazallit lhnna is only a few weeks away. If I am to be recognized as a warrior, it will be up to them to make it so."

"It is time for me to tell you something, my son. I never thought it would matter, but now it does." The look on his father's face was almost shamed, and it hurt Khulani to see it. "The Druids came to me secretly a few years ago. They said they were going to watch over you for a time and that I should not worry. Somehow, they knew you had the gift. Maybe they knew your mother did too. I don't know. They said they would decide whether or not to take you by the time you were of age to be sent to the Gathering. That time is now. They will be present at Tazallit lhnna, and if they decide not to take you, then it will be up to the elders to proclaim you a warrior. If any of them have doubts, then I will tell them everything."

"To where would the Druids take me, Father?"

Khulani's father shook his head. "They would not say. Only that you might have to go with them for a while for testing and training to understand your gift better."

"Then all I can do is wait."

~~~

Khulani was happy to have life back to normal. Three weeks had passed since the battle with the long-tooth and the death of Frinya. He mourned her for as long as he was permitted and then set her memory aside with that of his mother's. Imaziyen grieved for loved ones for ten days before accepting their passing. It would dishonor the deceased, who watched them from the stars above, to mourn for them longer.

Somehow, Frinya knew exactly how many skins of magically imbued milk the mammoth calf would need to fully recover and left them buried in her hut to keep them cool. To Khulani's amazement, none soured, and with Rebiku's help, he had the rapidly growing calf back to full health. Today, he planned to start the process of separation. The mammoth was growing too large to stay in the village, and it was time to reunite it with its herd.

Khulani began a daily routine of taking the calf down to the river to drink its fill, explore, and chase the birds bathing in the shallows. At first, the people of his tribe seemed unsure about him caring for the mammoth without Frinya until Tafrara assured them all that Khulani was caring for the spirit of the animal as much as its physical suffering. Khulani's ability to connect with animals was well-known, and by Tafrara's assertion, he could now attend to their spirits. He wasn't sure why she said it or if it was really true. Perhaps she knew something more of his gift than he did.

The next week, Khulani led the calf to a large parade of mammoths on the savanna. At first, the calf was reluctant to join the others. Coaxing it on, Khulani flooded the calf's mind with feelings of comfort and safety. Soon after, the calf hesitantly moved down to the group while Khulani watched from a nearby hill. He was relieved that the mammoths accepted the calf immediately and watched as mothers of other calves allowed him to suckle, and then he sadly returned to his village alone. He would miss his not-so-little companion.

Khulani rose early the following morning, expecting to join his Hunt Pack only to find the mammoth calf standing quietly outside his family hut. Initially, Khulani was happy for the return but worried about the mammoth's affinity for people rather than its own kind. The calf would need to learn to fear humans as a predator if it was going to survive. The Imaziyen would sometimes hunt mammoth when other sources of food were scarce.

Later that day, Khulani returned the calf to the same mammoth herd as the day before. The small mammoth was hesitant to join them, and Khulani felt emotions of warmth and kinship from it. He responded by returning the sentiments.

"I'm sorry, little one, but I have to protect you." Khulani felt tears streaming down his face. He had no choice. "Never fear me—you must fear my kind." He sent images and feelings to the mammoth calf with the impression of Imaziyen hunting and killing mammoth on the Ibhr Rrbi. Memories of his own hunts, the screams of the animals dying, the fear and panic they felt.

To his surprise, the calf did not flee from him in terror as other animals had. Its eyes, deep and intelligent, watched him with a steady gaze and then laid its trunk upon his arm as if in comfort. It understood. Flooded with sadness, the calf rambled down the hill toward the herd.

In the weeks that followed, Khulani visited the pride regularly to connect with the calf and monitor his progress. It was growing big and appeared healthy and content with its new home among the pride. The mammoth was always happy when he came to visit, and Khulani knew that for as long as they both lived, they would always know each other.

Chapter 5

Tazallit lhnna

Khulani awoke before sunrise to the sound of heavy rain falling on the roof of the hut he shared with his father. It would have been a comforting sound to wake up to if the weather had not also brought the heavy humidity. Only a few weeks before the summer solstice, and it was always the same—air so thick it stuck like wet grass to the skin. It was the time of year that random downpours from cloudbursts would leave the trails mussy and grasslands slick and sodden with water.

Despite the uncomfortable weather, Khulani was excited. Today he and Rebiku would depart for Tazallit lhnna to attend the Gathering. Quickly he washed himself with fresh water from a wooden bowl, ate a bite of dried meat with flatbread, and stuffed a few things he would need for the journey into a leather pack.

His father was already up and ready to go, as were many in the bustling village. Not everyone would go to the City of Peace; only the Elder Shamans, the Elder Council, the Amgar of his tribe, and any who, like Khulani, were coming of age. He was glad that his friend Rebiku would be with him on the journey. They had done almost everything together as boys, and they expected to become men together as well.

Those who were leaving gathered together in the Meeting Place with their mounts and travel packs. The rain had finally stopped, although the ground was thick with mud and would require smoothing after the travelers departed. The Elder Shamans, Tafrara among them, waited near the Amgar's hut with the Elder Council, including his father. Softly, everyone in the Meeting Place hummed the traditional travel song while they waited. They waited for the sun to rise, and as soon as Tafukt peeked the eastern horizon, the Amgar stepped out. He wore soft leather leggings and well-crafted leather boots fringed with the fur of rabbits, a thick belt of woven gold around his waist, layers of bejeweled necklaces, and a striped cape made from the hide of a great cat unknown to the Imaziyen. It was said that the Amgar received the hide as a gift from the Enlightened Ones many years ago and that it was magically imbued with powers no one but he and the shamans understood.

Without a word, the Amgar looked over the crowd that awaited him, and then he took to his mount, leading the way north out of the village. Still humming the travel song, the shamans, elders, and the rest slowly followed in a quiet procession close behind. There were many villagers who came to see their loved ones and friends off. They kissed the palms of their hands and waved in a gesture of good fortune to the travelers. There was neither cheering nor fanfare: they were Imaziyen people, and the time for celebration would be upon their safe return several weeks away.

Khulani expected that much of the journey would be along the River Shad and then through the savanna to the Uari Ssamal Mountains. That's where the City of Peace, Tazallit lhnna, would be found—within the mountain range that ran along the northern coast. It would take nearly a week by horse to travel there, but they were lucky. Some tribes trekked from distant locations, taking as long as a month to arrive, unless they could find a Capsian willing to sail them to the Little Shad, which would bring them within a few days ride over mountain passes from the coast.

Khulani knew all of this from the stories his father told him over the years. Every year he watched his father ride off with so many from his tribe, and he envied them. Now it was his turn, and he was proud, and by the look of his father, the older man was proud as well.

To the Imaziyen, Tazallit lhnna was the most sacred location for all their tribes and the only permanent city of their people, except for the Tasili n Ajjer, Plateau of the Rivers, far to the south. The night before they departed, Khulani's father reminded him of the purpose of the holy city.

"As I have explained to you many times, the annual tradition of the Gathering is for boys and girls from all the Imaziyen tribes to gather together when they reach your age and claim their right as a man or woman. What you must remember is that the right is not guaranteed, and if a boy or girl has not proven themselves in their Hunt Pack or by actions in their village, the Elder Council and shamans of their tribe may not support their claim to those rights."

His father did not need to also remind him of what happened to those who failed. Boys were compelled to immediately return to their tribe, alone in shame, until the next Gathering a year later. Sadly, most of the shamed ones never made it back to their village, preferring to live alone in the mountains rather than face their people. Sometimes they didn't survive their solitary trek home, falling victim to wild animals or accident. Khulani feared this outcome the most and understood how such rejection could cause despondence and sap a person's will to live. Girls were required to serve the shamans for a year and restricted from speaking to boys during that time if they failed.

"What is the matter, Khulani?" Rebiku was riding beside him in the long procession. "Your face looks dark, my friend."

"I was thinking about what my father has told me about the Gathering, and I am not certain that the shamans will agree to allow me the right of becoming a man."

"We will both receive the votes and return to the tribe with honor!" Rebiku was upbeat as ever.

Khulani tried to believe it in his heart as well, but he also knew that many of the Elder Shamans frowned upon his meddling with nature and might well wish to keep him back as an example to others. Frinya would have been a strong advocate for him and helped them understand why he was compelled to do the things he did. She understood, as his mother had. The Elder Shaman Tafrara had only taken a keen interest in understanding his gift after Frinya's death. Maybe she would take his side. Tafrara seemed to know something about it that she had not told him yet, but he was sure she would when she felt the time was right.

Rebiku changed the subject. "Did you know there can be no violence of any kind within Tazallit lhnna and tribes that are in conflict with one another must come to have their grievances judged by the Supreme Elder Council?"

"I did know that, my friend." Khulani laughed. "It is good that our people get along with everyone."

Four days later, they arrived at Tazallit lhnna. Khulani was amazed at what he saw. Twice in his youth he accompanied his father to the Capsian city of Capsa, so he was familiar with what the permanent settlements looked like, and he understood a little about the ways of city people. He heard that Tazallit lhnna was much like that, but seeing it now, he could hardly believe it. The city was much larger than he would have expected, with hundreds of stone and mud-brick buildings in neat rows separated by stone-paved streets. To his surprise, there were people other than the Imaziyen crowding the streets of their sacred city. He recognized the merchants from Capsa, TaMehu, and TaShemau; they drove caravans into the Ibhr Rrbi twice a year trading with the tribes. And there were merchants from other lands, selling their wares, that he was not familiar with.

"Impressed, my son?" Khulani's father rode up between him and Rebiku.

"I am, Father." Khulani pointed at the glowing pyramid in the distance. "What is that? You have never spoken of it before." Deep inside Tazallit lhnna he could see a narrow pyramid, the tallest structure in the city, with a crystal pinnacle that shone red in the failing light of evening.

"Ah. It is the dwelling of the Enlightened Ones, and the bright crystal on top symbolizes the eye of Tafukt by day and Ayur by night."

"Will we see an Enlightened One, Elder Boa?" Rebiku asked with no little excitement.

"I'm sure you will, Rebiku. We will be here for the next three weeks, and you will see many wondrous things." His father flashed Khulani a quick smile and a wink and then prodded his horse forward to rejoin the elders.

It was nearly dark, and torches lined every street, illuminating the way while throngs of people hurried about their business one direction or another. It appeared so chaotic and crowded to Khulani, and a little unsettling. He had never seen so many Imaziɣen together, and many even spoke the ancient tongue that his father insisted that he learn. The sharp clicks and tocks of the tongue echoed off the walls of the houses lining the street in distinct contrast to the modern language most Imaziɣen spoke.

"This will be a very busy city for the next three weeks." Rebiku observed.

Khulani nodded thoughtfully. "Yes, and then it will be abandoned to the spirits and the Enlightened Ones until next year."

The Amgar guided them to an area of the city near the central plaza that was reserved exclusively for their tribe. Every tribe was assigned a specific section where they would stay, and the closer their position to the central plaza, the more significant their influence among all the tribes. Khulani estimated that his tribe was honored to be among the top five. When they stopped at a cluster of several dozen residences, the elders immediately took charge and wasted no time assigning places for their people to stay.

Khulani and Rebiku ended up sharing one of the low, sun-dried brick houses that was farthest out in their tribe's section. Leaving their horses with a young stable boy, they entered their assigned dwelling. Khulani was impressed with the large single room that would serve as their living space, complete with a smaller room off to one side for storage. There was a warm hearth in a corner of the main room, providing the only light aside from a ventilation shaft through the ceiling. Khulani marveled at the idea of cooking inside rather than in an outdoor community kitchen like they did at home. The floor in the home was sunken and tiled with smooth stone. His father explained that it would remain cool in the daytime, and there was an abundance of furs, mats, and skins scattered about for comfort and warmth during the chilly nights.

Khulani's father came by shortly after they were settled. "The two of you will be on your own this week while the remaining tribes arrive. During the first and third week of the Gathering, the other Elders and I will be meeting with other tribal leaders to work out grievances, negotiate trade deals, and discuss other matters affecting all the tribes. The Naming Ceremony will take place during the second week. That is when you will be judged."

"What do we do until then, Father?" Khulani asked.

"Stay out of trouble." Khulani's father was staying with the other elders while in the City of Peace, and Khulani expected to see very little of him in that time considering his father's responsibilities to the tribe. "And don't get married."

Rebiku laughed and so did Khulani, but the look on his father's face was not one of jest.

Later that evening, Khulani and Rebiku walked along the streets, browsing at the merchant's stalls and taking in the city. They each had a strip of silver in case they wished to purchase anything from one of the foreign merchants. Khulani found that system of bartering very confusing. How could a small piece of silver have the same value as a pair of soft leather boots or the flank from a hartebeest? It was much easier the Imaziyen way—everyone knew that a hide from a lion was worth two well-crafted spears, especially since there was some jeopardy in obtaining it.

It was late afternoon when they strode near the narrow pyramid with the glowing crystal at its apex. Khulani watched two unusual men exiting the temple. They were strangely dressed in tight-fitting clothes with cloaks that had a pattern resembling wings. More striking than their dress was the unusual nature of their physical appearance. They were both taller than the tallest Imaziyen and absurdly lean, with elongated skulls, large almond-shaped eyes, and blue-tinted skin.

"Those must be the Enlightened Ones your father spoke about," Rebiku whispered to Khulani, although they were far enough away that he didn't need to.

Khulani nodded to his friend. "Watch how they move. It's like watching grey herons on a riverbank. Such grace and beauty," he marveled.

They stood and watched the Enlightened Ones from farther down the street. Khulani's father once told him that the Enlightened Ones were a balancing power in the world, benevolent to all cultures. They respected the Imaziyen beliefs and assisted the Amgar and shamans with advice about guiding their people. He sometimes called them by another name, but Khulani couldn't remember what it was. When the Enlightened Ones walked out of sight, it was like a spell was broken, and Khulani became aware of music and singing somewhere nearby.

Smiling mutually, Khulani and Rebiku set off at a run, following the sounds of merrymaking. Soon they were rewarded with the sight of premature celebrations of young people around the fires in the Central Plaza. There was tribal dancing and a special gift from the Praa of TaMehu—a sharp-tasting drink they called heqet that seemed to have everyone in especially good spirits. Khulani thought back to his father's comment about not getting married and understood why he said it. There were just as many girls as there were boys dancing around those fires, maybe more, and all of them were wild with excitement, expecting to be recognized as adults the next week. Rebiku ran to join the fun with Khulani right on his heels. Khulani would try to keep his father's words in his head, but soon they were forgotten, and his night turned into a blur.

A few hours later, when the fires became a glow of embers and the crowd began to thin, Khulani and Rebiku were exhausted from drinking and dancing all night. They half dragged each other back toward their stone hut. Along the way, they passed the pyramid with the glowing peak casting its crimson illumination over the city. At this hour, with the torches on the street burning low, the earth-toned building seemed painted red, and it sent a shiver down Khulani's spine.

A series of shadows flashed on the ground, suggesting something moving quickly overhead in the direction of the pyramid. Rebiku noticed it also, and they turned just in time to observe several large birds of prey—hawks, eagles, and other sharp-clawed avians—smoothly transform into humans just before landing in the deserted street.

"How is that possible?" Rebiku croaked.

Khulani held his friend from stumbling forward. "They are Druids," he whispered. They were just like the Druids who appeared during his struggle with the long-tooth. The cloaks with bright-colored feathers, the pale or tanned white skin, and the jewelry on their arms and fingers were almost a perfect match to the ones he saw that night. Two of them appeared to be women, one with fiery red hair like the one he saw before, but she was too distant for him to be sure. They didn't linger a moment and filed through the entrance at the base of the pyramid. The red-haired woman was the last to enter, and she hesitated a second and looked in their direction. Khulani thought she smiled, and then she was gone.

Rebiku was laughing and trying not to fall down. "Did we just see that, brother?"

Khulani held on to him to steady himself as much as his friend. "We did, brother. And I don't think it is for the last time."

If Khulani's mother was correct, then his gift had many similarities to that of a Druid's magic. He briefly wondered if there was some important meaning if that were true. At the moment he had trouble seeing straight, let alone thinking, and turned them in the direction of their beds.

~~~

On the night before the first day of the second week, Khulani and Rebiku skipped the dancing and heqet and went to bed early. The next day was going to be one of the most important days of their lives, and Khulani, for one, wanted to stand alert and ready before the Amgar as the Elder Council of their tribe voted on his claim to manhood. Lying on his mat, Khulani couldn't sleep. Although he felt confident that he and Rebiku would both pass, he was still nervous about the Elder Shamans' decision. Finally, he drifted off thinking about how proud his father would be tomorrow and how much he missed his mother.

> *"What am I, Father?" a young boy asked.*
> *"A beautiful bird," said the father.*
> *"How do I become the bird?" the child asked.*
> *"Simply will it," said the father.*

Khulani awakened. It was already late morning, and soon he would be standing in front of the elders for the first time. What was the purpose of such a dream, he wondered. He had not prayed for anything before he went to sleep. Maybe a spirit was trying to tell him something that he needed to know, or maybe it was just another dream.

Washing and dressing, Khulani could not help but adorn his lion cape with a few more colorful feathers he purchased the previous week at the market. In an odd way, he felt as if he were not just representing himself, but also nature when he went before the Amgar and the elders.

Khulani noticed that Rebiku was unusually quiet that morning as well. Did he also have a strange dream, or were his friend's nerves on edge like his own? Khulani would not ask him about it and let him be alone with his thoughts.

A few hours later, it was only he and Rebiku left standing in front of the elders. They were the last two, and it was Rebiku who was called first. One elder asked a question about why Rebiku chose not to lead his own Hunt Pack. His friend responded that it was because of loyalty, and the Amgar defended him by pointing out that Rebiku's first responsibility was to his Hunt Master and that he had performed his duties with excellence. Rebiku was passed unanimously with little debate.

The Amgar approached Rebiku and announced, "We name you a man with rights and a warrior of the tribe!" Taking a knife from a small table, the Amgar cut a thin line on his forearm, causing a trickle of blood to emerge. For many years, this Amgar had been the leader of their people, and his forearms were full of scars from all the warriors he had initiated into the tribe. He ran his finger through the blood and drew a vertical line on Rebiku's forehead to represent virility. Next he put a dab on Rebiku's tongue to represent the sign of menstruation and a blessing to find a fertile woman. This was the Sacred Blood Ritual Khulani had heard only vague rumors about. No one spoke of it openly. Finally, Rebiku was brought forward to receive blessings from the Elder Shamans.

They were standing in the courtyard of the largest house in their tribal section. The sun was high, and he could see only those assembled around them in the sunlight. Khulani knew others stood in the shadows— he could hear the frequent rustling of clothing and quiet coughs. He glanced at his father standing proudly with the other elders. This would be a great day for him as well.

Rebiku received his blessings and was then sent into another room to cleanse his skin with water as a representation of rebirth. It was only a moment later that Khulani's name was called, and he slowly walked to stand before the Amgar. The Elder Council voted to accept him with no dissension, but when it came to the Elder Shamans, they could not agree, and their debate degenerated into a heated discussion among the all of the elders. His father was his most ardent defender, pointing out how his son defended the tribe, nearly with his life, against the long-tooth and in defense of their own Elder Shaman Frinya. Some still doubted Khulani's story and wondered if Frinya might have sacrificed her life to save *him*. Khulani wished Frinya were there to speak the truth.

He cast his gaze around the courtyard looking, for Tafrara. She was not there, and he wondered why. He could use her help if she were so inclined to give it. If they didn't come to agreement soon, the Amgar would step in and forestall any decision until the next year.

Just when things were looking bleak, the Eriu Druid with red hair stepped from the shadows. Elder Shaman Tafrara and several other Druids stepped up silently beside her. Khulani caught his breath. *Why are they here? Have they come for him? No, they must be observing their rituals,* he surmised.

The elders still hotly debated his fate among themselves, but abruptly silenced their discourse when the Druid came forward. This was apparently highly unusual, based on the confused looks on the elders' faces. Still, they held their tongues to respectfully listen to what the Druid had to say.

The Druids made Khulani feel even more nervous. He knew he irritated the shamans with his constant intervention with nature, which they were ideologically opposed to. He flaunted his difference by bringing the wolf and the mammoth and many other wild animals among the tribe. What did the Druids think about that? Did they know? Did they offer advice on the matter? He was working himself up and needed to calm down. He sought his inner peace and waited to be called.

The Druid was not an old woman, but from the respect she commanded in the room, Khulani guessed she was an elder of her people. He recognized the Druid called Buadhach with her. The man's presence reminded him of the strange globe they trapped, the dark shadow that emerged from the dead long-tooth. Seeing the Druids for the first time in the daylight, Khulani noticed leather thongs around each of their necks supporting a colorful egg-shaped stone with a hole in its center. The stones looked smooth to the touch, and if he looked closely, the colors seemed to shift like storm clouds. Khulani was still enshrouded in his mental cloak of serenity, and his heightened senses noticed many more details than he might otherwise have.

The red-haired Druid scanned the courtyard before her gaze settled on Khulani. "This boy, Khulani, we have been watching since his mother passed. She was the one who brought his special abilities to our attention many years ago. It may go against Imaziɣen tradition, but we believe the spirits of nature are pleased and expect much more of him as he grows to understand what you call his gift. Your tribe has produced a most unusual boy—an Imaziɣen who is not only an Imaziɣen." Murmurs rippled through the group of elders. "We believe that he may be one like us, and we recommend that you pass him and allow that we test him in the proper ways to honor the spirits in the way he was created. This would be a great honor for your tribe if he were proven to be the first Imaziɣen Druid." The elder Druid scanned the elders in the courtyard a second time and then returned to her seat in the shadows.

No one spoke. It was plain that this was not something the elders ever considered or even imagined. With a quick gesture, Tafrara gathered the Elder Shamans together, and they spoke in muffled conversation. To Khulani's relief, it did not go on long before Tafrara surfaced from the discussion and looked to the Amgar, and with a quick nod it was over. Khulani passed with a unanimous vote.

"We name you a man with all rights and a warrior of the tribe," the Amgar announced and proceeded with the Blood Ritual and the blessings from the Elder Shamans.

While the dream was turning into reality, he barely noticed the Druids quietly filing out of the room without a word. They had saved him from disgrace, and not only that, they had given him something else. But what it all meant, he did not know.

Two hours later, the testing was over, and there were twenty new warriors and four new shamans accepted into his tribe, and not one presented had been refused.

In the mud-brick house, alone again, Rebiku and Khulani were ecstatic they passed the test of manhood and would be celebrated and respected as warriors at the Naming Ceremony that night.

"I still can't believe that the Druids think I may be one of them. Have you ever heard of an Imaziyen Druid? I have not." Khulani exclaimed to his friend.

Rebiku flashed his big smile, and Khulani could almost guess what he was going to say. "Maybe they just need someone to keep their elephants walking in a straight line!"

"Ha! This elephant walker is still a better wrestler than you!" Khulani dove into his friend, and the two rolled around on the mat-strewn stone floor, laughing.

Chapter 6

To Be Named a Man

"Be still, Rebiku," Khulani hissed.

Rebiku looked at him with a pained look on his face. "You know that I fidget when I'm nervous." It was true. Rebiku swayed back and forth like an agitated cat twitching its tail.

Khulani cast his gaze around Tazallit lhnna's vast central plaza. As one of the taller Imaziyen, he could easily see over the heads of the hundreds congregated for the Naming Ceremony. They were all young men and women, like him and Rebiku, who had reached maturity and gained the blessing of their tribal elders to be declared men and women. Most of them would be declared a warrior, a few might be chosen as a shaman, and then there were those who would be simply recognized as adults. This was the next generation of the Imaziyen, and they were gathered from every tribe that roamed the Ibhr Rrbi.

"Rebiku, look over there." Khulani elbowed his friend to get his attention. A small group of Eriu Druids stood next to a larger group of High Shamans representing each of the tribes, along with several of the Enlightened Ones. It was strange to see them together and even more peculiar how distinct each group looked from the others. Nevertheless, all of them were smiling and chatting as if they knew each other well. Odd that Khulani never considered that the Enlightened Ones had a sense of humor and typical social behaviors. They must not be so different from anyone else. The rumors always suggested that the Enlightened Ones were a very austere people, even a little scary. He wished again that he could recall their proper name. The next time he saw his father, he would have to remember to ask.

"They seem to get along well together." The buzz of the crowd was so loud with conversation that Rebiku had to nearly yell, despite being less than a handspan away from Khulani's ear

Khulani bobbed his head in agreement. "Can you imagine the power those few men and women concentrate in so small a space?"

"Can they stop the rain?" Dark clouds were forming above them, blown in off the Great Sea to the north. It would rain that night.

"I doubt it," Khulani conceded.

Rebiku wore his slyest smile. "Then what good are they?"

Khulani could only laugh.

The entire city turned out to watch the Naming Ceremony, the foreigners included, and they congested the perimeter around the plaza. The only place not packed with bodies was the center of the plaza where a huge bonfire illuminated the approaching darkness. There, the Grand Shaman stood in front of the fire with a clay tablet in his left hand and a stylus in the other. On each side of him stood several Elder Shamans as well as the Chief Amgar and the other Amgars and elders representing their tribes.

Khulani was aware that the titles of Grand Shaman and Chief Amgar were honorary and awarded each year at the Gathering by votes cast by all the tribes' elders. Their responsibilities during the event included leading all the public ceremonies, heading all of the council meetings, and arbitrating disputes within the leadership of the tribes. Khulani's father often complained that the selections were becoming more political each year and usually launched into a discourse about how they used to be based purely on merit.

Then, much louder than should have been possible, one of the Elder Shamans standing with the Grand Shaman stepped forward and spoke, "Welcome Imaziyen, Amgars, elders, Elder Shamans, and, of course, our honored guests from Eriu and Atlantis. I present to you this night, elected in the fashion required by our ancient laws, the Grand Shaman Badru and Chief Amgar Dia. May Ayur send blessings and watch over us this night."

The crowd responded with the traditional shout, "Saaaaaaaaaaaaaaa!"

That was it! Khulani exclaimed to himself. *The Enlightened Ones are from Atlantis.* His father's words came into his head then: *Atlanteans as they are called, or the people of the Emerald Isle.*

Grand Shaman Badru stepped forward. He was wearing the traditional colorful raffia robes of his rank with a wide multicolored necklace sewn of beads and an orange-striped skin cape. It was the same unusual skin the Amgar of Khulani's tribe wore. On his head he displayed a headdress of feathers from wild ostrich that was so long, it flowed down his back.

At first he spoke of Tafukt and Ayur and the primary spirits that were their avatars—creation, life, nature, the hunt, the stars, and others. Then he talked about the attributes that qualified an Imaziyen to earn the respect and title of shaman. Once he was finished speaking, the Grand Shaman began to call off a list of names. When a new shaman's name was called, that person walked from the crowd and received the Blessing of the Spirits and the traditional wide bead necklace from one of the Elder Shamans. Only one Imaziyen from Khulani's tribe was eligible and chosen this year.

The crowd responded to each name: "Saaaaaaaaa!"

Then it was the Chief Amgar's turn to come forward and address the crowd. He wore a short kilt of bark cloth, a wide bead necklace of seashells, and a lion skin cape even finer than the one Khulani had across his shoulders. The Chief Amgar was holding a long spear in one hand and a clay tablet in the other, and he spoke at length about the hunt that guided their migrations and sustained their lives. Khulani was familiar with it all, and still he hung on every word. The Chief Amgar spoke further about the courage of a warrior and the honor it was to become one. Then he began to read off names from his tablet. Like the shamans before them, each new warrior called was greeted by the "Saaaaaaaa!" cheer from the crowd and the Blessing of Spirits from one of the Elder Shamans. Instead of a necklace, the new warriors were handed a spear from the Amgar of that Imaziyen's tribe. When Khulani was called, he received a beautifully crafted spear that he knew was fashioned by his father. He was so proud in that moment that he was almost driven to tears.

After all the names had been called, there were nearly three hundred new warriors and shamans standing in the center of the plaza, spread out in a ring around the fire. The Grand Shaman and Chief Amgar stepped up together and began to sing. It was a song of thanks Khulani knew well from birth, as did every Imaziyen, and after a moment everyone in the plaza joined in. When the song ended, the crowd cheered wildly and surged forward to join those in the center to offer congratulations and well wishes.

The rest of the night, Khulani and Rebiku spent drinking and dancing around the bonfire, breaking at times to hear old stories told by some of the Elder Shamans and Amgars. Khulani couldn't believe the day had finally come that he would be considered a warrior of the tribe, and more importantly, no longer a boy, but a man. This was one of the best days of his life.

After a while Khulani lost track of Rebiku. *He was likely dancing and flirting with the pretty girls.* Khulani had no doubt that if his friend were not careful, he would find himself happily tied like a wild boar to a woman within the year. Women and wives were the last thing on Khulani's mind. He was intoxicated from the heqet, with adrenaline fueled by the music and dancing coursing through his veins. Full of energy, he felt the need to run, and his inebriated brain agreed that it was a wonderful idea.

Breaking from the crowds and into one of the main boulevards, Khulani ran. He was always a good runner, with speed and endurance to rival any of the Imaziyen of his tribe, and he didn't hold back. At first dodging this way and that to avoid people walking to and from the plaza, he was soon approaching the outer perimeter of Tazallit lhnna. Rather than running into the darkness on unfamiliar mountain trails strewn with rocks that could cause him to lose his footing, Khulani stayed on the dimly lit street that encircled the city. He ran and ran, losing himself in the motion and the crisp mountain air that held just enough of an edge that it burned his lungs. It reminded him how good it felt to be alive. The few people he passed waved and smiled, seemingly unsurprised by his swift passing. Maybe they were used to seeing drunken warriors running about Tazallit lhnna after Naming Ceremonies. He laughed out loud like a fool, but he didn't care.

By the time he reached the midpoint of the city's perimeter, Khulani was running as efficiently as he ever had. Once in a while he would pass a long avenue or boulevard that ran straight to the city center, and he could see the silhouette of bodies eclipsing the raging bonfire in a rhythmic orbit. It surprised him that he could see detail in the outlines of those dancing figures, and he wondered if the heqet somehow improved one's vision. He looked down the street ahead of him. Not even the smallest movements escaped his attention—a rat scurrying along the side of a building, a leaf dancing in the light breeze—he saw it all, despite the darkness that surrounded him. And his hearing was heightened as well. Khulani could feel his ears twitch in the direction of the lightest sounds.

He thought it was odd that his ears could twitch in a direction and pick up sound better.

Before long, Khulani realized that he was running faster than he could remember having run before. Within a single pace, he passed a couple walking hand in hand down the middle of the street. He must have startled them when he passed, as the woman screamed in fright and the man moved in front of her protectively. Khulani tried to call back to them an apology, but it came out as a strange grunt. Then, from the periphery of his vision, something caught his attention, and he was compelled to look down at his feet. He felt no surprise. What he saw was like living a waking dream. He ran on all fours, his arms and hands altered and unfamiliar as a part of himself. Still, he recognized their shape and the color of the thick fur as that of a golden wolf from the Ibhr Rrbi and realized that he was no longer a man

~~~

The morning after the Naming Ceremony, a messenger from Tafrara woke Khulani. He was being summoned to the shamans house. Khulani did not want to get up. It was barely daylight, and it irritated him that they would send for him so early after what the elder must have known was a night of celebration.

What a strange dream, he mused while he splashed water on his face. *Was it a dream?* Khulani didn't have time to ponder the strange events of the previous evening. The Elder Shaman didn't like to be kept waiting. He quickly dressed in his best leather and donned his lion-hide cloak adorned with feathers. *Just like the Druids,* he realized for the first time.

A loud snore echoed through the small room. Rebiku was still sound asleep in a corner covered in warm furs. In a small fit of jealousy, Khulani couldn't help but dump the wash bowl of cold water on him before running out of the house.

Khulani of course knew the Elder Shaman Tafrara, mostly because of his attendance at tribal ceremonies at home and his most recent experience. He did not have a personal relationship with her like he had with Frinya, although his father seemed to know her well. Perhaps he was being summoned for congratulations on becoming a warrior to honor his family and the memory of his mother. Of course, Khulani was sure she could have done that later in the day without consequence.

When Khulani arrived at Tafrara's house, he was led through dark corridors to the same courtyard where he and Rebiku had stood just the day before. He was surprised to see Elder Shamans from many other tribes, his father, the Amgar, and . . . Druids. While he stood silently in front of them, the shamans discussed his gift for a long time, never once asking him his opinion, and then the Druids stepped forward and asked many questions. Grian and Buadhach were clearly the elders of their group, and they were the ones who interacted with him the most. They began with what Khulani could only describe as probing magic, and then they observed his gift with different animals brought in to test his ability. Only the Druids seemed to understand this last part. Khulani knew that to everyone else, including the Elder Shamans, he and the animals just seemed to stare strangely at each other in silence.

Finally, Grian turned to the shamans and proclaimed, "This boy will be a Druid."

The announcement was very startling to the Imaziyen. Khulani heard gasps from around the room. In their oral histories, there had never been an instance of a Druid from among their people.

The Druid Buadhach stepped forward. "We suggest that Khulani travel south to the Nabta people, where there is a mission of Druids from Eriu. They will be better able to guide him on his journey to understand his gift and determine the true potential of his Druidic talent."

Tafrara glanced at the blank faces of the Elder Shamans around her and the Amgar. It was clear that none of them knew what to say. She rolled her eyes and stepped forward. If Khulani was not so stunned himself, he might have laughed.

"There is nothing more to discuss in this matter." She addressed the Imaziyen in the room. Then she nodded to the Druids, and she set her gaze squarely on him. "Go to the enclave in the lands of the Nabta people and explore your gift. If it is true, then you will be the first Druid of the Imaziyen people. I cannot express to you the honor that would hold for all of our people." She paused just a moment after a glance at his father. "You will leave in three days."

Khulani was dismissed and sent from the room with no further ceremony. His mind was whirling with a million thoughts on his walk back to the house he shared with Rebiku. Was it true? What did it mean? When would he be able to go home again?

Rebiku was waiting for him anxiously when he returned to the house, and Khulani told him everything about the meeting with the Elder Shamans and Druids.

"Will you go?" Rebiku asked him.

Khulani never considered that he even had a choice in the matter. "I will go."

Rebiku hesitated, then smiled, "Then I will go with you."

"What about the Hunt Pack? They will need you to lead them while I am gone."

"They are doing fine while we are here. They will do fine a little while longer." As silly as Rebiku could be sometimes, once he made up his mind on something, pulling a warthog out of its burrow was easier than changing it.

"Thank you, my friend. Having you with me on this journey gives me great comfort." In truth, Khulani was more than a little relieved that Rebiku decided to go with him. With his best friend by his side, he always felt confident that they could overcome any obstacle along the way.

Later that evening, his father returned to the house. Khulani and Rebiku were there and eager to discuss the day's events. Khulani's father agreed that it would be good for him to learn about his gift from the Druids, and that if he turned out to be one of them, it would be a great honor to his tribe that he would be the first.

His father was also familiar enough with the lands of the Nabta people that he could help Khulani work out the best route to take on the long journey south. "The most direct route through the Ibhr Rrbi will take about fifty days on a good mount." They were sitting in the small interior courtyard that connected with several other dwellings. Khulani's father drew a rough map in the dirt and marked their location. "You could also take the mountain passes to the Capsian city of Thipsu, board a coastal ship to Thunis in TaMehu, take another up the Aur River to the TaShemau city of Nekhen, and then ride the rest of the way across the grasslands to the city of the Nabta people. This last route has more steps, combining land and sea travel but should take ten days less." His father glanced over at Rebiku. "Either way has its dangers. My only worry is that you will go alone."

"I won't be alone," he told his father. "Rebiku will be coming with me."

"Shouldn't you consult your father first?" Khulani's father asked Rebiku.

"I am a man now, so I will tell him of my decision when I return to the family house later tonight." Rebiku puffed out his chest. "My mind is made up, Elder Boa." It was odd to see Rebiku so serious.

Khulani's father gave away a small smile. "Very well. I know how stubborn you are, so I will not try and dissuade you. Besides, there is no one better to be at my son's side on this long voyage. So which route will you boys be taking?"

Khulani looked at Rebiku. "I would like to see the cities and lands along the sea route. Besides, neither of us has ever been on a ship before."

Rebiku agreed excitedly. "I must go see my father before it gets too late and while my resolve remains strong." With a grin from ear to ear on his face, Rebiku left the house nearly at a run.

"There is something I need to tell you about your mother," Khulani's father told his son after Rebiku was gone. "It was never important for you to know this until now."

"Tell me, Father."

His father had a faraway look in his eyes. "Your mother had the same gift as you do, but she never told anyone except me."

Khulani was stunned at this news. "Why did she keep it a secret?"

"She wanted a normal life with children and as a shaman. She knew that if she told the Elder Shamans, she could be sent away for years to learn from the Druids. We were young and happy, and she didn't want her life to change. To cover the unusual nature of her gift, she was careful not to engage the animals she longed to be near unless she was alone. Along with her magical talents as a shaman, she was able to enhance her talents with her gift and conceal them at the same time. That's why she was so unusually talented."

Reflecting back on the times he spent with his mother exploring his gift, she seemed to understand it better than anyone, but he was too young to make the connection. After a long moment, Khulani said, "I remember how easy it was for her to teach me about my gift. I wish we had more time together . . . and not just because of my gift."

"I know, son. Me too," his father responded sadly.

"Do you think I will be away from home for years as Mother might have?"

"I think you will." His father nodded. "But you will be bringing great honor to our family and all the tribes of the Imaziyen. Besides, I will be here when the Druids have finished with you, and I know you will bring back stories of your wonderful experience."

Khulani kept his father up late into the evening with questions about his journey. It wasn't that Khulani needed every detail he could gain from his father's knowledge. He also wanted to extend the time there was left with him as much as possible before he departed. So much of his time was spent with his Hunt Pack over the last year that he somehow forgot the value of spending time with his father. There was no way to make it all up now, yet he would regain as much as he could tonight in case he never returned.

Chapter 7

Unexpected Company

Three days passed too quickly, and Khulani found himself standing with Rebiku saying goodbyes to friends and family before departing the City of Peace. The Amgar of their tribe was next to Khulani's father, and with him the Elder Shaman Tafrara. She came forward and marked his head and then Rebiku's with a sacred blessing— a white line vertical between his brows that was a sign to the spirits to guide them with safe travels.

"You will be the first of our people to take this journey." Tafrara's eyes were intent on him, much like Frinya's the night of the long-tooth. "Do not take your responsibility lightly. The gift you carry is destined to reside in the Arch-Druid of Eriu one day."

Khulani was confused. Did she have a vision? Was she saying that *he* would be the Arch-Druid of Eriu someday? He wanted to ask the Elder Shaman, and then he realized the Amgar was speaking to him.

"The people in the lands you will travel are not as generous as the Imaziyen." He opened one of two small pouches he held, revealing a string of colorful jewels and a few strips of gold and silver that reflected the light of the morning sun. "You will need these to barter for food and transportation." The Amgar handed a pouch to him and to Rebiku. Although Khulani was somewhat familiar with the practice conducted by city dwellers, the previous night his father explained in detail the care he should take bargaining with the merchants and traders.

Khulani's father hugged his son and wished him well while Rebiku and his parents wept like children. That was the way of Rebiku's family—quick to laugh and quick to cry and sometimes both at once! Finally, Khulani mounted Wind Dancer, and with Rebiku alongside, he rode out of Tazallit lhnna for perhaps the last time.

The route they followed wound roughly north through the mountain passes of the Uari Ssamal, forcing them to alternately ride and walk their horses depending on the difficulty of the terrain. The last thing either of them needed was a horse to take a misstep and break a leg. The small horses were bred to run the flat grasslands rather than climb the treacherous inclines like goats over loose rocks and sand. Once they managed to get through the mountains, the land would flatten again all the way to the coast, and it would be easy going east to Thipsu.

"Are you afraid?"

Khulani considered the question. "Apprehensive, I think. How about you?"

Rebiku hefted his spear over his mount's head. "Not as long as I have this." He smiled.

"Then I am glad to have you as my protector," Khulani teased. He knew that both he and Rebiku were equally adept in their fighting skills.

"You just tell me where to find the rabbits when we are hungry!" Rebiku laughed.

On the second night in the Uari Ssamal, Khulani helped Rebiku set their camp on a small plateau overlooking the Little Shad River. He hoped that, with any luck, they would follow the river out of the mountains the next day and camp on the coastal plains in the evening. It was cool but not cold. Since their descent from the higher passes into the ravine cut by the river, the wind had died down to a comfortable breeze. Khulani started a small fire and placed the fish Rebiku caught from the Little Shad under heated rocks.

It was a quiet, pleasant evening, not quite dark yet, and he chatted idly with Rebiku while they waited for the fish to cook. Already, the delicious aroma of the meat was making Khulani's stomach rumble. They had not stopped during the day to hunt or fish, relying only on the flatbread from their packs to stave off hunger.

Khulani was enjoying a funny story Rebiku was telling about a girl he met on a recent night dancing around the bonfire when an unexpected sound reached his ears from below, near the river. Khulani thought he heard what might have been a youthful laugh. Hushing Rebiku, they listened together. It came again, a female by the sound of it, except this time he could hear a second female voice. Quietly, Khulani motioned to his friend, and the two crawled to the edge of the plateau and looked over. From the corner of his eye, Khulani could see Rebiku smile broadly. In the shallows of the river below were two young women, about their age, bathing. It was hard to see them in the fading blue light, but it was light enough to appreciate their athletic figures and natural beauty as they frolicked in and out of the water, their clothing lying neatly folded on the river bank.

Rebiku whispered to Khulani, "They are more beautiful than any woman in our tribe. Do you think they are water spirits?"

"No, I think they are real enough Imaziyen" replied Khulani, "but I didn't know there was a tribe of our people in the mountains."

Just then, one seemed to be looking in their direction, and the men scurried out of sight. A few moments went by, and the laughter continued. Khulani peeked over the edge again. "Rebiku, you must see this." The women below were no longer in the water. They were standing on the riverbank scraping the water from each other's body with tree bark and rubbing in oils that glistened on their perfect ebony skin.

"We should not be watching them." Khulani felt embarrassed.

"Of course, you are right, brother." Rebiku nodded, still smiling, but neither man moved. Their eyes were firmly fixed on the erotic scene below.

Taking their time, the women dressed in their short bark-cloth skirts, fabric tops that tied around their breasts, and colorful beaded necklaces. Then, before they walked into the shadows of the rocks, they picked up long spears and were lost from view.

"Were they carrying spears?" asked Rebiku.

"I think so," said Khulani, "but I have rarely seen a woman carry one."

Returning to the fire, Khulani commented, "I heard a story from an old shaman who said there was a tribe of women warriors that lived in the mountains. Perhaps we have seen them."

The two men laughed about their experience for a while and finished their happily interrupted meal. When they were done, Khulani set a small clay pot on the fire to boil water when he sensed a sweet fragrance in the air.

"May we share your fire?" a calm, feminine voice asked.

Khulani nearly jumped out of his skin, and in a fraction of a second, he and Rebiku were on their feet, holding their spears defensively.

Entering the firelight strode the two young women they spied at the river earlier. They also held spears, casually, and stood staring askance at the men. "What is it about men and their spears?" one asked the other. "I like the one who likes to smile." The smaller woman giggled, indicating Rebiku.

Khulani lowered his weapon and relaxed. "We were not expecting anyone to walk into our camp." Khulani was still annoyed at being startled.

"We did not expect anyone to watch our bathing this evening," the taller one retorted with a smug smile.

Khulani glanced at Rebiku, whose cheeks reddened with intense embarrassment just like his own must have. Rebiku managed a reply, "We apologize for that."

"We didn't mind." The smaller one smiled mischievously. Her eyes almost never left Rebiku.

Khulani leaned his spear against the nearby rocks. "Please, join us at our fire. I am boiling water for tea."

The women expertly stuck their spears in the ground and sat by the fire. The taller one addressed them. "My name is Asha, and this is Binah."

"I am called Khulani, and this is my friend Rebiku."

"I have a local herbal mix that will make a good tea, if I may?" asked Asha.

"Please," replied Khulani. "Our journey is all about trying new things." Asha removed the herbs from a small bag on her hip and added them into the nearly boiling water.

"Tell us about this journey of new things," chirped Binah in a cheery, high-pitched voice.

Rebiku spoke enthusiastically. "My friend Khulani here is going to train among the Druids!" Khulani shot him a dark glance, but it was too late.

"An Imaziɣen Druid? I've never heard of such a thing. Are you a shaman, Khulani?" Asha was staring at him curiously.

"No," he replied reluctantly. "I am not a shaman. I am a warrior. The Elder Shamans of our tribe seem to think I have some Druid talent within me. Probably some little thing." Khulani was quite sure that he had Druid abilities, especially after he learned about his mother, but with strangers he preferred to downplay the oddity.

"A warrior who wants to be a Druid," Asha teased. "You are on quite the journey."

Binah looked at Rebiku. "Are you going to be a Druid as well?"

"Not a Druid!" Rebiku's infectious smile was wide. "I am going to be a great warrior one day!" They both laughed.

Asha passed around the tea, first to Khulani, then to the others.

"What tribe are you from?" he asked Asha. "I do not know of any Imaziyen who live in the mountains.

Asha glanced at Binah. "Our tribe was ancestrally Imaziyen, but we left the savannas generations ago. Our people prefer a more solitary life in the serenity of these peaks."

Khulani was starting to feel unusually content. Never having been in a relationship with a woman before, he assumed that what he was feeling was natural. He had heard that this was the way women made men feel sometimes. He glanced over at Rebiku sitting close to Binah. He had her laughing at his funny jokes and stories.

Khulani accepted more of the tea offered by Asha. "Is your village nearby?"

"Less than a day from here," she confirmed.

"You carry a spear like a warrior, but I know very few women to be warriors among the Imaziyen."

"In our tribe, all the women are warriors," Asha replied proudly. "Tell me more about your people of the grasslands. We rarely meet, as our people never venture out of the mountains."

Khulani's mind was swirling while he chattered about his people, and before he realized it, Asha was sitting very close to him. She was a beautiful woman with dark brown eyes and full lips. Her long black hair trailed in tightly braided rows stacked with beads over her ebony shoulders. They clacked together softly when she moved. She smelled of fresh lavender and would often touch his arm, sending a thrill of arousal through him every time. With nightfall enveloping the camp, he was vaguely aware that Rebiku had moved off into the darkness with Binah and his blankets.

Khulani couldn't tear his eyes from Asha's beautiful face. Were the effects of a woman so strong? Neither he nor Rebiku had ever been with a woman and for the most part avoided the young girls in their tribe before being recognized as men at Tazallit lhnna. He was not sure what was proper for or expected by this woman. For a moment he felt proud that his friend had figured it out. While he was talking, Asha prepared more tea, which he eagerly accepted to quench his parched throat.

Time passed slowly, or was it fast? Khulani was not sure; everything was a blur. All he knew was that he was enjoying himself, his new feelings, and the closeness of Asha. The next thing he knew he was lying on his blankets still talking. Why couldn't he shut up? Asha lay next to him, so close. With a start, he realized she was not wearing any clothing and that she was removing his. Apparently, his response to her was appropriate, and he was pleased that she was pleased. He wanted nothing more than to please her in ways had he rarely considered. She felt so soft and warm and comforting. Her scent was intoxicating, and he felt bold. The next hours Khulani spent learning things he could never have dreamed as she guided him through increasing apogees of pleasure. It was not clear, but the last thing he remembered before he fell asleep, exhausted was her whisper, "I, Asha of the Amazigh, thank you for donating your seed, sweet Druid."

The light of dawn awoke Khulani the next morning. He was feeling refreshed and energized. Looking around, he realized that he was alone. Did he dream the things that happened the night before? What a fantastic dream. Where was Rebiku?

He rose to his feet, naked, and dressed quickly before looking around for his friend. He had a vague memory of Rebiku cheerfully following another woman into the darkness on the north side of camp. To Khulani's relief, he found Rebiku in his blankets under the shadow of a boulder not far away, still blissfully sleeping. Kneeling close, Khulani shook him by the shoulder and his friend awakened, smiling and stretching his limbs.

"Did you have a dream about a woman called Binah?" Khulani wasn't certain that was her name.

"Yes, it was a wonderful dream." He smiled and then sat up, suddenly alarmed. "How do you know my dreams? Is this a new Druid power you have discovered?"

"I don't think so, it must have been real, but they are gone now." Khulani sat down next to him, shaking his head. "I think they were of the Amazigh."

"The Amazigh!" Rebiku exclaimed. "I thought they were just a story the old men told around the fire."

"Some stories are true, it seems," he told his friend.

Rebiku jumped to his feet and spoke urgently, "We should leave before they decide to come back and enslave us."

Rising more slowly, Khulani tried to calm him. "If they wanted us, they could have taken us. I believe they already have what they came for, if the stories are true."

Taking no chances, Khulani agreed that they should leave right away and quickly went about clearing the camp. They were still many hours away from escaping the mountains, and he was determined not to spend another night in their cold embrace. Although he was confident the Amazigh women would not harm them if they returned, he also did not wish to be their extended guest.

It was well after sundown when Khulani and Rebiku made their final descent from the lower valleys of the Uari Ssamal Mountain Range. They followed the Little Shad River all day until they sighted the grassy plains below and the line of azure on the horizon that revealed the first glimpse of the Great Sea. Khulani could not have been happier, and before the moon reached its zenith, they were on the flatlands, sitting at their campfire.

"Are you unwell, Rebiku?" His friend had been uncharacteristically quiet the entire day.

Rebiku forced a half smile. "I must shake the Binah woman off my skin. It is all I have thought about today."

"Me too." Khulani admitted. It didn't matter that he felt used and abandoned. He still thought of her fondly and desired to see Asha again if it didn't mean running the risk of being enslaved the rest of his life. Although, in truth, his spirit already felt enslaved just sitting in his camp with freedom all around him.

"Perhaps we will see them again on our return," Rebiku said hopefully.

"Perhaps." Khulani knew in his heart that he would never see Asha again. He was to become a Druid, and the spirits only knew where that would lead him. It was best for them to forget about the beautiful Amazigh women and go on with their lives.

~~~

The Imaziyen god Tafukt rolled the sun over the horizon, bringing the first light of day to the world. Khulani awoke with the dawn and roused Rebiku to break the night's fast and pack up their camp. It would take at least ten days of riding to reach the Capsian port of Thipsu if the weather was good, and they still needed to get closer to the coast before heading east. Fortunately, the prevailing wind was keeping the rain farther inland, and Khulani thought they would remain relatively dry on their journey despite the humidity.

By midafternoon they rode less than a league from the coast, and the slight slope of the plains toward the sea allowed them a clear view of the water. This was a rare thing for most Imaziyen considering the tribes settled along the interior of the Ibhr Rrbi, far from the coast. Only once in his life, when he was a young boy, did Khulani cast his gaze over the Great Sea. At the time he was learning to hunt with his father, and they strayed near the coast southeast of the mountains the Capsians called home. The weather was not good, churning the waters into violent whitecaps that crashed loudly on the boulder-strewn beaches, and he was overwhelmed by the vastness of it. That was one of the most frightening experiences of his childhood even though they were never in any real danger.

"The Great Sea is beautiful," remarked Rebiku. He had never seen the sea before, and Khulani was glad for his friend that the weather was good. "I hope someday we may cross it together."

"I wish the same, but I am in no hurry. I have seen the spirit angry." He laughed, but Khulani was only half joking.

Over the next few days they made good time. The land they crossed was flat and clear of rocks, making the going easy for their horses. With fewer breaks to rest the animals, they crossed the leagues swiftly. Once in a while they would see the silhouette of a ship under sail or oar moving along the coast in one direction or another. Khulani didn't know much about ships or the people who built them, so he had little idea as to where the ships might be from or where they were going. Unless they were Capsians, with whom his people traded on a regular basis, yet even then it was always by land caravans.

Khulani often consulted the rough map drawn for them by his father and the tribal elders on papyrus from TaMehu. He calculated the distance they already traveled and determined that they were still at least a week away from their destination. Khulani didn't mind. He and Rebiku were having the time of their lives, and the small game was plentiful.

Two nights prior to arriving in Thipsu, a strange thing happened late in the evening after the fire burned down to embers. Khulani awakened to relieve himself when he noticed a strange light hovering in the air far out and above the Great Sea. At first, he thought it was a star or a light from a ship, but it was too high and too close. He awoke Rebiku, and they watched the glowing white orb for some time moving this way and that. At first it moved slowly, and then it abruptly accelerated to impossible speeds. After several minutes of watching this eccentric dance in the sky, Khulani was astounded when two more orbs emerged from the waters below the first and hovered together. A moment later, the third joined them, and they streaked straight up into the air and disappeared among the black ocean of stars above.

"Do you suppose those were spirits?" Rebiku was scanning the sky in case they returned.

Khulani, still shocked by the whole experience, didn't know what to think. "They must be water and air spirits," he answered weakly.

This journey was turning out to hold many unexpected surprises. Khulani sat down on grass that was lightly damp from overnight dew and wondered if this was the way of his life now. Maybe he had been too eager to leave his tribe and family for this adventure. Rebiku plopped down next to him, and together they kept watch over the sea and stars for another hour before returning to sleep.

Chapter 8

Thipsu

Khulani gazed far across the bay at the Capsian port city of Thipsu. He watched the ships moving in and out of the large open port. The walls of the city rising just beyond. Because of the Capsians' unique position as the Imaziɣen tribes' main trading partner, Khulani was familiar with their people and the products their merchants often brought to the Ibhr Rrbi. He recalled the excitement in their village when the traders arrived once or twice a year. They celebrated for a week with festivals and games while his people traded furs and livestock for metal implements to make tools and weapons, dyed textiles, and dried fruit.

He recalled when he and his father visited the capital city of Capsa on two occasions in his youth and was impressed by the endless hills outside the city lined with orchards bearing delicious olives and dates. Capsa was a beautiful city in the mountains that his people referred to as the yellow city due to their ostentatious use of yellow marble from the quarries of Simitthu a few leagues north.

Khulani hoped that Thipsu would be just as grand and impressive, and from the looks of it so far, he would not be disappointed. "Thipsu looks much larger than Capsa," he remarked to Rebiku, who sat astride his horse next to him.

Rebiku agreed. "My father told me it is a very vibrant trade center for merchants from lands on the east side of the Great Sea to trade with those in the west."

"I suppose if everyone is coming to them for trade. That is why there are so few ships out there bearing Capsian colors." Khulani recognized the banners that identified the Capsian and TaMehu vessels, but few others.

"I am happy we are finally here, brother." Rebiku's voice inflected with excitement.

Khulani felt more nervous than excited, especially with the thought of getting on a ship to take them to TaMehu. "Remember that the city people are not the Imaziɣen. We must be cautious not to offend them or act in a way that will draw unwanted attention."

Skirting the wide bay, the men traveled through rolling farmland and a small village before crossing the river on a ferry powered by a single row of oarsmen. Regaining their mounts on the other side, they approached the crowded west gate set into the massive stone wall that surrounded the city. Warriors wearing polished bronze metal armor and gray-plumed helmets directed them to a stable just outside the wall to leave their horses. Near the stables there was an open corral that served as a market for the animals held in rows of holding pens awaiting their turn at auction. There was an array of livestock to be sold, including sheep, goats, aurochs, pigs, and geese, among others. Khulani was relieved not to sense any suffering among the penned livestock. Instead, they seemed to have a domestic contentment unlike what he might distinguish in a wild animal if it were constrained in the same way. The stench, however, was nearly overwhelming, and he was glad when they handed off their horses to the stable boy and entered the city.

Passing through the gate on foot, Khulani was immediately struck by the flows of people streaming to and from the port. "The whole world must be in Thipsu."

"Well, we can stand here and watch them all day or jump in with the herd and try not to get trampled!" Rebiku was always more spontaneous than Khulani cared to be, but he was right.

"OK, follow me!" Khulani carefully merged into the multitudes.

Even where the streets were wide there was the congestion of numerous chariots and wagons that moved people and trade goods throughout the city. He was used to wide open spaces, and the tight press of people made him feel more than a little uncomfortable. It reminded him of the Shad fish when they were migrating to their spawning territory during the summer.

Keeping up with the crowd, Khulani was amazed at the abundance of goods they passed that were making their way to and from the direction of the docks on carts or in baskets carried on a porter's back. He recognized carts filled with olives, dates, timber, ore, and yellow marble. Still, there were many products he was not at all familiar with from other lands. Given the dense population of the city, he was glad that livestock and unharnessed horses were required to be penned outside the walls. Khulani couldn't imagine how crowded and filthy the streets would be if there were goats and aurochs to share them with.

Nearly all the buildings they passed were two or three levels and constructed with stone. Khulani knew something of stone from Frinya, who specialized in elemental magic, and he recognized that the residential and trade buildings were made from limestone, sandstone, or both, while the more impressive administrative buildings and affluent citizens' homes used facings of yellow marble. It was so very different from the mud-brick houses he knew from Tazallit lhnna or the grass huts in his village.

Following the flow of people deeper into the city, Khulani appreciated the Caspian's unusual style of creating figurative and abstract rock art. The pieces ranged from very small personal items sold by street merchants to large statuary displayed in front of walled courtyards of the wealthy residences they passed. Some of it was painted in shades of ochre to match the colorful wall paintings, sculptures, and decorative art that were abundant everywhere he looked.

Among the most notable structures was an enormous pyramid topped by a rotating red crystal pinnacle that hovered just above where the pyramid would naturally peak. It was very similar to the one in Tazallit lhnna, except that this one was far larger. He remembered seeing a small one like it in Capsa when he was a boy and recalled stories told by the elders about similar constructs built in nearly every city around the world. All of the pyramids and towers were overseen, at least in part, by the mysterious Atlanteans known to the Imaziẏen as the Enlightened Ones.

Ahead of them, the crowd somehow managed to part enough to allow a patrol of warriors—some riding chariots and others following closely behind on foot— to pass. They wore layers of padded armor cuirasses, with yellow-dyed leather pauldrons and skirts. The ones on foot carried spears and single-edged blades in belts on their waists, while the warriors riding chariots hung short bows across their backs. Each archer vigilantly kept an eye on the crowd while another warrior guided their vehicle along the road.

The Capsian people were dark-skinned, with slender frames much like the Imaziẏen's. What they lacked was the athletic hardness of their build; their softness betrayed them as city dwellers who shopped at markets rather than hunting for food on the savannas. They also dressed in an array of colorful clothing and fabric materials available through the abundance of trade with foreign merchants. Khulani idly wondered if he would soon look and behave as they did if he lived in a city. The thought made him shudder—he would always be a child of the Ibhr Rrbi.

He tried to focus on the people around him. As quickly as he recognized a Capsian, a foreigner would replace them in the winding press of bodies. There were people from many lands with very different styles of dress and cultural distinctions. Khulani easily recognized traders from TaMehu, TaShemau, and Kerma. They resembled the Imaziyen physically, like the Capsians, except that they wore white linens from the flax plant, lots of gold jewelry, and cosmetics on their faces. He also recognized the traders from Hellas with pale tanned skin and wearing cottons and silks, some dyed with striking colors, and flashing silver jewelry on their arms and ankles. Then there were many peoples that were unfamiliar to him, most with light skin, hair, and eyes that had very different facial features than the Imaziyen. It was exciting to see so many different people from lands he could only dream of visiting in his lifetime.

With the crowds eventually dispersing in various directions, he and Rebiku continued down the main avenue in search of what his father called an inn. Khulani was relieved. No longer were they being swept along with a river of people, and they could take in all the wonders around them.

"This place is amazing," Rebiku remarked when he could be heard above the noise in the street. "I did not think there were so many people in the world."

Khulani ran a hand over his short black hair to displace his nervous sweat. "Thipsu is only one city among many, and according to the Amgar, it is not even the largest."

Before long they found a small inn where they rented a room for the night. It was on the second floor and had an open window accepting the breeze from the sea. There were thick mats and blankets stacked in the corner for sleeping, a small hearth for heat, and a hole in an opposite corner for relief. To men that were used to sleeping under the stars and in small huts, the experience of an inn was new and exciting.

"We don't have to look like we come from the Ibhr Rrbi do we?" Rebiku set his spear in a corner and placed his travel pack next to the wall. "Since we will be traveling through many lands over the next few weeks, why don't we try to fit in better? I wish to go to the market and buy fabrics to wear."

Khulani pondered a moment. "You are right, my friend. People here watch us like hyenas that accidently stumbled into the city on two legs, and I have not seen a single Imaziyen since we arrived. We can get more supplies at the market as well. Just remember the Amgar's advice—nothing too distracting or expensive."

Thanks to the Amgar, they had more than enough gold, silver, and jewels to get them to and from the Nabta people, and Khulani planned to prudently enjoy their journey to the fullest. The last thing their Amgar cautioned them about was the greed and manipulation present in many city-dwelling peoples, and he warned the two about flaunting their small wealth and living above their means. Two men from the savannas would likely draw attention anyway, but if they were assumed poor, no one would bother them.

The men left their spears and supply packs in their room and went downstairs to find the innkeeper to get directions to the market.

~~~

Khulani stood with Rebiku at the edge of the broad central plaza, staring into the market. For some reason, he imagined the market to be a larger version of the caravans that came to his village every year. It was nothing like that. The market was crowded with colorful merchant stalls in long, winding rows with wide breaks every so often so patrons could cross over into adjacent rows. It was very busy, especially around the stalls selling rarer commodities, and loud with the din of negotiations and hawkers selling their wares. Khulani understood negotiating very well since the Imaziyen tribes would often come together to trade tools, weapons, furs, produce, livestock, and a hundred other items. The negotiations between his people were genuine and not nearly as aggressive as what he witnessed here, and he worried that this might be over their heads.

Khulani nudged Rebiku with his elbow. "Are you ready for this?"

His friend's eyes were wide when he dragged his gaze from the market to look at him. "I would rather hunt an Istsa snake with my teeth."

Khulani laughed. "Then let us go into this den of vipers."

The stalls they passed were not well organized by the products that they sold. There was a stall selling produce next to another selling inexpensive jewelry or clay pottery, and it took some time for them to find a stall selling the plain linen clothing they were looking for. The merchant was a thin ebony-skinned man from TaMehu. He was wearing a traditional brown, pleated shendyt with a leather belt; light, yellow linen tunic; a striped nemes on his head; lots of metal rings on his fingers; and dark cosmetics around the orbs of his eyes. He eyed them carefully when they stopped in front of his stall.

"Ah . . . People of the Savanna, Imaziyen, yes?" he asked.

"We are." Rebiku smiled, doing his best to turn on his charisma. "And we would like new clothes."

"What do you bring in trade? I don't want rabbit pelts and hartebeest furs. As fine as they may be, my country is warm this time of year, and furs hold little value."

"We have a little silver if you have what we want," Khulani stated flatly.

The merchant's eyes lit up. "Perfect! Tell me what you need, and I will find it for you." He was smiling broadly now. The Amgar told him that the people of TaMehu and TaShemau valued silver more highly than gold as it was much rarer and more costly for them to obtain.

"We would like linens like what you wear, but with less designs and less color," Khulani said.

"Maybe just a little color," cut in Rebiku. Khulani shot him a quick look, but Rebiku only shrugged innocently.

"I have just the thing for you!" the merchant exclaimed. He strode to the back of his stall and rummaged through the stacks of organized linens on tables and mats. "You two are taller than usual, but I have what you want." He presented two linen tunics with a simple design on the collar and two shendyt without the pleats.

"Would you like a nemes as well?" asked the merchant.

"What is that?" asked Rebiku.

"What I am wearing." The merchant slapped one of the flaps on his striped headdress.

"No, no. Thank you. How much for the tunics and shendyts?" asked Khulani.

The merchant looked at them closely and then scrunched his face. "Five marks on the scale."

"Five marks. Then you must intend to include a pair of sandals for each of us and belts." countered Khulani.

The merchant feigned a shocked look. "How could I feed my children if I gave away what you ask for such a price?"

"Very well, we will seek another stall." Khulani turned to leave.

"Wait!" the merchant said hurriedly. "I will do the sandals, but the belts will be a half mark each."

Khulani half turned. "A half mark for both belts, and the sandals must be good leather, not the papyrus your priests wear."

"But . . ." the merchant started, and Khulani began to turn away.

"Done!" the merchant shouted and quickly gathered the belts and sandals.

Khulani brought out his scale and measured five and a half marks of silver shavings. The merchant verified the weight on his scale, and then they gathered their purchases.

"You have opened my eyes to the sophistication of your people." The merchant spoke with a hint of admiration, and then added, almost as an insult, "Looks can be deceiving."

Rebiku barked a laugh and said, "And we didn't know the people of TaMehu had humor!"

The two men walked away with the merchant staring after them with a confused look on his face, as if he was not sure if he had been insulted or complimented.

Returning to the inn, Khulani was dismayed to find their belongings in complete disarray. Their supply packs were emptied of their contents and scattered all over the floor. Their mats and blankets were tossed around, and their spears lay on the floor. Someone had ransacked their room while they were out.

"I closed the door when we left," Khulani grumbled while he picked up their things.

Rebiku regarded everything scattered about the room. "Did they take anything?"

"I don't see anything missing. They must have been looking for valuables. Good thing we keep those with us."

"Then all they did was make a mess," Rebiku replied angrily.

Khulani shared his friend's anger. Theft was unheard of in the Imaziyen culture. "I bet the innkeeper tipped off a thief or maybe even did this himself after he saw the strip of gold we paid him from."

"Then I will confront him about this disrespect." Rebiku headed for the door.

Khulani grabbed Rebiku's arm as he passed. "Let it be. Nothing is taken, and we did not see the theft. I doubt the innkeeper has the honor to admit his intent and would probably throw us out. Besides, we should not be here long."

After putting everything back in order, Khulani walked to the window and looked toward the port. He was still not used to the idea of a second floor. It was almost evening, and they would not have enough time to find a ship to TaMehu until the next morning. Looking down, he saw the roof of the first level of the inn close below.

"I know how the thief came into our room," he said to Rebiku, who joined him at the window. "From the roof of the lower level of the inn, they could have jumped high enough to reach this window and crawl through."

"Ha!" laughed Rebiku. "Maybe it was not the innkeeper after all! We will have to bar the window when we leave tomorrow. It seems that there are high-jumping hares in the city as well!"

Khulani couldn't help but laugh with him at the silly joke.

The Imaziyen awoke just before dawn, far earlier than most city dwellers, it seemed as they made their way through the nearly deserted streets that were so congested the afternoon before. Barely a light shone in the dwellings they passed, and of the few early risers on the street, most looked to be farmers or bakers, with a few drunks stumbling about.

Khulani was shivering in the light clothing they purchased the day before, and he could see that Rebiku was as well. It was chillier near the sea than on the savannas, especially with the constant wind coming off the water. He regretted leaving their warm capes in the room, but they instantly identified the men as tribal people, and they were trying not to look out of place.

"We will need to buy warmer covers when the merchants open," remarked Khulani between chattering teeth.

Rebiku agreed. "Yes, brother, we must."

Khulani's father had advised him to seek out the dockmaster at any port to find out what ships were going where they wanted to go. He inquired with a cluster of warriors standing near the entrance to the port, and they waved the two men to a rough wooden structure nearby that seemed to have been rebuilt many times in its history. He wondered absently why the dockmaster would not build it with stone if it fell down so frequently.

Entering the small building, they immediately felt comforting warmth from a hearth in a corner of the room. A burly young man sat at a desk, and when they entered, he briefly looked up from a papyrus ledger where he was writing figures. "Greetings, travelers. You are welcome at my hearth this chilly morn."

Like many of the Capsians Khulani had seen, this one wore a heavy colorful top cover and a necklace of shells. His skin was ebony, like their own, and while the tight corkscrew curls of his hair were cut short, they were still thicker than their own hair.

"The light of Tafukt shine on you and your hearth," Khulani replied.

Looking up from his writing, the man carefully put aside his quill. "Our sun god is Ammon, Imaziɣen, but I take no offence. There are many who believe the two are the same and known by different names. If you are here to see the dockmaster, he will not arrive for another hour. You may return to see him then unless I can help you."

Khulani felt embarrassed and realized that they would need to be much more careful interacting with others in their travels. He knew that there were others less forgiving and far stricter in their views about the gods and spirits. His father tried to help him understand that there were many people outside the lands of the Imaziɣen who had very different views about the gods and their relationship with them.

He decided not to touch on that subject and went straight to the point. "We are looking for a vessel that can take us to TaMehu."

The man riffled through the papyrus pages on his desk, and then pulled one from the pile. "There is a merchant ship going to Thunis in two days. It will be laden with yellow marble, olives, some livestock, and other trade goods, making the ship very crowded with the crew and a few passengers, but they may still have room for you. The captain's name is Uetu, and his vessel is in dock nine."

"We thank you." Khulani said, and they turned to leave.

But before they reached the door, the Capsian stopped them. "One moment." Had they done something wrong?

Turning to where the man still sat, Khulani asked politely, "Yes, brother?"

"It is tradition in our land that when one does another a service they respond with an appropriate gift, unless you are paying for the service, which in this case, you are not." He said casually.

Khulani had no idea what to offer the man and his father had not given him advice on the matter. "My apologies, brother. As you have already shown us, we are not familiar with Capsian traditions. Would you tell us what an 'appropriate gift' would be?"

The Capsian was very matter of fact in his reply, "If you have gold or silver, a quarter mark shaving will do."

Rebiku brought out a silver strip, approximated a quarter mark, and handed to the young man.

The Capsian took the shaving and put it in a pocket under his top cover. "A little advice to you. If you are going to TaMehu, the traditions will be similar, but don't flash around strips of silver. Instead, carry shavings so you don't show how much you have. Otherwise the cost of everything will go up, and you might get marked for robbery."

"Thank you for your advice." Rebiku smiled, and the Imaziyen left the building.

The sun was already above the horizon when they were outside again, and the air was beginning to warm up. Khulani expected that it would be very warm and humid again by the afternoon. There were many sailors moving about their ships now, and the docks were becoming busy with the loading of goods and livestock.

"I've never felt such a fool until we took this journey," Rebiku remarked. They strode down one of the long piers toward the mooring where they expected to find Captain Uetu and his ship.

"Even wise men were once fools." Khulani chuckled. "There is hope for us yet."

They found dock nine easily enough; however, there were three ships tied up to moorings, and they were not sure which it might be. Fortunately, several sailors were about, and they were sent to the ship at the end of the dock, the largest.

The TaMehu ship was long and wide, with a single square sail hoisted only partway up the mast and a single bank of oars. There were only two sailors on its deck. They absently worked on lines and ties connected to the sail that needed repairing. The sailors looked much like the merchant they purchased their garments from the day before, except the fabric of the shendyt they wore was less fine and far dirtier. Like most sailors they had seen, these men were lean and muscular, with shaved heads, and went about barefoot. Unlike the others, these carried plain nemes tucked into their waistbands. When Khulani and Rebiku waved from the edge of the dock, one of the sailors walked over to speak with them.

"Beer and bread," said the sailor.

Khulani, confused at the words, responded, "We do not have any."

Looking at them closely, the sailor's eyes narrowed. "You are dressed like people of the Aur, but you're not of them. Where are you from, and why are you trying to deceive?"

Khulani was startled by his words, it seemed as if they were insulting everyone they met. "No brother, we are Imaziyen, and we do not intend to deceive anyone. Only to fit in."

Surprisingly, the stern-faced sailor smiled. "Imaziyen. Yes, I have met one of your people before. He was a good man. I do not cast any blame upon you for your dress. The city dwellers would seek to take advantage of those unfamiliar with their ways. It is the same in TaMehu."

"What did you mean about 'beer and bread'?" Khulani asked.

"It is a traditional greeting among the people of TaMehu and TaShemau, unless you are wealthy."

Khulani nodded his understanding. "We were told by a man in the dockmaster's house that your ship is sailing to TaMehu soon. Do you have room for us?"

"The ship will be crowded with stone, livestock, and a few other passengers, but I think we have room for two Imaziyen and your horses." He gave them a toothy smile, although many teeth were no longer present.

"We thank you. Are you Captain Uetu, then?" Khulani asked.

"I am the Second to Captain Uetu. Call me Musa. We will depart at this time in two days. Bring enough food for two weeks and only one bag each. The captain will probably want two marks from each of you for the journey, and I will take one mark each to keep your space."

Rebiku cut two marks off a short strip and bid Musa farewell until they returned.

"I look forward to our voyage!" Rebiku said excitedly when they walked back up the pier.

"I as well." Khulani smiled broadly. "But we have much to do before we leave, and before we go to another merchant we should take the Capsian's advice and cut a few strips of our gold and silver into smaller sizes."

Rebiku agreed and then smiled wryly. "It is strange to feel like prey among so many predators."

"Then we must scurry unnoticed like the Rrbi mice and keep our teeth sharp. I doubt we could know much less about the unseen dangers lurking among the city dwellers."

Chapter 9

Seafarers

TaMehu and TaShemau, the two brothers of the Aur. So much alike that to travel from one to the other will leave one wondering at the distinction. Even still, they are great builder cultures that will leave monuments that will last the ages with mysteries never to be unraveled. It is a sad commentary on two great civilizations that their lasting impression will be buried in time capsules of death and the riches packed with them on a journey to nowhere.

—Wodanaz the Wanderer

Khulani and Rebiku stood on the forward deck of the TaMehu merchant ship. There were others gathered there with them, and it looked as if it was the best place to watch the city change to land and the land change to the sea. Slowly, the single bank of rowers propelled it out of the Bay of Thipsu and into the expanses of the Great Sea. The sizable yellow marble blocks they transported took up much of the open area of the main deck, leaving little space to accommodate the livestock and passengers. A vessel this size had very limited cargo space belowdecks and no cabins, even for the captain. Khulani noted that there were four other passengers besides him and Rebiku who would share the shade of a small shelter covered with animal skins and fabric. It was sufficient for good weather, but since it was open on the sides, there would be little protection from the rain and wind. The captain had not spoken to them apart from requesting payment for their passage. He was busy getting the final goods aboard and then guiding the ship out of port—too busy for idle conversation.

An hour later, the ship was well into the open waters of the Great Sea, and the captain approached them with a grand smile. "Welcome aboard the *Rom*! Once we push a little farther out to sea, we will set the sail and enjoy a strong wind pushing us east. This voyage will be long and possibly dangerous, as it will take nearly fourteen days to reach Thunis, with no ports in between." The captain clearly had a flair for the dramatic, and it was obvious to Khulani that he had repeated this speech many times in the past without losing his passion for presentation. "These waters are rife with pirates and slavers seeking easy prey. They are mostly from the Lukka lands, but there are others from as far away as Tartessos who would profit by the goods we carry and the slaves they could make of us." The captain looked over the faces of the passengers gathered around him. "Have no fear! My crew are not only the best sailors from TaMehu, they are trained warriors capable of defending the ship and your lives!" With a histrionic flourish of his nemes, the captain turned and strode amidships shouting orders to his crew to ready the sail.

Khulani cringed when he heard the predictable laugh that came from Rebiku. His friend couldn't contain himself when it came to the absurdity of the situation. The other passengers nervously laughed with him, although it was doubtful they knew why. This was going to be an interesting two weeks at sea, and Rebiku made no secret that he hoped for more of a show from the captain to keep them entertained.

Just as Captain Uetu foretold, the wind was at their backs as soon as they turned east, and the heavily laden ship moved faster than Khulani thought possible—faster than a running horse, if he could make the comparison. The wind was warm and comfortable against his skin, and the sun was high but not too hot. He felt a little unease in his stomach from the rolling movement of the deck under his feet at first, and he found himself grateful and relieved when the sensation passed.

The crew was constantly busy with the endless tasks of running the ship and appeared to be highly experienced, from what Khulani could tell. Fortunately, their infrequent and curt conversation loosened up after a few hours, and they became quite friendly with the passengers. Khulani had to believe that being out on the open water, on a ship of any size, must be constricting to the crew. No one was a stranger here, and indifference toward others, as in a city like Thipsu, was happily absent. Khulani and Rebiku, especially Rebiku, enjoyed distracting themselves from the never-changing seascape by getting to know individuals of the crew, understanding the dynamics of the ship, and observing the role of the crewmembers' individual efforts to keep the ship functioning and efficient. Khulani was attentive but stayed out of their way. He was curious about their work and was already becoming restless before the end of the first day at sea.

By the next afternoon, Khulani was tired of staring at the water and the passing coastline. He started to take an interest in the tasks of the crew, no matter how menial, and it wasn't long before crewmembers were teaching him and Rebiku about the different kinds of nautical knots. At first, the captain expressed aggravation and grumbled about the intrusion on his crew's duties, but soon he was quieted by the crew's open remarks about how competent and hardworking the two Imaziyen were, and he allowed them to help out as long as they didn't get in the way.

On the third afternoon after leaving Thipsu, Musa confided to Khulani that Captain Uetu was one of the few from TaMehu who had been able to avoid conflict on the seas in the years he plied this highly profitable route. They were always fortunate to have favorable winds, which kept them moving at a fast, steady pace day and night with rested oarsmen. The real danger, he told them, was the route back to Thipsu, which was very slow going, taking twice the number of days and for the most part under oar.

After four days, the captain announced that they would anchor for a few hours off the coast and let the crew bathe in the water and go onshore to look for fresh water and a hare or two. Khulani and Rebiku took the opportunity to do what they did best. They quickly disappeared into the grasslands and returned less than an hour later with two hartebeest, which they field dressed and cooked for the enjoyment of everyone on the ship. There was enough meat to last at least three days, and they turned it over to the captain to dispense fairly until it was gone. After that, the captain let the Imaziyen do as they wished onboard, even teaching them the basics of navigation at sea using the sun during the day and stars at night. Khulani was beginning to enjoy himself and wondered why anyone would find this way of life so demanding.

When they stopped again a few days later, the Imaziyen came through once more with an aurochs. The captain had to send half the crew to drag it to the beach to cook up. It was a massive beast that Khulani and Rebiku showed the crew how to clean and properly butcher. Their efforts would provide the ship with meat for at least another five days.

"In all my years on the sea between Thunis and Thipsu, I don't think we have ever eaten so well!" Musa happily told Khulani. "We should bring Imaziyen with us on every voyage!"

"Ha!" Rebiku snorted with glee. "You would never be fortunate enough to find enough Imaziyen willing to step on a boat."

Musa thumbed his nose. "You two managed to do it!"

"Ah, well. We are the bravest of them." Rebiku showed his widest grin.

Khulani just laughed. He was starting to really like Musa.

Just after dawn the next morning, there was a commotion on the vessel. The crew rushed to the starboard bow of the ship. Some of the men carried gaffs and plunged them over the side and into the water. Khulani followed Rebiku out of the small shelter and sprinted up next to the captain, who stood looking over the water in front of his ship with sadness in his eyes.

Floating in the water ahead was the smoldering wreckage of a ship and her crew. The men with the gaffs vainly reached out to prod and turn the bloated bodies, hoping to find one with life—there was none. The debris all around them made it difficult to navigate, but the captain was determined to check each man.

"This was a ship from TaMehu," said Captain Uetu. "They must have been attacked by the Lukka before dusk last night. Only the Lukka burn the ships they attack as a way to instill terror in anyone who finds them."

"What kind of people are these Lukka?" There was anger in Rebiku's voice. Khulani felt it too.

The captain's face altered to form a scowl, and he spit on the deck before answering. "The Lukka, or Sea People as some call them, are from lands across the Great Sea. I have heard that they live in huts and do little to support themselves with their lands, but I have only seen them in the small ships they sail when they are chasing down a merchant, so I don't know if that is true. Their ships are small and swift, and they ply the sea in packs, easily overtaking any unlucky merchant vessel they find under oar. Everyone knows the fate of those they capture." He gestured toward the bodies in the water. "That is why they are so feared."

"Are they still nearby?" Khulani asked with concern.

"Not likely. Whatever they looted from that ship would make their small vessels too heavy and slow to continue their search. They are probably on their way back to their cursed villages to unload and resupply."

Khulani shook his head. "Did you know this ship and its crew?"

"No, but they were like us, simply trying to make a living bringing trade between two cities." Captain Uetu spoke a blessing to the fallen sailors, then turned to his crew. "Leave off!" he commanded. The crew put away their ropes and gaffs and went to work setting the sail to get the ship back up to speed. Within minutes, the soggy remains were left far behind them.

~~~

Captain Uetu navigated the *Rom* against the northward-flowing current of the first major distributary of the Aur delta. Fortunately for their progress, the wind was still with them, and the great square sail kept the ship moving forward at a respectable clip.

It was the afternoon of the thirteenth day at sea, and Khulani craved the feel of green grass between his toes and solid ground that did not constantly shift to stand upon. In spite of his discomfort, he was very pleased with the lush terrain they passed sailing up the Aur River. The marshes that dominated the delta flourished with life, and he could sense the wild freedom of the animals that inhabited the region. Everywhere, as far as his eyes could see, there were red lotus blooms floating on still water and huge flocks of water birds resting or in flight from one area to another.

Musa turned out to be quite the talkative sort and spent the hours diverting their attention from the long voyage with stories about his people, trade, agriculture and religion. *TaMehu*, he informed them, meant, *the land of papyrus* in his tongue. Khulani could understand why, since the banks of the river where thick with it from the moment they entered the delta.

As they sailed farther inland, the ground became less saturated, and crops appeared, tended by local farmers living in small villages that dotted the landscape. Musa pointed out that barley, cereals, grains, papyrus, and flax were some of the more common agricultural products they grew.

"The dirt here is the blackest I have ever seen," Rebiku remarked to Musa. "What is the reason?"

Musa raised a dark eyebrow and whispered in mock confidentiality, "That is the secret of our bountiful harvests! Every year the Aur River floods, depositing black silt rich with sedimentation carrying life-giving nutrients for our crops. It is the seed of Atum for serving him well." He pointed to the many canals and trenches that stretched far into the distance, segmenting the farmland. "There you can see the irrigation that brings the waters of the Aur far into the fields. Soon it will be time for harvest and the festivals that come with it!"

Khulani nodded his appreciation. "The Imaziyen know little about farming. We grow only leafy vegetation in small gardens and hunt the Ibhr Rrbi for mainly hartebeest and roots. And when the herds move on, so do we."

"I heard there was a city far to the south where the Imaziyen lived. Is this place real, or is it like your City of Peace, Tazallit lhnna?" Musa asked.

"No, it is inhabited all of the year, and the only village of the Imaziyen that never moves." Khulani replied. "But they have changed and are no longer exactly Imaziyen, according to our elders. The village is called Tasili n Ajjer, and few of us who live on the Ibhr Rrbi have ever been there.

"Look!" Musa shouted abruptly. "You can begin to see Thunis ahead!"

Indeed, the walls and a few of the higher structures behind them could be seen in the distance. Watching the city slowly grow larger as they approached, Khulani was surprised to see that Thunis boasted a very busy port.

Captain Uetu joined the three of them at the bow. "I suppose you two will be happy to find your legs back on land again."

Rebiku nodded vigorously. "The gods did not make the Imaziyen to ride the sea well." He laughed.

"Captain, the port appears to be thriving. Why is it then that we have passed so few vessels on the river?"

"Those ships were mostly foreign traders that go only as far as Thipsu to pick up goods brought from as far away as TaShemau and the kingdom of Kerma." Uetu shrugged. "Like this ship, they are not built to navigate the hazards of the Aur farther south. Beyond Thunis, the Aur is very busy with river trade moving up and down from one city to another."

"So you never sail south of Thunis?"

"Not on the *Rom*." The captain scratched the darker stubble on his ebony, sweat-laden bald pate. "I will offload my goods for my trade partners to take farther south on their river boats. Most of what I carry is reserved for specific customers. The rest will go to market."

The port of Thunis was built along the east bank of the Aur down the length of the river. Although it was hard to tell, because it was spread out so far, Khulani thought that this port might be larger than the one they left at Thipsu. Not far from the docks, high white limestone walls with flat-topped towers along their length stretched into the distance. The walls appeared to encompass the entire city. A large wooden gate was open to the port allowing trade to flow in and out between the city and the docks. On each side of the entry, great symbols with sideways-oriented figures of people twice the height of a man were carved into the walls. The captain translated the symbols as the city's declaration that it was dedicated to the god Hu, who represented the deification of the Word of Creation.

Spying an open mooring, Captain Uetu quickly took his leave and shouted orders for his men to prepare to dock. Musa was right behind him, making sure the crew did as they were told quickly enough. Before long, the *Rom* was skillfully docked and tied down.

A member of the crew brought over their horses while Khulani and Rebiku gathered their belongings. Then there was hand clasping, back patting, and blessings from the crew for their continued safe journey. They had all grown close over the past two weeks, and Khulani wondered if he would ever see them again. He hoped so. Captain Uetu was very appreciative of the supply of fresh meat during their journey as well as their hard work learning the ropes of the ship and giving the crew a hand where they could. He recommended a safe inn for the two to stay at while they were in the city and the name of a captain he knew who would likely be willing to take them farther up the river. With sincere smiles and waves, the Imaziyen departed the ship with their mounts and walked the crowded road into the city.

Thunis was a cluster of mud-brick and stone buildings separated by narrow alleys off the central road through the city. There were stalls of merchants along the road rather than an organized market district. The palpable stink of penned animals filled the air almost to distraction. In the center of the city, Khulani could see a short pyramid that rose just above the one- and two-story buildings packed tightly around it. This pyramid, like the others they had seen, also displayed at its apex a rotating red crystal. Based on some of the stories the crew of the *Rom* had told them, pyramids carried different meanings for different cultures. Some cultures believed they were religious symbols of the gods or holy places to inter their kings and serve as temples. Others, like the people of TaMehu, believed that they were not only holy places, but also served as tools to study the movement of the stars. Musa told them that besides the TaMehu priests, only the Neteru, representatives of the gods, and their priests were allowed in the pyramids. The Neteru were considered living demigods, respected by the highest and the lowest in TaMehu. It was only when Musa described their odd physique that Khulani realized the Neteru where the same people the Imaziyen referred to as the Enlightened Ones.

Musa further explained that the Neteru were highly revered among the people of the Aur and were said to never make demands, but offer only guidance to the rulers of TaMehu and TaShemau. According to Musa, it was written in the ancient sacred texts that the Neteru were "sent forth from heaven" by the god Atum to guide and instruct the people of the Aur. It was said they first arrived on a flying ship in ancient times and stayed to counsel TaMehu's rulers over the generations. They were currently present to advise the Praa of TaMehu, their king, in the capital Inbu-Hedj and had the benefit of complete access to all of the temples, sacred places, and royal palaces in TaMehu. From the time of their arrival, it is said that their kingdom was blessed with peace and prosperity.

Musa told Khulani and Rebiku about ancient stories of misguided Praa who tried to manipulate the Neteru into helping them to gain lands and conquest over their neighbors, but the Neteru declined and even thwarted TaMehu's aggressive efforts. The most well-known example of a Praa's folly occurred many decades earlier during a war between TaMehu and TaShemau. Known as The War of the Brothers, the bloody conflict lasted for ten years and devastated the economies of both kingdoms. The Neteru refused to support either side and abandoned both countries for many years thereafter, leaving them to face famine and foreign invasions on their own. When the Neteru finally returned, the Praas from both kingdoms begged them not to leave again and promised to negotiate a lasting peace. The two kingdoms had been true brothers ever since.

Khulani was going to miss the conversations they had with Captain Uetu and Musa about their people's culture and tradition, and most especially the deep historical knowledge they savored so much.

Just like in Thipsu, there were people from many different lands in Thunis. The most disturbing sight to Khulani were the slaves, dressed in simple white shendyt and nemes, running from place to place doing their masters' bidding. TaMehu and TaShemau were known for their tradition of slaves and slave labor. Slaves were common, consisting of captured enemies, debtors, and criminals. Most were slaves for a specific period of time and then released, usually after ten or twenty years. Then there were others with severe enough crimes that they would be slaves their entire lives. Another tidbit from Captain Uetu: slaves could purchase their freedom if they or their families had the resources to do so. The whole idea of slaves did not sit well with Khulani. In his tongue, *Imaziɣen* meant *free people*, and slavery was unheard of.

The Imaziɣen found the inn without too much trouble and spotted a stable boy to watch and care for their mounts. Now that they were dressed similar to the people in the city, they barely got a second glance. The people of TaMehu were likely to see them as local villagers rather than foreigners. Most of the populace had probably never seen an Imaziɣen anyway.

The inn's common room was filled with a few locals lounging on stools, mats, and tables. Khulani had been warned by Captain Uetu that seating was determined by wealth and status, with the people of higher ranking sitting at the tables, lower status on the stools, and the lowest on mats or bare floors. The captain suggested that the best way to determine what status they fit into was to simply do as others wearing similar clothing did. In this particular tavern, they would sit on stools.

One thing Khulani knew of TaMehu and TaShemau was their talent for brewing a barley-based heqet. Every tavern had its own specialty, but only the heqet produced by the royal brewery in each city had any real consistency. It was also the most expensive. They first tried the royal brew onboard Captain Uetu's ship when they made stops on shore. It didn't take long for them to realize how much TaMehu people loved heqet, which inevitably led to dancing, singing, and more drinking.

This tavern was owned by Captain Uetu's cousin, Intef, a pudgy, jovial man wearing a permanent smile and a laugh on his lips. "My cousin sends you! How is Uetu? Will he be coming by this time?" Intef was constantly moving, and the Imaziyen followed him through the common room as best they could.

"Uetu sends his best and promises to come by before he returns to Thipsu," Khulani said quickly on Intef's heels. "He suggested you might have a room to rent with clean mats?"

"Uetu never sends his friends to my inn! He must really like you! Of course, a room for you is no problem." He laughed. "And the mats are even clean!" Intef led them through a door into the back, where he barked orders to the kitchen staff. He closely watched the various plates filled with emmer wheat breads flavored with coriander seeds; fruits platters; bowls of dried dates, raisins, and cucumber; as well as lots of heqet, perfumed liquors, and varieties of wine that were sent out to the taverns patrons.

"Go upstairs to the room with red mats. You can leave your things there safely. No one will bother them here," Intef told them absently before he rushed back into the common room with two cups of heqet meant for an impatient customer. "Come back down if you want anything to drink or eat!" He laughed, nervously while threading his way through the increasingly crowded room.

Rebiku shrugged at Khulani, and they looked around for the stairs leading to the second floor. With a bit of searching, they found the stairway in the back of the room behind a wooden partition. At the top a large man was sitting in a chair, wearing a decorated nemes, and carrying a club.

"We are looking for the room with red mats?" Rebiku inquired with a smile.

The man pointed with his club down the hall. "Second room."

Khulani saw only four doors. This inn was more of a tavern that had a few small rooms to rent. The first doorway they passed had a wooden door, and the second was covered only by a curtain. Looking inside, they discovered clean red mats on the floor, a hole for relief, and a narrow window too thin for anyone to crawl through. The window cast the only light into the dim room. Khulani was not disappointed. The room was cool and comfortable, the mats were thick, and there were more blankets in a square chest in case it got cold.

After resting most of the afternoon, Khulani and Rebiku went back down to the common room, intending to have a light meal. It was louder and more crowded than earlier. Patrons crowded the common room and spilled out onto the street, where Intef had set up tables, stools, and mats for those who wished to enjoy the cool evening.

There was nowhere to sit, and they would have to push through the entire room to get outside, so they decided to stand near the kitchen where a server brought them clay cups of house heqet. Almost immediately, Intef rushed by and noticed them standing. Urgently, he beckoned for them to follow. They hurried to keep up through the kitchen and out into an open courtyard in the back. There were a few patrons lounging on fine furnishings, listening to entertainers playing the arghul and sistrum accompanied by beautiful dancers who wore sheer silk kalasiris and clicked castanets. Servers with trays of dates, fruits, and bread circulated among the patrons, offering delicacies and filling empty cups.

Intef stopped and turned to them. "I apologize for my ignorance. Only an hour ago did I receive a message from Uetu that you were princes of the Imaziyen and that he would personally cover your expenses during your stay." Without waiting for a response, he turned to the room and announced to everyone there, "Presenting Khulani and Rebiku, princes of the Imaziyen!" Then he rushed off to his next task. There were polite nods and smiles from the clearly affluent patrons of this exclusive room. Rebiku immediately burst out laughing, and Khulani, too startled to think of anything else, joined in. The patrons in the room looked on politely and laughed with them, which only heightened the absurdity of the situation. The captain had a fine humor, it seemed. Soon the drinks were flowing freely, and the Imaziyen were enjoying lively conversations with the other inebriated patrons.

The next morning, Khulani woke up to a pounding headache and a naked companion curled up next to him on the mat. Glancing across the room, he noted the presence of another companion under the blankets next to Rebiku. As best he could remember, they were two of the beautiful dancers in sheer clothing who were entertaining the private room the night before. He wished he could remember more than a few hazy images from when they came back to the room.

Intef again proved his diligence by leaving a covered pot full of steaming boiled cabbage and flasks of cool water for when they awakened. Khulani got up first and went for the cabbage right away. Rebiku and the two women followed a little while later. After the meal, the women dressed and said their goodbyes, promising to see them again soon.

Alone in the room again, Rebiku smiled broadly. "You should have become a Druid a long time ago."

"I have to admit that I did not expect to enjoy this journey so much." Khulani leaned back on his mat.

"We should probably leave soon."

Khulani didn't see why they should be in a hurry. "Why is that?"

Rebiku was smiling as if he were about to tell the greatest joke ever. "Before the dancers return with their fathers."

"Why would they do that?"

"I vaguely recall that they think we are princes, and we might have promised to marry them."

Khulani sprang from his mat. This was no joke. If the TaMehu people were anything like the Imaziyen when it came to their daughters, then they could be in serious trouble. "Get up, Rebiku! Captain Uetu said he knew a captain who would take us south. It's time we found him!"

Chapter 10

Dancers

The sun was still low over the waters of the Aur when Khulani and Rebiku arrived at the busy office of the dockmaster. They were looking for Captain Hepzefa of the river ship *Mew-Hanej*, and after an hour wait, a clerk informed them that the ship was still in port. Just barely. It was scheduled to depart that very afternoon with a full cargo to the TaMehu capital city, Inbu-Hedj. Without delay, the Imaziyen sprinted down the dock in search of the ship that would be their salvation from Thunis.

"Uetu sent you? Very well, we leave in two hours. Be on board. We will not wait." Captain Hepzefa exhibited a more severe countenance than Captain Uetu, but he was willing to take them as far as Inbu-Hedj, and that was good enough for Khulani. Mindful of their time, they hurried back to the inn to retrieve their packs and mounts.

Intef was scurrying around the common room when they arrived, and Khulani quickly walked over to speak with him. "Thank you for your hospitality," he told the innkeeper. "You have made us feel at home during our brief stay."

"You are leaving?" Intef sounded disappointed. Khulani wondered if he might be charging his cousin premium rates to cover their expenses.

Khulani matched the innkeeper's expression. "We have urgent business south that cannot wait, I am afraid."

"And if anyone comes by looking for us, please express our sincerest apologies for our hasty departure." Rebiku chimed in.

Khulani wanted to smack his friend in the back of his head. It would have been better to have just quietly departed. Now the innkeeper might think they were fugitives. Maybe that's just what they were, for all Khulani knew about the TaMehu laws regarding promises of marriage. Remembering the lesson they learned from the Capsian, Khulani pressed a few marks of silver into Intef's hand to the man's surprise and appreciation. Hopefully, that would buy his silence, at the very least.

Once they had their horses penned onboard Captain Hepzefa's ship, Khulani followed Rebiku to an open spot on the deck near the bow. The *Mew-Hanej* was very similar to the *Rom*, except that it seemed to ride higher on the water. Just like Captain Uetu's ship, this one was outfitted with a single square sail and one row of oars. On this voyage, they were the only passengers on board, and Khulani had the distinct impression that it was highly unusual for this vessel to have any passengers at all. The captain informed them curtly that they would arrive in Inbu-Hedj on the evening of the third day on the river assuming that the winds stayed strong and they did not stop. After that, no one spoke to them. The crew went about the ship efficiently preparing to depart.

Just after midday, Captain Hepzefa ordered the crew to cast off, and the oars men pushed the *Mew-Hanej* away from the dock. When they were barely away from the moorings, Khulani heard shouting above the noise of the crowds along the waterfront and looked up to see a group of men pushing toward them through the throng.

"Tafukt burn me," Rebiku muttered. And then Khulani saw two familiar women trailing behind the knot of rushing men.

The dancers.

Rebiku turned and shouted to Captain Hepzefa, who was standing amidships, distinctly unsure of what was happening. "Will you be stopping for our friends, Captain?"

"There is no room for them," the captain growled.

"Too bad, then." Rebiku was all smiles then and leaned over the portside railing. "We will miss you!" He waved cheerfully at the dancers and the men running parallel with the ship on the dock. Their shouts and calls for the captain to stop the ship fell on deaf ears. "So sorry we couldn't stay longer! We will remember your beauty forever!"

Finally, the ship gained enough speed to leave the angry men behind, and Rebiku sat back down next to Khulani.

"Your humor can be cruel sometimes, brother." Khulani was more embarrassed than angry.

Rebiku shrugged. "They were intent to take advantage of Imaziyen royalty. As if there was such a thing. If they caught us before we departed then we would have been forced to marry their daughters and likely stoned to death when they found out we weren't really princes."

Khulani could only shake his head. It seemed like stumbling in and out of trouble because of their ignorance of other cultures was becoming a common theme of their journey.

~~~

Just as with Musa and the crew of the *Rom*, Khulani attempted to lend a hand with the crew of the *Mew-Hanej*. After what he and Rebiku learned from Musa, he thought they would be grateful for their help. Captain Hepzefa would have none of it. He stiffly ordered the pair to stay out of the way. Feeling a little dejected, Khulani sat with his friend at the bow and watched the fertile land pass in front of them. It didn't take long for Rebiku to regain his humor, and before long he had them both laughing over their nearly tragic nuptials to the pair of Thunis dancers who thought they were princes.

Khulani's mood improved considerably after that. "Before our journey is over, we will have some very interesting stories to tell our pack mates," he remarked.

Rebiku's smile stretched across his face. "I certainly hope so!"

During the night, their ship passed the city of Pe-Dep. Khulani knew they were close by the red glow that radiated from what he guessed must be one of the Neteru structures with the rotating red crystal on top. Although Pe-Dep did not have a wall surrounding it, there was an entryway of sorts that faced the river, separating the port from the city proper beyond. The most notable things about the entryway were two giant cobra statues with sparkling red eyes. They stood on each side of the arch, with a wide roadway passed between them. He could see the dark silhouettes of houses and buildings, some with torches illuminating a small area outside and others with dim light peeking from between curtains. It was late, and Khulani didn't bother to wake Rebiku to see it, which he would regret later, knowing how enthusiastic his friend was to experience everything in this strange land.

While he watched Pe-Dep slip into the darkness behind the ship's wake, a crewman working the night shift whispered that the city was originally two smaller settlements that grew together over time. Khulani, having lived his entire life with his tribe following the hartebeest herds, wondered at the significance of the sailor's statement.

He supposed the city dwellers found comfort in a less transitory lifestyle that depended on trade and agriculture to subsist.

Khulani enjoyed the quiet serenity of the night, watching the stars that glittered above him. It was a time for him to think without the distraction of the ship's crew and the constant chattering of Rebiku. Of course, he loved Rebiku like a brother. It was just a nice opportunity for introspection and peaceful contemplation with no interruptions. He looked over at his friend slumbering on the deck near the bow with only a blanket for shelter, like all the other crewmen of the *Mew-Hanej*. He spoke a soft prayer of thanks to the moon goddess Ayur above him, who floated in the dark cosmos like a yellow beacon of hope.

The next afternoon they passed the cities of Merimda and Iunu. Merimda was also not a walled city and featured a symbolic gate similar to Pe-Dep's for the main entry. Rather than cobras there was a huge stone falcon, which the crew claimed represented the city's primary deity: Horus, the god of war. Khulani also learned that Iunu translated to *the place of pillars* and was considered the first city of creation by Atum, creator god, father of the gods, god of the setting sun, and the father of all Praa.

In a rare moment of conversation, Captain Hepzefa pointed out what appeared to be a temple built on the highest hill in the center of the city clearly visible in the distance. "The temple of Atum is known as the Per-aat."

Khulani was awestruck by the massive structure. Hundreds of tall pillars covered in the hieroglyph writing of the TaMehu priests supported heavy stone slats, offering the appearance of a stone column forest.

"We call the hill where the Per-aat sits the Benben," the captain continued. "It is where Atum first landed on this earth and created the first gods and humanity." The captain made a sign of respect to the temple as it receded into the distance before going about his business.

Khulani would have liked to stop at every city along the way and explore it thoroughly, save for Captain Hepzefa, who was on a strict timetable and expected to arrive in Inbu-Hedj on schedule the next day. As luck would have it, the crew were opening up to conversation with him and Rebiku, and they eagerly provided descriptions and explanations of the interesting places they passed.

During the day the river was crowded with trade and fishing vessels, nearly all local to the closest city or village. At night it was a different story, as only the long-haul trade vessels were still on the river. Once in a while they would pass another river ship laden with cargo going in the opposite direction. A trader from TaShemau passed one afternoon, and Khulani could not tell the differences between the ship, the people, or their dress from those of TaMehu. The only reason he even knew the ship was TaShemau in origin was that he happened to be in conversation with a crew member at the time.

During their voyage, Captain Hepzefa mostly kept his distance from Khulani and Rebiku. He was not rude or inconsiderate of their needs, quite the opposite, simply unwilling to converse beyond the need of the moment. It was disappointing to Khulani, because he was sure the captain must have fascinating stories to tell and experiences to share in this new world he and Rebiku were plunging into.

The night before their arrival in Inbu-Hedj, Khulani enjoyed a ration of royal heqet allowed by the captain with Rebiku and some of the crewmen. They all sat together at the bow of the ship.

"We are very excited about visiting your capital tomorrow," Rebiku remarked. "Can you tell us something of the city that may help us find our way around?"

A few of the crewmen chuckled, and one spoke up, "You want to find the best tavern for heqet?"

Another continued the inevitable, alcohol-inspired thought, "Or the best whorehouse?"

They all laughed at that and laughed even harder when Rebiku replied, "Both!"

One old crewman, more serious and possibly soberer than the others, broke the jovial mood with his gravely, deep-throated intonation, "Inbu-Hedj is the greatest city in all of TaMehu. It has the highest walls and grandest temples. The people of the city recognize Ptah, the creation god, patron of sculptors, painters, builders, carpenters, and other craftsmen. The main temple to Ptah is known by all who care as Hewetkaptah, but the temple is not located within the city, rather, it is on the other side of the river, in the Necropolis."

Khulani noticed some of the crewmen shifted uncomfortably at the mention of the Necropolis. "I thought Atum was your god of creation?" *Can there be two gods of creation?* he wondered.

The old sailor snorted loudly. "The priests of Ptah believe that Ptah was the original creator god and Atum was his agent. Of course, the followers of Atum dispute this idea, but they all get along well enough, and there is even a small Per-aat to Atum within the walls of Inbu-Hedj. It's a little confusing to foreigners. Anyway, if you want to see what makes Inbu-Hedj the wonder that it is, then go to see the palace, the outside, anyway. It is grand in scale and a vision of beauty."

Khulani was still thinking about the Necropolis. He had some idea of what it was, but he was puzzled by the idea of a temple located within one. "Why is Ptah's temple, the Hewetkaptah, located within the Necropolis while the other temples are in the city?"

The crewmen appeared uncomfortable again, glancing at each other and making signs of protection or kissing religious symbols to one deity or another that they carried. The old sailor drew his gray eyebrows together and appeared annoyed at his fellows. "Don't act like feral goats," he scolded. "Everyone knows that the Necropolis is safe enough during the day."

"What about at night?" Rebiku asked apprehensively. The old man smiled wickedly and lowered his voice to almost to a whisper. Khulani was sure the act was for the benefit of his superstitious fellows. "The night is not for the living in the Necropolis." He seemed smugly entertained watching the crewmen nearly go through contortions asking their gods for blessings and protection.

"It is true," a deep voice from behind them boomed. Khulani nearly jumped out of his clothes he was so startled by the unexpected sound. The sailors around him erupted into wild laughter. Captain Hepzefa had walked up behind them while everyone was engrossed in the old crewman's words.

For his part, the captain had a satisfied look on his face. "The dead are said to populate the Necropolis from dusk until dawn. They cannot leave the Necropolis, and anyone living who is foolish enough to enter at night is at their mercy. It is the sacred burial site of the royal family, high priests, temple architects, affluent citizens, and military leaders. Generally, the larger the tomb, the more important the person interred there. The Hewetkaptah is attached to a huge pyramid near the center of the site, and they are the only structures occupied by the living." He paused to wet his throat with a draught of heqet. "Just as some of the others you have probably seen, the very top of the pyramid is shorn flat and has a large red crystal hovering a little above it, cut to form the pyramid's apex. It is also symbolic of the Benben and a subtle reference to Atum. The crystal rotates slowly and shines with such intensity that its glow can be seen leagues away in the black of night. The pyramid is known as the Crystal Pyramid to the locals, but all similar pyramids in TaMehu and TaShemau are referred to in the same way. There is a huge wall around the pyramid, encompassing more buildings for the priests of Ptah, servants, administrators, soldiers, and the Neteru. The pyramid, its wall, and all the buildings of the complex are made from limestone and granite and finished with an enchanted powder causing the surfaces to appear bright white during the day and produce a soft white glow at night. It is truly beautiful to behold." he paused again.

No one said a word.

"During the day many people from the city visit the tombs of relatives to honor their memories with prayers and periodic official rituals conducted by the priests. It is at night, however, when no living soul should enter the grounds. Only those behind the white walls surrounding the Crystal Pyramid or on the long earthwork causeway that extends from the main entrance on the eastern edge of the Necropolis are safe from harm."

Khulani was intrigued. "What is the danger?" he whispered.

"There have been many reports over the years of the dead walking the Necropolis at night. Patrols from the pyramid complex keep grave robbers away during the day, and at night it is left to the dead themselves to secure their earthly valuables. Occasionally, a morning patrol will come across the bodies of thieves daring the legends or a widow desperate to be close to her deceased spouse. It is said that the Crystal Pyramid was built in the center of the Necropolis for just this reason—as added protection from robbers and raiders. You see, several generations of Praa have their tombs in the depths of the pyramid. It is where our current Praa, Khamet, and every future Praa of TaMehu will be entombed when he dies. It is absolutely unimaginable the wealth that must exist inside that pyramid."

Khulani hadn't hardly moved the width of a blade of grass the whole time the captain spoke. And as far as he knew neither had Rebiku or the other sailors. They all sat motionless, completely enthralled with Captain Hepzefa's words even though Khulani suspected the crew had likely heard the information many times before.

After waiting a moment in case the captain said more, Khulani finally broke the silence. His voice cracked from dryness, forcing him to speak just above a hoarse whisper, "How do you know so much about the Necropolis?"

The captain smiled. "My brother is a priest of Ptah and spends most of his time in the Crystal Pyramid and adjoining temple grounds. He has a number of great stories to tell, some of which I may not repeat here."

"We will have to see this amazing Necropolis," Rebiku declared. Khulani was eager to see it as well, and apprehensive. Something about the Necropolis reminded him of the dark night he fought the long-tooth.

By late afternoon on the next day, the great white-stained limestone and granite walls of the TaMehu capital, Inbu-Hedj, came within sight. The pure white of the walls and towers was striking against the beige stone buildings within and the green landscape that surrounded the city. Farther southwest, Khulani could observe the top third of the Crystal Pyramid that Captain Hepzefa spoke about with the red-glowing crystal on top. It was the most impressive of its kind that he had ever seen.

The port of Inbu-Hedj was large enough to easily dock half a hundred river ships. Musa grumbled that it was always busy with traffic moving in and out of the congested harbor, forcing them to wait for a wide enough mooring to open up. An hour later they were securely tied up to the dock, and Khulani carefully walked Wind Dancer off the ship after saying his farewells to the crew. Rebiku followed closely behind him.

Inbu-Hedj, which Captain Hepzefa translated as *the White Walls*, was an agricultural center, with crops stretching in every direction away from the river for leagues. The walls of the city extended to the edge of the river, where they terminated in high watchtowers to the north and south of the port. Khulani could see there was an inner wall separating the port from the main city. It was covered with hundreds of huge carvings depicting service and rituals to Ptah as well as the usual hieroglyphic symbols that seemed to cover everything. Smaller carvings inset near the top of the wall were overlaid with polished copper that gleamed brightly in the intense sunlight. Near the center of its length, a wide entrance flanked by several smaller entrances at measured paces led into the city. On each side of the wide entrance stood two colossal bulls, their great heads facing west, with horns enrobed in polished copper and easily three times the height of a man.

During their river voyage, a crewman mentioned that they would see many statues and murals of bulls around the city. The symbol of the bull was revered as the earthly representation of Ptah. At first Khulani found it odd that a people would use so much symbology in their lives until he realized that it was no different than the spirits his people worshipped. The spirits were represented by wind, water, stones, grass—there was a spirit for everything in his culture. The Imaziyen symbols consisted of painted animals on their pottery and hides. They had no walls or carved representations of their spirits.

The main entrance was closest to where he and Rebiku disembarked from the merchant ship, and although it was crowded, it appeared to be the best option. Leading their horses, they walked along the wide thoroughfare through it.

The beige stone buildings inside were as high as three stories and appeared to serve as residences, trade shops, mercantile, or taverns with no particular organization. Unlike in Thunis, however, the streets and avenues were planned and led more or less in straight lines. There were also a number of effigies, and not just of Ptah. Several Gods of TaMehu were represented throughout the city. Some were adorned with copper inlays that reflected the light from the late afternoon sun. Obelisks that were of various heights and covered with hieroglyphs appeared in public courtyards, temples courtyards, and adjacent government buildings.

"What does the writing on the obelisk mean?" Khulani respectfully asked a priest standing near one.

The priest was a young bald man wearing a long unadorned white tunic cinched by a plain leather belt at his waist and simple sandals. He had a kind face with eyes outlined with black kohl and cheeks that appeared pinched red. "This one is a prayer to the gods, not any particular one." He gestured to other obelisks nearby. "Some have stories of the gods cut into them, while others list important laws proclaimed by the Praa as a reminder to the citizens."

With all the architectural and sculpted beauty in the city, nothing compared to the royal palace situated at its center. The complex was surrounded by another high white wall with more towers. Beyond the wall, Khulani could make out multiple levels of pure white stone buildings with chiseled carvings, statuary, columns, and obelisks. Most were inlaid with copper and gold, some painted with vivid colors. Softening the severe lines of the construction, white awnings and trees were visible on terraces and rooftops, providing shade and comfort to those within. Captain Hepzefa informed them earlier that this was the palace of Praa Khamet, ruler of TaMehu, and residence to his family.

"Could you imagine the Amgar demanding such extravagance?" Rebiku jested.

Khulani barked a laugh. "He would thrash us just for the suggestion!"

Unfortunately, the wall surrounding the palace was as close as anyone could get to the splendors inside, unless they were royalty or invited, and the Imaziyen were neither. Instead, they walked farther into the city in search of a tavern renting rooms. It didn't take long to find one that was not very busy. The taverns they passed by near the port were far more crowded with rowdy sailors and merchants than those farther into the city. This one appeared to be patronized by locals more so than foreigners, and as such was quieter and more subdued. Regrettably, the accommodations closer to the palace were more expensive than the ones near the port, but at least this one included a meal every day, which they spared no time requesting. Over the last several days on the river, the standard fare was hard bread, salted meat, and heqet that had the distinct taste of saltwater. A good barley stew with warm, flat crusty bread was a delicious luxury that Khulani considered money well spent, not to mention the fresh house brew that wasn't stale.

Khulani cast his gaze around the open room. Like others where they had stayed, this one had a low ceiling, dim lighting, and a mixture of tables and mats on the floor. Most of the people here looked as if they worked all day and simply wished to unwind and enjoy quiet conversation with a few cups of heqet before they started all over again the next morning. The loud clatter of cities was more than a little disruptive to Khulani's feeling of balance, and the muted nature of this tavern made him feel less on edge and more relaxed.

They still had a long distance to go before they reached the Nabta people. Captain Hepzefa said that the TaShemau city of Nekhen was another one hundred and thirty leagues south of Inbu-Hedj and that they would be lucky to find a river ship going straight there. Khulani was not eager to return to the port the next morning after spending so many days within the confines of small ships. Inbu-Hedj was a large and exotic city that promised many interesting sights and experiences that he was enthusiastic about exploring. He was sure Rebiku would be too. Perhaps a few days on land would be good for them.

"Let's go visit this Necropolis tonight and see this Crystal Pyramid," Khulani suggested.

A wide smile stretched across Rebiku's face. "You should drink heqet more often, brother. You are finally starting to make sense!"

After finishing their meals, the two men went to their room. It was on the first floor near the back of the tavern, and like their previous room, this one had a long, narrow window that was open to accept the cool breeze but too narrow for even a child to slip through. The mats and blankets were clean, and there was even a small table with stools. It was still several hours until dusk, which allowed the Imaziyen to rest for a while before they strolled over to the causeway.

Just as the light was starting to falter, Khulani woke Rebiku from their short nap. The innkeeper gave them directions to the ferry dock where they could traverse the Aur and land directly at a dock connected to the long causeway that crossed over the Necropolis. It was a fair distance to the ferry with a few wrong turns through crowded streets and nearly dark when they finally arrived at the ferry dock. Fortunately, there was a ferry about to depart with several priests and a Neteru in the process of boarding. The Neteru seemed to be tolerating the presence of the young priests, who had been obviously drinking heavily that afternoon. It was not clear to Khulani if they were actually traveling together or not.

"This must be your first time in the capital," the Neteru remarked to Khulani when they were standing on the deck of the ferry boat. Like all Neteru, he was tall and slender, with strange blue-tinted skin and an elongated skull. This one wore long tan robes and a heavy gold chain with a medallion hanging from it. Engraved on the medallion was the symbol of a wave.

"Yes, Enlightened One," Khulani replied respectfully. "This is our first time in Inbu-Hedj. The captain of the ship that brought us here recommended we see the Crystal Pyramid and Necropolis while we were here."

The Neteru nodded. "You will find many people on the causeway at night. Some are here for the first time, like you; others are here every night. Everyone wants to see the dead walking at night, but they almost never reveal themselves to the people watching from the safety of the causeway. They wait for those whose curiosity, or intoxication, overcomes their sensibilities to venture into the city of the dead. Never are they heard from again. So take care, young Imaziyen, and don't let your own curiosity blind you."

Khulani was surprised that the tall Neteru knew where they were from. "How do you know we are Imaziyen?"

"Haven't you heard? I am from the City of Atlantis on the Emerald Isle—we know everything." He smiled at them mischievously and walked over to the now singing priests.

Khulani laughed, then stifled it quickly, not knowing if the man was serious or not. He remained silent after that and watched the opposite bank growing closer. In the near darkness that surrounded them, the red glow from the Crystal Pyramid was indistinguishable from the last rays of the setting sun behind it. Below the luminescence, he could see the torches that lined the causeway and the high wall surrounding the Necropolis, which appeared as a darker black outline against the fading daylight. Once the ferry reached the other side, they followed the loud priests and the patient Neteru from the landing to the well-lit incline up to the causeway that would lead to the temple grounds encompassing the Crystal Pyramid.

Just before the causeway, the road they followed split. The right fork led to the causeway, and the left fork led down along the dark wall of the Necropolis to somewhere unseen. Rebiku looked at Khulani. "Which way shall we go?"

Khulani knew his friend was making a joke. "Let's go to the causeway tonight."

At the top of the causeway, Khulani was surprised to see that there were a number of couples strolling or holding each other close while looking into the darkness. He would not have guessed that the Necropolis would be a destination for a romantic stroll, although from the perspective of a man, this might be the perfect place to take a lover to get them clinging and seeking comfort and protection.

Aside from lovers, there were several priests moving along the causeway toward and away from the temple complex, going about their business or heading into the city for the evening. The sun, below the horizon now, left the light from the Crystal Pyramid alone to cast its crimson light upon the taller structures in the Necropolis that surrounded the temple complex. There were hundreds of tombs of different sizes arranged like a city with streets and avenues. It was an eerie spectacle to behold, as he could just make out the shadows and shapes of tombs bathed in the red light of the crystal. To Khulani, it looked like a vastly scaled-down version of the stone cities they had experienced in TaMehu so far. At the opposite ends of the Necropolis, he could make out the shadowy shapes of two huge Sphinx—one facing east away from the Necropolis, and the other facing west. The body and head of each was sculpted in the fashion of a jackal, the animal that represented the Guardian of the Dead, Khulani learned from the sailors.

At the southeast edge of the Necropolis, very close to the Sphinx, was a wide harbor connected to the Aur by a wide channel. It appeared to be primarily used to bring in heavy blocks of limestone and granite via barge, as those were the only boats docked there.

Khulani looked down the side of the causeway into the darkness of the Necropolis and wondered why the corpses didn't just walk up the side of the causeway to accost the living. There was no barrier to stop them other than the causeway's slope. There must be some other method of restraint, he thought, unless the whole story was a deception to keep grave robbers away. Next to him, he was vaguely aware of Rebiku idly spinning something around his finger.

In the relative quiet, Khulani experienced a strange sensation—an intuitive tingle that suggested powerful magic at work, although he could not determine from where. It seemed to surround them, and he guessed that it was either the Crystal high above or the force that kept the dead at bay. Whatever it was, he was fascinated by the phenomenon. There were so few times in his life when he was cognizant of it, the last time being in the presence of the long-tooth. While he stood pondering his strange feelings, he suddenly realized that Rebiku was in some distress.

"I dropped it," Rebiku was saying.

"Dropped what?" asked Khulani.

"The charm. The charm she gave me." Rebiku was peering desperately along the side of the causeway.

Khulani was confused, "Who gave you a charm?"

"Haven't you been listening? I dropped the charm that Binah gave me! I must keep it until we meet again."

"Where did you drop it?" Khulani couldn't understand why his friend was so agitated. Neither of them had much interest in trinkets.

Rebiku was very upset. "Down the side of the causeway."

"Forget it. It was just a charm; you don't want to go down there." Khulani feared Rebiku's impetuous nature might cause him to do something foolish.

Rebiku took a light globe from its sconce on the causeway and attempted to peer into the darkness in vain. "I cannot leave it! She said it was important and I must have it when we meet again." He rolled the light globe down the steep incline of the causeway. At the bottom, near where the globe came to a stop, glittered the golden charm. "There!" he said. "I will slide down to the bottom for it and come back up right away."

Chapter 11

The Necropolis

Before Khulani could say a word or move to grab his arm, Rebiku was in a controlled slide to the base of the causeway. When he reached the bottom, Rebiku scrambled forward and retrieved his precious charm. It took him only seconds, and he turned to clamber back up the steep incline, his feet slipping on the loose gravel, unable to find a solid foothold. Khulani watched him thrust his body forward, going on hands and knees to find minimal traction. With every span of progress, he slid back down again. There was no way for Khulani to reach him, even if he had his spear. Rebiku was simply too far down the hill.

"Rebiku! Use our long knives to help you climb," Khulani tossed his long knife to the bottom of the causeway.

Rebiku scampered to where the long knife lay near the edge of the illumination of the light globe, which still lay where he had rolled it. Just as he bent to pick it up, something flickered out of the darkness, impacting his head with a *crack*, and his body dropped to the ground, unmoving.

Khulani's body physically jumped at the shock of the blow to his friend. "Rebiku!" he screamed.

There was no reply.

At the edge of the causeway, Khulani prepared to slide down to help his friend. Before he could push himself over, someone grabbed him by his shoulders and pulled him back. He struggled to free himself, but the grip was powerful—he felt like a small child in the grip of a giant.

"It's too late," a voice said from behind him. "There is nothing you can do for your friend now."

It was the Enlightened One, the Neteru, the Atlantean. Rage filled Khulani. How could he let Rebiku die down there? He struggled more violently and thought he might wrestle himself free, and then the voice hissed in his ear, "Look!"

Khulani froze. Something else had entered the light below.

It was a man, or was once a man. Now it was no more than the skeletal remains of a man draped with rotten and torn fabric that was once its clothes, and it held a heavy club. The creature looked up at Khulani. Red orbs that glowed from within its eye sockets somehow held life that animated the creature. It held no expression, but somehow Khulani felt he was being mocked. And then it slowly raised its club to strike Rebiku with a final blow.

Khulani felt helpless. The Neteru still held him in an iron grip. All he could do was watch his friend die. And then the impossible happened. Rebiku fluidly turned and deflected the downward thrust of the heavy club angling toward his head. Without interrupting his motion, Rebiku kicked his foot forward and sent the skeleton tumbling to the ground. Then his friend was on his feet, and he crushed the skeleton's skull with a heavy stomp.

Rebiku staggered back toward the base of the causeway. A trickle of blood on his right temple revealed a nasty wound that would need attention soon. Both long knives in hand, he attempted to climb up again.

Suddenly, Khulani was released. "That won't work," the Neteru told him. "I will run back to the dock and find a rope to pull him up." The lanky Neteru turned and sprinted down the causeway with surprising swiftness.

"Rebiku, are you OK?" Khulani called down to him.

Rebiku glanced up and nodded while wiping blood from his face. "I will be a little better when I am back up there."

Khulani was encouraged that his friend still had his humor. The feeling didn't last long. There was an unnatural hiss from the darkness, and another skeletal figure entered the light five paces away from Rebiku. His friend heard it too, and he slowly turned to face it.

"Oh no," breathed Khulani. Rebiku was going to stand and fight. He suddenly felt like everything was spiraling out of control. In a fit of desperation, Khulani quickly slid down the incline of the causeway to stand next to his friend. There was no way he was going to stand on the causeway and watch Rebiku get torn to pieces. They would die standing shoulder to shoulder, together, if it came to that.

"I don't think you heard me correctly." Rebiku smiled and handed Khulani the long-knife he had thrown down earlier. "It's definitely not better down here."

"The Neteru went to find a rope to bring you back up." Khulani shrugged. "He might as well bring us both up."

Out of the darkness, two more skeletal figures appeared. Now they faced three. The figures were similar to the first, each with clothing tattered to different degrees, a bit of leather or metal armor here and there, and a rusted sword or spear. Khulani thought they may have been warriors when they lived and he stood close by Rebiku gripping his long-knife and waited for their inevitable attack.

It came quickly.

The Imaziyen beat the assailants back mostly through the force of jabs, kicks, and punches. Their blades were largely ineffective and tended to get stuck in the dry bones when they made contact. Two more dead came at them from the dark, and Khulani's long knife was pulled from his grasp when it stuck fast in a skeleton's thigh bone. Still crouched, he picked up a club—the one dropped by the skeleton that initially struck Rebiku—and quickly realized that it was far more effectual than the knife he lost. He glanced over to tell Rebiku, but it wasn't necessary. His friend already found a spear and was spinning and striking the skeletons with its shaft, breaking off parts of their bodies with every hit.

The hissing intensified, and several more appeared from the darkness. Once fine garments, now tattered and rotting, hung from their skeletal frames. Some wore tarnished pieces of metal that could have served as armor in better days. Most had clearly been dead a long time. But there were a few—the worst of them—that stank of pungent decay, with skin blackened by rot and decomposition. They moved slowly and deliberately with the single-minded intent of nothing less than stripping him and Rebiku of their lives.

Khulani moved closer to Rebiku and waited for the next assault. With his free hand, he rubbed at his temple. He was experiencing a strong buzzing in his head that he couldn't shake and tried hard not to be distracted by it. Then the dead were upon them again, more this time and with others coming. In the darkness Khulani could hear the chittering and clacking of more of the monsters arriving, and he knew they could hold them off for only so long.

They barely beat back a group of the creatures before the next wave appeared. There had to be at least eight or ten, and it was all the men could do to fend them off again. Khulani expected the next attack would be the last, and he and Rebiku would fall to their numbers. Both of them were already bruised and bleeding from several injuries and breathing hard from the effort to survive. The buzzing in Khulani's head grew louder, and he felt pressure building that needed release, if he only knew how.

It had to be the magic. He tried to concentrate and release it like he had against the long-tooth. He visualized fire, and a flame ignited in his hand. It wasn't enough. Gritting his teeth hard, he tried again. The top portion of the club he held burst into flames so suddenly that Khulani almost dropped it. That was better, but the buzzing diminished by only a little.

The skeletons continued to advance toward them. More than two dozen crowded into the circle of illumination cast by the light globe at their feet. And then they stopped.

"Why have they stopped?" Sweat glistened from lines that ran down Rebiku's face and dripped from his hairless chin.

"I don't know, but I think there are many more of them that we cannot see in the dark behind them." Khulani was glad for the pause to catch his breath.

There was a disturbance in the darkness. Something big was moving toward them. The night was nearly silent, and Khulani could hear its heavy footfalls coming closer. The living dead parted in front of them to reveal a creature straight from images Khulani recently saw on the wall of a temple in Thunis. The thing was tall, taller even than the Enlightened Ones, and it had the body of a human man—bare-chested, lean, and muscled—with skin blacker than the night. It wore gold sandals on its wide feet and a gold-trimmed shendyt fastened at his waist in the style and fashion of a Praa. In one hand it held a heavy gold scepter with a rounded, bulbous dome atop it that Khulani had no doubt would be a dangerous weapon and in the other a heavy flail. Worst of all was the creature's massive jackal head with a protruding snout full of razor-sharp teeth, long ears that twitched toward the slightest sound, and blazing red eyes that glowed from within like the skeletons' that surrounded them.

"Be careful, Rebiku. This is no dead thing. It may well be a TaMehu god," Khulani whispered.

"Then we shall see if their gods bleed." Rebiku took a step forward.

The jackal-headed man's gold scepter began to glow, and the buzzing intensified inside Khulani's head. He knew it must be magic. Before he could shout a warning to Rebiku, a flash of light illuminated the night around them. In that brief moment, Khulani could see hundreds of the dead gathered around them, and his heart sank. They were going to die here tonight and become one of the creatures. Then, everything in front of them erupted in flames. The jackal roared in pain and anger, while the dead endured it silently and burned.

"Run!" a voice from above them called urgently. "Grab the rope and run up the causeway as best you can! Don't look back!"

Without hesitation, Khulani took hold of Rebiku's arm and pulled his friend along with him. They clutched their way up the steep slope to the top of the causeway, slipping and sliding even with the benefit of the rope. Khulani did as he was told and did not turn to see if they were pursued, but he imagined that if the dead had breath, he would have felt it on the back of his neck. As they ascended, more flames passed over their heads and exploded behind them.

Rolling over the top of the causeway to safety, Khulani was confronted by the angry visage of the Neteru. He lifted Khulani effortlessly to his feet with one hand and demanded, "Why didn't you destroy them, Druid?"

Khulani was baffled. How could the Neteru know about his gift? "I don't know. I didn't know how."

The Neteru's expression softened a bit. "Learn your craft, and learn it well. You could have easily destroyed them all."

A quick glance at the base of the causeway showed Khulani the charred remains of several skeletons near the light globe and others walking aimlessly while they burned. The jackal-headed man and the rest of the dead had fled back into the darkness.

Khulani crouched to help Rebiku to his feet. "Forgive me, Neteru, and thank you for your intervention. We are on our way to the Nabta people so that I may receive proper instruction from the Druids there. I have only recently become familiar with my potential."

"Be careful, Druid, otherwise you and your friend will never make it to your destination."

Khulani knew only too well the truth of that statement. "We will take much better care in the future." He paused a moment before asking the question that was burning to be spoken. "What was that creature with the jackal head? It looked much like an image I have seen on a temple wall."

"That was Anapa, Protector of Graves," the Neteru replied. "Sometimes he appears as a colossal, full-bodied jackal, and other times, like tonight, he appears half man. Pray to your spirits that you never meet him again in any form. Even I would be no match for him down there."

Rebiku laughed nervously. "Then we were lucky you were nearby to save our hides!"

The Neteru studied them for a moment. The drunken priests of Ptah with him were still jovially shooting magical flames into the darkness. With a scowl and single word from the Neteru, they ceased their play and sobered up enough to hurry off toward the pyramid.

Turning back to Khulani he said, "My name is Deezigre of House Osris. I am the high priest of the delegation from the City of Atlantis responsible for the Orichalcum Crystals. Leave this place and resume your journey. In the morning I will have to explain to the Praa why I nearly burned down his Necropolis, and it would be better if you were long gone from Inbu-Hedj. He is not very forgiving when it comes to disruptive foreigners. Return when you have received instruction from the Druids. Or not—it's up to you." Without waiting for a response, he strode unhurried after his drunken entourage.

Khulani sighed. "He is right. My gift is rapidly turning into a nightmare. I need to learn how to control it before I end up getting us killed."

Rebiku patted him on the back. "We are alive, brother, because of you. It wasn't your gift that had me chasing that silly trinket."

"What is all that about anyway?" Khulani felt a little annoyed by the whole thing. "You never told me about it."

"I don't know," Rebiku admitted. He looked as embarrassed as Khulani had ever seen him. "It seemed so important to Binah that I not lose it. She called it our little secret. I am sorry."

Khulani slapped his friend on the chest. "Don't worry, brother. My father says women make a habit of causing men to do crazy things."

Within an hour they were back in their rented room. Khulani was anxious. "That Neteru priest was right," he said. "We should have been killed by those things tonight."

Rebiku nodded silently before he responded. "How did he know you have the gifts of a Druid?"

Khulani shook his head, "He was a Neteru, and they seem to be very sensitive to magic and those with the ability to use it. When we were fighting the dead things, I felt there was something that I should do, something I knew I should have done, but I had no idea how." Khulani was frustrated. "As much as I want to see the cities we travel through and enjoy their culture, we must waste no more time in our journey to the Nabta people. And not just because of the Praa of TaMehu. I must know how to control these feelings inside of me and how to properly use this gift I have."

"Patience, brother," said Rebiku, "You will learn everything soon. And I agree that you have been more fidgety than a pregnant aurochs expecting a calf."

Khulani could at least find humor in that. "You always make me laugh, Rebiku, and it reminds me how foolish I am acting. Tomorrow we will find a ship to Nekhen and try to stay out of trouble!"

~~~

Khulani slept well and awoke refreshed early the next morning. As agreed the night before, they went straightaway to the port to seek out the dockmaster. He hoped to find a ship to take them as far south as possible without stopping at other cities along the way. However, considering their haste to leave Inbu-Hedj, they would take what they could get.

Rebiku chuckled, "For two ignorant Imaziyen, we are leaving a string of urgent departures in our wake."

"We are, my friend. Soon, our reputation will precede us!" Khulani pulled at Wind Dancer to keep him from biting the people they passed. His horse was less happy than they were to be pressed by unfamiliar crowds in a city. He imagined that they would both be happy and relieved to be back in the open savanna of the Ibhr Rrbi.

The dockmaster was a fat, sweaty man wearing a white silk shendyt trimmed in blue, with a matching silk tunic and a blue-and-white striped nemes to keep the sun off his neck. The morning was cool, yet the silk stuck to the man in places where he sweat the most, causing him to constantly pull at the fabric to release it from his skin. The official's eyes bore heavy cosmetics, and Khulani wondered if it ran down his face with the sweat off his bald head when the sun was actually hot. Apparently too busy and self-important to be bothered, the dockmaster distractedly brushed them off when Khulani inquired about a ship, telling them to see his assistant who kept the daybook of arrivals and departures.

The assistant was a slave and far friendlier than the dockmaster. He suggested they talk to the captain of a TaShemau trade vessel expected to depart to Nekhen that morning. If they hurried, they might catch him before he cast off. Quickly they navigated through the crowds of the busy dock to the mooring indicated by the slave. Earlier that morning Khulani made sure that they were fully supplied for a two-week voyage in anticipation of leaving as soon as possible. He didn't believe that the Praa of TaMehu would be sending a troop of soldiers to intercept them at the dock, although considering their luck lately, he might not have been surprised. They hurried in any case.

The captain of the river ship was supervising the loading of the last of the trade goods onto his ship and was happy to have them as passengers to Nekhen. As with the TaMehu ships they traveled on recently, this one was long and narrow, with a flat bottom and no keel.

The vessel employed a sail and oars for movement up and down the river and like the others utilized a set of three rudders on each side of the aft section of the ship for precise maneuvering to avoid any hazards in the Aur. Once the ship's cargo was loaded into the shallow hold, the planks and rowing benches were replaced on the deck, and they were permitted to embark. Soon enough, the ship was underway and they were sailing south down the river.

The captain's name was Khuy, and he had a far more jovial and conversational personality than Captain Hepzefa. And as far as Khulani could tell, the TaShemau crew attended to their tasks as efficiently as their TaMehu brothers.

"We will stop to offload a portion of our cargo and pick up more in the city of Naqada three days downriver, but we won't stay overnight unless the weather turns bad. If we're blessed by the gods, the entire voyage to Nekhen should take about five days. Don't worry, the weather is always good this time of year!" The captain was the optimistic sort.

That night the captain was forced to anchor in the reeds for hours while a torrent of rain soaked them all to the bone. The captain laughed the whole time and shouted appeals to the gods for forgiveness for being right so often. Khulani and Rebiku were the only passengers on board the ship, and they sheltered among the stacks of cargo on the aft deck of the ship until the next morning.

The next three days were filled with conversations with the captain and his crew. Khulani learned quite a bit about TaShemau and the next city they would be stopping at, Naqada. As they did to everyone they met on their journey, Khulani and Rebiku presented themselves as the sons of Imaziyen tribal leaders traveling to the lands of the Nabta people to develop stronger trade relationships. After their encounter with the Amazigh women in the mountains so many weeks ago, they decided to keep the details of their travels to themselves. The stories they told about themselves now were real and exclusively about their experiences in their savanna homeland.

Khulani discovered that the TaShemau people were very similar to those from TaMehu. They based their culture on the raising of crops and the domestication of animals and used copper extensively for decoration as well as utility. Near Naqada there was substantial mining of gold and a very rare, rich purple-red porphyry stone that appeared dusted with the stars when polished. It was highly valued by those around the Great Sea who could afford it. Hellas was the most popular destination for export, and they used it primarily for columns, statues, sheeting for the chambers of royalty, and commissions of art.

Quarries of sandstone and granite were farther south, near Nekhen. The massive raw stones were sailed down the Aur by barge to building sites across TaMehu and TaShemau. Often, Khulani witnessed these massive river barges built specifically for transporting huge blocks of stone and obelisks headed to ports north on the river. Farther south were diorite and amethyst resources that were in a disputed area between TaShemau and the kingdom of Kerma. It was currently controlled by TaShemau. Captain Khuy described several impressive fortresses along the Aur and the land border to protect the mines from raids by the Kerma tribes. When not fighting with the Kerma, the TaShemau aristocracy valued their rival's gold ore, livestock, and hardwood resources. The captain pointed out trade ships from Kerma, which were not so different from those from TaMehu and TaShemau, moving under oar with the benefit of the north flowing current. It was apparent to Khulani that there was a very brisk trade between the northern and southern kingdoms in times of peace.

In the early-morning hours of the third day on the river, they passed the TaShemau city of Tjenu. The imposing city presented very high walls studded with fortified towers built with a combination of stone and mud bricks. With the dark shadows moving along the walls, silhouetted against the predawn night sky, it was obviously a very well-protected city. The captain, up early with Khulani, explained that Tjenu was known as the City of Temples. The city eared its name due to the numerous temples dedicated to nearly every deity worshipped in TaMehu and TaShemau. It was also the closest port to the porphyry quarries only two to three days' ride east.

Khulani knew a little about quarries from his travels with his father when he was a child. The Capsian mountain city of Capsa boasted quarries as well. Khulani couldn't imagine working as a slave or freeman under the ground where the sun god and wind spirits could never touch his face. Captain Khuy knew something about quarries as well and explained that the ones east of Tjenu were practically small cities of their own. Each was built with permanent residences, a trade district with a sizable market, and a barrack for the garrison that protected them.

Farther south of Tjenu, Captain Khuy pointed out the royal necropolis of TaShemau that they called Abydos. It was protected from tomb robbers and cared for by the priests serving the various temples associated with the deceased Praa and their royal families.

"Is the necropolis at Abydos protected by the dead at night like the one in Inbu-Hedj?" Khulani asked.

The captain roared with laughter and slapped Khulani on the back. "No, young Imaziyen, my people are not nearly as superstitious as our brothers and sisters in TaMehu!"

Khulani felt embarrassed by the response, but he knew the truth.

Late on the third day out of the TaMehu capital, they arrived at the port of Naqada. The captain cautioned Khulani and Rebiku not to stray too far from the ship as they would depart as soon as their cargo had been unloaded and new cargo brought on. Rebiku suggested they accompany the crew members not required to load the ship to a local heqet house, and a few hours later they were sailing south on the river feeling a little more buoyant than when they arrived.

That night while eating the evening meal with the crew, the sailors began to gossip. Apparently, the big news in TaShemau centered on a cult of priests devoted to the serpent god, Apep.

"The cult is outlawed by the Praa," one sailor explained, "and they don't have public temples."

"What have they done that they cannot worship their god openly?" Rebiku asked.

"Deplorable acts of ritual," the sailor shifted uncomfortably, "including human sacrifice."

Khulani was shocked. He had never heard of such a thing. The Imaziyen believed that the spirits of the animals they hunted sacrificed their bodies for the nutriment of his tribe. What would be the purpose of sacrificing a human, unless . . . "Do they eat them?"

It was the sailor's turn to be shocked. "If they do, I have not heard stories of it."

"Why doesn't your chief, the Praa, put them in chains like your slaves?"

"No one knows who they are," another sailor replied. "It is said some hold office, even high office of every industry—military and trade—planting the seeds of chaos and destruction where they can."

The first sailor spoke up again. "Naqada is rumored to be their religious center, although they have been discovered practicing their blasphemy in every city of TaShemau and even cities of TaMehu. Fortunately, it is believed that there are not so many to cause any serious threat to the kingdoms."

"Until recently, so few have been accused that many believed them to be only a legend to frighten children," a third sailor added.

Khulani could feel the tension from the sailors. This was more than just idle gossip shared with a few cups of heqet. "Something has happened? What is it?"

"Snakes," one of the sailors blurted.

"Big snakes," another echoed.

"None of us has seen them with our own eyes," a sailor admonished. "But there has been talk in Waset, Nekhen, and Naqada about giant snakes hunting the streets of the cities at night."

"We may not have seen them ourselves, but what about all those who have gone missing? Even the armed patrols?" a sailor countered.

Khulani had seen many snakes in his life. Many feared them, even in his tribe. He had removed countless snakes from huts over the years. They weren't so bad. They were just misunderstood. A snake would almost never strike unless it was cornered and had no other choice. Most people would be surprised to know how much they feared humans. "How large are these snakes? Do you know what they looked like?"

"Longer than this ship and half as wide."

Khulani couldn't believe it. He was expecting a snake like the large constrictors that lived near the wettest parts of the Ibhr Rrbi. "Why do you think these snakes are associated with the cult of Apep?"

The sailors were quiet for a long moment before one finally spoke up. "Because the priests who have been captured recently say their god has returned."

Chapter 12

The Zoo

Weary of so many days on the water, Khulani was grateful that they were on the final leg of their journey. Once they reached Nekhen there would be no more ships to board, and the only sea they would be crossing would be the southernmost region of the Sea of Grass the Imaziyen called the Ibhr Rrbi. Seafaring and river boat voyages were exciting in their own way, but Khulani craved the open expanses and freedom to ride Wind Dancer wherever he pleased. He was certain Wind Dancer would appreciate the change as well. Horses were not well suited to spending their days on ships either.

On the morning of the fourth day from Inbu-Hedj, they passed the walled city of Waset, or, as the people of TaShemau referred to it, the City of the Was. A crewman described the meaning of a Was as a scepter of the Praa—a long staff with an animal's head above a forked base. It was also the ruling symbol of the patron deity of Waset, Amana—god of the sky and air. The captain pointed out that the city was the primary waypoint for trade going up and down the Aur River. Fortunately, Captain Khuy had no cargo to exchange at this port, and they passed it by. Khulani was glad for it, considering that the port of Waset was much like the one in Thunis, with a long port that stretched well beyond the entrance of the harbor. It was packed with vessels.

"Looks like we should arrive in Nekhen by midday," the captain announced in his usual jovial manner. "We will celebrate our voyage with heqet this evening!"

The crew cheered and called out praises to the captain. Khulani was pleased as well. This captain sailed with a much better quality of heqet than any of the others they traveled with so far.

A little while later, Khulani approached Captain Khuy with Rebiku. "Captain, would you mind telling us a little about our destination?"

"It would be my pleasure!" the captain eagerly assented. "Nekhen is the capital of the kingdom of TaShemau and home to the Oracle of the Shrine of Nekhbet. Prior to TaShemau's advance south and the building of fortresses along the Aur, Nekhen was the kingdom's only defense against invasion by the Kingdom of Kerma farther south. That is why the city is surrounded by a massive stone and mud-brick wall that extends protectively to its port and why it has been the site of numerous battles in our long history." The captain paused a moment as if considering whether to say more on the subject, then his eyes lit up. "You must visit our famous zoo while in Nekhen! It is filled with exotic animals like hippos, hartebeest, elephants, baboons, wildcats, and many unknown creatures from around the world!"

Rebiku's eyes lit up as well, but with curiosity. "What is this zoo you speak of?"

The captain chuckled. "It is a marvelous thing. Animals are collected for display to anyone willing to pay a small fee. There are creatures there one could only imagine from stories and legend!"

Khulani wasn't sure he liked the idea of a zoo. It sounded too much like unnatural confinement. He determined not to debate that with the captain, unwilling to offend him, and changed the subject. "How far are the lands of the Nabta people from Nekhen?"

Captain Khuy paused a moment, considering the question. "I have never been to their lands, but there is some bit of trade between our kingdoms. From what I have heard, the grasslands are fairly flat with copses of trees here and there. If you follow the trade route to their city, it will probably take about five days considering you have fit horses. I'm sure you two can handle yourselves appropriately, but be careful. They are said not to like outsiders very much."

Khulani smiled. "It is our hope that we will be expected."

As the captain promised, they arrived at Nekhen just before midday. After the usual goodbyes, Khulani and Rebiku walked their mounts toward the gates leading into the city. The people of TaShemau looked identical in physical features and dress to the people of TaMehu. According to Captain Khuy, they also had a Praa that resided in the royal palace with his family, and with the exception of some of their gods, they had many of the same rituals as their northern neighbor. Even their laws and culture were nearly identical. Captain Khuy informed them that the name of the kingdom, TaShemau, meant *Land of the Reeds* and was symbolized by the hedjet, or white crown, worn by their Praa during official rituals and ceremonies. Khulani thought it made sense that the two kingdoms were considered brothers throughout their history given their similarities. It made him wonder if perhaps the kingdom of Kerma might be considered a third brother, even if they didn't always get along.

The portside entrance to Nekhen was through three wide gates set side by side with high towers on the defensive walls between them. There were bronze armor–clad soldiers with spears manning the towers, the walls, and either side of the gates, keeping a close watch on the masses of people crowding in and out of the city. Of all the cities they passed through in their long journey, Nekhen was, by far, the most militarized.

Inside, the city looked much like Inbu-Hedj, with stone and mud-brick buildings as high as three stories and walls decorated with murals or carvings inlayed with copper. Unique to Nekhen were many representations of vultures in art and sculpture throughout the city and predominant on the main gates from the port. Khulani was aware that the vulture symbolized Nekhen's patron deity Nekhbet, and occasionally they would pass one of her priestesses, the people called Muu. Either from fear or reverence, the crowds parted for them, making hand gestures of respect. Captain Khuy was very adamant about respecting the Muu, and Khulani intended to follow his advice.

"I hope we can manage to leave this city without an encounter with a vulture-headed goddess." Rebiku laughed nervously after passing an entourage of the Muu wearing their long flowing robes of vulture feathers.

Khulani knew his friend was joking except that the smile didn't quite reach his eyes. "In their tongue, *Muu* means *mother*. How bad can they be?"

"On the Ibhr Rrbi, vultures eat dead things."

Khulani stifled a laugh. "Let's find an inn."

The royal palace was surrounded by a tall wall chiseled with hieroglyphic symbols that Khulani guessed were probably religious writings or prayers to the vulture goddess. At least he supposed they were dedicated to the deity considering the number of symbols in the writing that looked like a vulture. This was not surprising, as Captain Khuy explained that Nekhbet was considered the iconic mother of the Praa of TaShemau.

By chance, they found what appeared to be a comfortable inn not too far from the Nekhen Zoo. Rebiku was eager to visit the zoo and suggested that since they were in the city until the next day anyway, they could experience something new without delaying their journey or getting into trouble. Khulani agreed, but he wished he had found out more about what a zoo was before they left Captain Khuy's river trader.

After stabling their horses and dropping their supply packs in their room, they walked the short distance to the zoo. Even before they saw it, they could smell it. Although Nekhen allowed penned livestock within the city and the smell of animals was always in the air, this was much stronger by far. Khulani began to worry about what they were going to see.

The Nekhen Zoo was enclosed by a high mud-brick wall with a stone-framed entryway that could be closed at the end of the day with two massive wooden doors. Standing at the entrance was an official-looking man wearing the traditional nemes and white shendyt of flax linen. Next to him stood a large bald man armed with a club and two slaves who just stared meekly at the ground. It still infuriated Khulani to see people stripped of their freedom and dignity and forced to serve others against their will.

A line of visitors walked by the man wearing the shendyt, pausing to hand him a small copper coin before they proceeded inside. Khulani had coins from TaMehu that he hoped the man would accept. He and Rebiku stood in the short line of people a short time and were waved through without a word when Khulani handed him two of the TaMehu copper coins. He assumed the coins must be of similar weight and value.

Beyond the walls, Khulani was immediately confronted by a long row of small pens and wooden cages containing typical small furry animals, snakes, large spiders, and lizards they had seen many times on the savanna. As they passed by, he could feel the anxiety of the animals. They felt trapped and cornered. The enclosures were small and the noises foreign and frightening. It was all he could do to stop himself from attempting to release them. The next row was lined with cages of various birds, and the one after that held larger pens of small herd animals.

The pens became larger with each row and soon included zebras, a mammoth, several lions, wolves, and a striped beast similar to a lion that the tending slaves called a tiger from some far away land he did not know. Khulani recognized the striped pattern from a hide worn as a cape by the Amgar of his tribe and wondered if even he had seen the elegant feline from which it had come.

There were many unusual creatures Khulani had never seen and apparently many of the zoo's visitors had never seen either, since these were the most crowded exhibits. To Khulani, the entire concept of caged animals was disturbing, and from the moment he stepped into the walled enclosure, he could sense the fear, suffering, and rage from so many of them that it was nearly overwhelming.

"There is a cruelty done to the animals held here," he told Rebiku. "They are not fed enough, they have barely enough room to move about, many are sick, and they are in constant fear of their handlers and the people who pay to see them. I can feel it all."

"Is there anything you can do to give them comfort? Like you did with the mammoth that one time?" asked Rebiku.

"I don't know. I wish I did know, but I don't know how to make the magic work in me. Perhaps if we can find a less crowded place I can reach out to them with my mind. I don't know." Khulani was upset, and he knew that his distress was weighing heavily on his friend as well. For as long as they had been friends, Rebiku had always known him to be very sensitive to nature and balance; he was the only person that Khulani shared everything with. There were no secrets between the two.

Rebiku found a bench near the outside wall where they could sit without many people walking by and the noises from the animals were muted. Khulani closed his eyes and concentrated. Within a few moments he was calm. His breathing slowed, and he sat against the wall perfectly still and at ease. He reached out with his mind to connect with those animals closest to him. It seemed so much easier when he was helping animals. It was natural, as if the spirits of the animals chose this as his purpose. One by one he reached farther and farther into the rows of pens around him, connecting with them and connecting them with each other like some massive web that he was spinning invisibly between every animal in the zoo. Khulani felt disconnected from his body, yet he could still hear and feel the physical world around him. He heard the animals become quiet with his mental touch and felt them calm. He could also hear the muttering of people who found the sudden change curious. Still, he wove his web. Khulani would not stop until every imprisoned creature, big, small, of fur or feather or scale was connected.

Then he touched something unexpected, and the web almost collapsed, he was so astonished. He recovered quickly and maintained his focus and connection before reaching out again to his unexpected find. It was an animal, but not like the others. This one confronted him with . . . intellect, and he could feel the seething anger and hatred it felt for its captors, its cage, and the people that sought to stare and jeer at it. The creature was the main attraction that everyone came to see and watch in amazement. Terrified and angry, the creature chose to remain still and hidden in the shadows until driven by its handlers with sticks and prods to move to another corner of the cage. It enraged them when it did not give the paying goats the show they wanted, and it delighted in those small victories even if it got a beating from their sticks. Yes, they were goats, and so much more so if the creature could get to them. It hungered for them. Gawking and watching and throwing stones to get its attention. Khulani had the distinct impression that the creature was a caged predator trapped by its prey.

But there was more.

There was sorrow, deep sorrow as the creature thought about others it loved, a family, children that it would never see again. The hopelessness the creature felt was deep and . . . almost human. So much so that he was certain the creature would have preferred death.

Khulani tried to force himself out of the web, disconnecting the creature from it as well so not to infect the others, but he did not know how. His eyes were open, and he was staring straight at Rebiku, who looked back at him with intense concern. Khulani had been pulled into the consciousness of the creature to such a deep level that he could hear its thoughts. Nothing like this had ever happened before. Not even close. Then he was conscious of Rebiku saying something and shaking him.

"Khulani? Khulani! Are you well? Speak, Khulani!" Rebiku was almost in a panic.

Khulani finally broke through the mental quagmire and forced himself to blink. He was back. "I, I am well my friend. Have no fear."

Rebiku heaved a sigh of relief and hugged his friend. "What happened? You were calm until the end and then you began to twitch so much that I thought you might fall over."

"There is something caged here that I have to find. I don't know what it is, but it is important that I find it. The creature has intellect, Rebiku, like us, but it is also an animal, and it is in great emotional pain. There was nothing I could do to help it." Khulani rose from his seat. He was surprised at the approaching evening; he must have been "away" for a while.

The zoo was open to the sky, and as it darkened, slaves lit hundreds of torches to keep the light. If it were not for his distress, the torchlight reflecting off walls, creating long shadows of people and animals, might have been beautiful.

Rebiku stood next to him. "You were able to touch the minds of the animals?"

"Yes, somehow I was able to provide them some comfort, although I don't know how long it will last. By tomorrow they may be just as stressed. I also found others, and there were a few, that were . . . beyond calming. They no longer had self-awareness or identity. Their minds were chaotic as if they had passed into madness. This is a terrible place, Rebiku."

They walked the rows of wooden cages and pens looking for the being that Khulani found in his trance. In the last row there was a pen walled on three sides with high metal gates that made it look like a giant birdcage. In front of it, a crowd of people gathered to gaze into the pen. One man shouted something and then threw a piece of fruit through the open space between the wooden bars. The crowd gasped and then went silent again.

"This is it." Khulani told Rebiku. Patiently, Rebiku took care to weave his way through the crowd until he was standing at the edge of the massive cage. Khulani followed him closely and took a place at the edge of the cage right up against the bars. At first, he did not see anything. There was a deep moat on the other side of the fence, an overturned log, and several items lying about intended to entertain whatever was housed here.

Khulani stood at the fence for a long time, allowing his eyes to adjust to the darkness inside. He detected movement. Slowly at first, something was standing and looking around as if this were the first time it noticed its surroundings. The thing was behind a boulder and hard to see. Then, the tall outline of a man slowly began to emerge from the darkness. At first, Khulani thought it was another animal handler checking something inside the cage. A gasp rippled through the crowd behind him when the creature walked into the light. It stood directly in front of him on the other side of the moat. As close as it was in the dim light, Khulani could not believe that what he observed could existed.

The creature stood taller than a man by half, and its body was covered with a leathery, scale-like skin of olive green over a muscular build. It wore no clothing and appeared anatomically correct for a man. The head—Khulani wanted to look away—was dominated by a long snout, which revealed a wide mouth filled with sharp teeth, under large oval eyes with slits for pupils, like a snake. The best way Khulani have could described this creature would be serpent-like or reptilian in nature. The slave attending the pen proudly announced it as a serpent man from across the mountains beyond a land called Kur-gal.

To look at the creature was startling in itself. It was an unbelievable monstrosity of nature that could not have been better imagined to incite terror in a dramatic narrative. Khulani heard the stories about these creatures and whispers about their penchant for human flesh. If his worst nightmare were ever to come true, he believed that he was looking at it now. Most shocking was that it was staring directly at him as if no one else were there.

Khulani stared back at the creature, mesmerized by what he was seeing until he noticed that it was moving its mouth in an effort to communicate. Strange sounds like grunts, growls, and deep hums were what he heard, but he understood none of it. After a moment, Khulani realized that the creature no longer had a tongue, if it ever had one. The gestures it made with its hands and arms were erratic and made no sense to him either, yet it seemed to know him or be familiar with him somehow. Although Khulani was unable to understand anything it was trying to say, he understood the desperation and fear it was feeling. This was the poor creature that he found with his mind earlier, the one that was fraught with despair for another. It seemed hardly possible that Khulani could feel sympathy for the horrid creature, but he did.

The snake man was clearly irritated that he couldn't speak and becoming increasingly agitated that he couldn't convey whatever message he so desperately wanted Khulani to understand. The handler, a large man who sat outside the cage, started banging his stick on the bars and shouting at the creature to calm down. The idiot had no idea what he was doing. The reptilian was only getting further worked up. Finally, with something that sounded like an angry curse, the reptilian man ran forward and sprang over the moat, landing on the other side of the wooden bars from Khulani.

Everyone standing near the cage screamed and surged backward and away, terrified at the sudden closeness of the horrific creature—except Khulani. He didn't even flinch. Even Rebiku took a reactive step back. The bars were wide enough that the reptilian reached through and grabbed Khulani's left hand and held it firmly but not enough to cause pain. With a cough the lizard man regurgitated something into its long-nailed claw and pressed the slimy object into Khulani's hand, where he held it a moment before releasing. Khulani instinctively closed his fingers around the object so not to drop it.

With his other hand, Khulani held tightly to one of the cage's wooden bars. They were not thick and probably never intended to keep a creature like the reptilian confined. The buzzing in his head returned, and this time Khulani was aware that the magic he detected was coming from within himself. And it was strong.

He locked eyes with the creature again. It stood quietly still and calm as if it were expecting something. Khulani opened his mind, and images flooded in. He gripped the bar tighter. It felt soft. They traded images in rapid succession for several moments. There was a commotion nearby, and Khulani was vaguely aware that Rebiku was struggling with the handler who was so disruptive earlier.

Anger filled him . . . and compassion. He received a message and he sent one. He showed the reptilian an image of the soft wooden bar that he gripped and images of fire. More images followed, and in those seconds an agreement was reached that would change both of their lives forever.

Khulani was suddenly pulled from the bars, and handlers appeared inside the enclosure with long sticks to beat the creature back to the other side of the moat. Without a single glance back to Khulani, the reptilian retreated behind the large rock where it came from earlier, and the dark shadows hid it from view again.

Khulani was profoundly affected and exhausted by the experience. "Let us leave this place," he told Rebiku. "I am tired and need to rest."

On the way out, many of the onlookers asked him if he was injured by the creature, but he waved them off, nodding that he was fine. Without hesitation, Rebiku took Khulani by the arm to support him on the walk back to their inn. Not a word was spoken between them until they were safely in their room.

"Rebiku, the lizard man gave me something." Khulani washed his hands and the object vigorously in a bowl of fresh water.

Rebiku stood from his mat and walked over to where Khulani was standing, "What is it?" he asked.

Holding the object in the light, they could see that it was a gold ring in the shape of a snake that looped itself twice over the finger when worn, and there were two clear jewels that appeared to be diamonds in its eye sockets. The ring was large enough to fit a finger larger than Khulani's thumb.

"Why would it give that to you?" Rebiku voice rose in alarm. "Do you know what it means?"

Khulani held the large ring in the dim yellow light cast by the light globe and watched the reflection on its scales and glittering of its eyes. It was almost hypnotic. "I promised to return this to his family, in exchange for his life."

Chapter 13

Nabta People

Fire raged within the walls of the Nekhen Zoo. Screams of men and animals panicked and dying echoed off the walls to where Khulani stood on the roof of the three-story inn. He was alone watching silhouettes against the backdrop of flames frantically moving back and forth outside of the walls that encompassed the zoo. They desperately threw water-filled pottery on the flames from the outside, as none would enter the enclosure where their efforts would be more effective. Those who had entered earlier never returned. They died horribly and not by smoke or flame. Many of them could still be seen through the charred remains of the wide wooden entry. Their broken and disfigured bodies attested to their violent end.

Khulani withstood the suffering of the animals, knowing that their spirits would be gratefully released from the years of purgatory they faced inside the zoo. There were a few that escaped—mostly birds and smaller critters that could swiftly take flight. The rest succumbed to asphyxiation from the smoke before their remains were incinerated by the fire that followed.

All except the men who came to put out the fire. That was the doing of the reptilian. Khulani could feel him from the moment he sent his mind out from the rooftop when the city was still and quiet. He knew when the creature triumphantly broke the bar that Khulani had somehow weakened enough to become brittle, and he knew when the first cage was put to the torch. The reptilian could have escaped over the wall and out of the city without setting the zoo ablaze. He didn't have to keep his bargain with Khulani. He could have been free. There was a sense of honor in the reptilian that was unexpected, and there was also a sense of rage and vengeance that was not surprising at all.

Then the reptilian was gone.

Khulani did not know if the creature was dead or if he had successfully gotten beyond the walls and away. The distraction of the fire would give him cover to escape the city if he did. Khulani would likely never know.

Khulani felt at peace watching the blaze from afar. The zoo's high stone walls would keep the fire from spreading to the city, and by morning only a smoldering pile of bones and ash would remain. He would honor the animals that left those bones behind. It pained him to put them through the horror of the death they faced. He mourned them profoundly already in his heart, and the emotion began to bring about a change.

It did not happen fast, but it was not slow either. His point of view changed, and his eyesight and hearing sharpened. He found himself on all fours in a body covered in brown fur and the paws of an animal. It did not feel unnatural. Then the grief that he knew would come for what he had done overwhelmed him, and he pitched his head to the sky and howled a long and sorrowful wail under the unblinking eye of Ayur.

~~~

Tafukt cast the first rays of the morning light through the narrow window and onto Khulani's sleeping face. His first waking thoughts were about the animals, the zoo, and the unexpected transformation he experienced the previous night. It was the second time that it had happened to him, and he was unsure what to think about it. He knew that the Druids often changed their physical state to that of an animal, in fact, he witnessed it the night of the long-tooth. Now it was happening to him spontaneously, and he needed to learn how to control it before it occurred at an inconvenient time and place.

Rebiku stirred from his rest and sat up on his mat. "What happened last night? I awoke and you were not here."

"There was a fire at the zoo. I watched it burn from the roof." Khulani wanted to tell Rebiku what happened. He wanted to tell him what he had done, but his friend might not understand, and it could irrevocably harm their friendship. In this, he would have to be alone.

"Did it have anything to do with the lizard man? Yesterday after we left the zoo, you were a little delirious and you mentioned something about a sacrifice." Rebiku was washing his face in a wooden bowl across the room with his back turned to Khulani. It was a good thing. Khulani could not bear to lie to his friend's face.

"I don't know. It is probably dead now anyway, as are many of the animals that were trapped in their cages."

Rebiku turned to face him. "That must be painful for you. I am sorry."

"It is"—at least that was the truth—"but I cannot linger on such thoughts. It is time that we found the Druids in the Nabta lands. I am feeling the energy inside me more and more, and I must learn to control it soon."

Rebiku nodded and began packing away his personals. "Then we leave now."

Khulani followed Rebiku to the stables, where they gathered their mounts, and then made their way toward the westward-facing gates of the city. The street traffic was light so early in the morning, allowing them quick passage along the narrow backstreets leading to the broad avenue that would take them out and away from Nekhen. Along the way they passed a strange procession of what Khulani could only characterize as Little People coming from the direction of the port. There were twelve of them, each no taller than a man's waist. They had fine facial features, dark reddish complexions, narrow braided beards, long hairstyles, and eyes framed with cosmetics. They dressed in an opulent fashion, wearing fine fabric shendyt; capes produced from the hides of giraffe, panthers, and cheetahs; and jewelry on their fingers, ankles, and wrists. Some wove unusual silvery gold-toned jewelry into their hair that Khulani was unfamiliar with. Near the center of their entourage, a man held the leash of a creature resembling a monkey that was nearly as tall as the man himself and covered with fine yellow hair. To his relief, Khulani sensed that the animal was well cared for and unperturbed by the collar around its neck connected to the leash.

Khulani was so struck by everything about these unusual people that he stopped to gawk at them without realizing. He vaguely acknowledged that Rebiku had stopped his mount next to him.

"You have never seen the people of Punt?" a woman's voice asked from behind him, nearly making him jump.

Turning around, Khulani realized that he had stopped in front of a merchant's stall where an old lady was preparing to open for business. She had a kind face and a smile that made him feel embarrassed for staring at the small people so openly. Looking over, he could see that Rebiku's cheeks had reddened a little as well.

Sputtering at the start, Khulani said, "We have never seen people like those before. Are they Dwarfs? We heard stories of the Dwarfs when we were children, but we did not dream that they were true."

The old woman cocked her head and laughed as if he had made a joke. "There are Dwarfs in TaShemau, mostly where there are mines, but those you see there are the People of Punt. They are small, yes, but their land resides near the Utjenet—Gods Land—where also lie the Pleasure Gardens of Atum and all the wondrous things that they bring from those lands."

"Was that the ruler of their kingdom that passed by?" Rebiku asked.

The old lady laughed again. "No, no, they are merchants on their way to the palace to present themselves to the Praa. The royal family will have first opportunity to purchase the goods they bring before they are offered at the market."

"Sister," Rebiku spoke up, "what was the yellow creature the one man had on a leash?"

"That, young man, was the sacred Cynocephalus brought as a gift to the Praa, I'm sure." The old lady never stopped moving while she spoke to them, setting out the baubles and trinkets she intended for sale. "Now, how about you each buy one of my charms? They will protect you from sickness and disease." She held up two simple necklaces with uneven yellow stones on leather thongs.

"That is yellow crystal," Khulani laughed. "You can find it all over the Ibhr Rrbi. It is worthless."

"Is it?" The old woman squinted her eyes at him. "As I said, it is a charm, and it holds strong protection magic. When you leave here with them, you will also bear the knowledge about the People of Punt, which I have given freely."

Khulani sensed no magic from the trinkets but handed her a few coins anyway, enough that she seemed satisfied, and gave one of the charms to Rebiku. They both put them around their necks before biding her farewell.

Khulani thought back to the day he and Rebiku departed Tazallit lhnna. The Amgar of their tribe knew the route that they were taking to their destination and had offered some advice. According to the Amgar, the journey from Nekhen to the lands of the Nabta people was expected to take less than a week on horseback. He also explained that traditionally the Imaziyen tribes and Nabta peoples had occasional contact, a few trade missions back and forth, and rarely any conflict. However, he warned that the Nabta were a solitary people who did not trust outsiders. He stressed more than anything that Khulani and Rebiku should treat the Nabta people with respect and represent their tribe honorably. Khulani resolved to make sure he followed his Amgar's advice.

The nights they spent camping in the open savannas, where they felt right at home again. Rebiku was his old self, joking and laughing more casually than he had since they left their people to undertake this journey. It was almost as if they were home again. As sleep would overtake them each night, Khulani watched the stars and considered his future. Once in a while a star would shoot across the sky, and he would smile. *Another spirit is born,* he thought. That was the tradition of his people. And he felt comforted.

During the day they followed a rough trail that led west and south. Oddly, there was almost no traffic, not even a merchant along the ancient path through the hills, copses, and grasslands. Khulani suspected that there was very little trade that traveled west from TaShemau.

On the fourth day out of Nekhen, Khulani observed several small villages and settlements along their route in the distance. He guessed that by now they must be in the lands of the Nabta and suggested they skirt them widely to avoid unnecessary contact. From what little detail he could see, the structures in the villages appeared to be huts made of wood, reeds, and other natural materials. There were people moving about who paid no attention to their passing, yet he had the distinct feeling that unseen eyes were upon them the whole time.

The next afternoon Khulani could see the outline of a large lake to the west with a number of villages along its shores, a forested area farther south, and the main city of Nabta itself ahead of them. Almost a league outside the city they encountered a solitary old man standing in the center of the dirt path they had been following for the last five days. It was almost absurd to see the lonely figure on the trail that was so absent of people over the last several days. And his posture was that of a man intent to bar their way.

"Welcome, visitors. Why do you approach the city of the Nabta?" he challenged. Wearing a plain flax robe, the old man was not as he appeared. Khulani could sense the magic that he wielded and surmised that he was probably a shaman of their people. It surprised him a little that he was certain about the sensation. It was almost as if the more he was exposed to those who wielded magic, the more sensitive he became to its presence.

"I am Khulani of the Imaziyen, seeking council with the Druids of Eriu who have a mission in your city, and this is my friend Rebiku."

While he spoke, Khulani became aware of the sudden appearance of several warriors around them. Quickly, he shot Rebiku a look to stay calm. From where they came was hard to say—the Nabta warriors were known for their legendary use of concealment within the natural environment. Khulani's father spoke admirably of their ability to attack and defend from camouflaged positions and move quickly to confuse or outflank their enemies. It was rumored that they used a vast network of subterranean tunnels and burrows to move silently and quickly around their lands.

The Nabta warriors who surrounded them wielded mostly bows and spears with only small shields for protection. Khulani's father had told him tales of the Nabta people as exceptional bow makers. Their bows were stronger, lighter, and claimed farther distance and accuracy than any other in this part of the known world. Bows from the Nabta were highly sought and prized and nearly impossible to obtain. They were so durable that they were traditionally passed down from one generation to the next and almost never sold. Especially to an outsider. From everything Khulani had heard about these people, if the Nabta were hostile toward them, they would already be dead.

The old Nabta shaman apparently accepted Khulani's explanation for visiting and waved the warriors away. They melted back behind brush and rock as if they had never been, and for the life of him, Khulani could not tell if they departed the area or stayed and watched. He didn't have long to consider before the old shaman waved at Khulani to follow. "I will take you to the Outsiders Camp." He guided them to a flat, open space outside the city to make their camp among the other foreigners.

The Outsiders Camp was almost the size of a large village situated around a central well. There were merchants in small wooden structures selling fabrics, clothing, food, and supplies, and even an open-air tavern covered by spans of wide waxed fabric in case it rained. From what he could guess, there were at least two hundred men, women, and children from many lands doing business with the Nabta people: he recognized Imaziyen from other tribes trading goats and sheep; Capsians with olives and dates; Kerma traders with gold trinkets, carnelian, and incense; and a group from TaShemau with livestock and gold ore.

Khulani and Rebiku made their camp near the other Imaziyen in the camp and changed into their native clothing. Khulani was glad to have his lion-hide cape back on his shoulders. He found the garb of TaMehu comfortable as well except when it was cold in the night and early morning. At the edge of the camp they found a wide fenced enclosure operated by stable hands where they penned their horses before continuing on to find out where the Druids stayed.

The Nabta city had no walls or towers surrounding the buildings inside, and there was only one wide avenue that marked the entrance. Venturing deeper into the city, Khulani noted the abundance of Sacred Cow symbols in the form of large and small statues, chiseled bas-reliefs, and painted art on the walls. He guessed that, like the people of TaMehu and TaShemau, the Nabta worshiped their gods through iconic representations.

The homes they passed were highly organized sandstone structures built in perfectly straight rows, including a few with pens of domesticated cattle and deep wells that were dug in precisely the same locations in each row to supply the residents with fresh water. Beyond the homes there was a large open market dominating the central square, bustling with mix of local and foreign traders. Khulani gazed over the assortment of wild sorghum, fruit, legumes, fish from the lake, millets, tubers, livestock, tools, and cooking implements that were among the many products available in the market. Most of the foreign merchants occupied temporary wood stalls open at the front with no doors; however, a few of the more prosperous traders, particularly those selling more valuable products such as gold, copper, and precious gems, had built more secure stone structures similar to the houses that clustered near the corners of the market square. On the east side of the market loomed the larger public buildings, including a temple of considerable size and what appeared to be the palace.

Oddly, there were very few horses about. It seemed the Nabta people preferred to go on foot rather than by mount. He always assumed they were a tribal people like his own, except that they lived in city, planted, and fished a lot. Even the Imaziyen who lived in Tasili n Ajjer still hunted the herds, and they needed their horses to do so proficiently. Maybe the Nabta people were more like their neighbors to the east than he thought. Khulani supposed he would find out if he stayed here long with the Druids. He suspected he would.

"Let's go to the temple," he said to Rebiku, gesturing across the market. "That is probably the best place for us to start if we are going to find these Druids." Khulani didn't know much about the Druids and anticipated that they must have a temple or meeting place somewhere in the city.

Rebiku nodded in agreement. "Or at least a shaman that can tell us where they are."

The temple was an impressive sandstone structure with wide steps that led up to a broad set of open double doors flanked by the hulking sculptures of two gold-plated Sacred Cows that stared over the city and into the eternal distance. Shamans wearing the cowhide of the animals they worshipped across their shoulders lectured temple acolytes with robust gestures or spoke quietly with devoted followers on the steps or in the shade of the golden cows.

When they entered the temple, it was cool and dark, with no windows. The only illumination was from the hundreds of candles on the walls and altars and from dim light globes that floated freely throughout the grand room. The light reflected off high columns, and cowhides trimmed with gold or adorned with precious stones hung from the ceiling. Most impressively, at the far end of the temple stood an elevated altar with a huge golden cow positioned sideways with its head turned to the left, as if gazing over the people gathered in the room. It was easily twice the size of the ones outside and commanded attention in a room that was large enough to hold at least five hundred people during religious ceremonies. At present, the room was bustling with dozens of shamans and citizens going about their daily tasks. Khulani observed no few of them shooting disapproving glances at the two foreign Imaziyen who gawked at the symbols of their sacred place of worship.

Almost immediately a middle-aged man wearing a cowhide skirt similar in style to the shendyt worn in TaMehu and a long, open cowhide cloak approached them. Like all of the Nabta people Khulani had seen so far, this man had a lean build, dark ebony skin, sharp features—especially in the nose, cheeks, and chin—and a partially shaved head interrupted by long braids studded with beads.

"Greetings, Imaziyen. It is not proper for those not of our faith to linger in the holiest of temples." The shaman was polite but firm as he ushered them back toward the front doors.

"Please forgive our intrusion, holy shaman. We are looking for the temple of the Druids, and we thought someone here could help," Khulani replied once they stepped back into the bright light of the day.

With a laugh the shaman spoke to them as if they were children. "The Druids live in their enclave outside of the city somewhere deep within the forest. No one knows exactly how to find it, not even us, but you will see them around the city once in a while, and they perform sunrise and sunset ceremonies daily at their sacred stone ring near the eastern edge of the city."

"We have only arrived today, and we know little of the Nabta people's traditions. Will you tell us of your practices so that we may honor your people properly?" Khulani asked, sympathetic to the people of the land they were in.

The shaman appeared to gain a new respect for them and paused a moment before responding. "We worship the goddess of fertility and nature, and she is represented by the Sacred Cow. We keep pens of domesticated cattle inside and outside the city for our consumption. Their milk and beef are considered sacred by our people, and the ritual act of consuming them is what brings the goddess's spirit into our bodies. Women who desire children will consume milk and meat from the Sacred Cow more frequently to increase their fertility."

Khulani spoke as reverently as he could manage, "You may know that our people think of all animals in the same way—protected and guided by the spirit of the animal to bring them to safety or sacrifice."

"Yes," the shaman agreed, "there is a similarity, but also a vast difference in our beliefs. Do not forget." The shaman smiled and walked back into the temple.

"Since we are near the market, we might as well refresh our supplies." Rebiku was always enthusiastic about shopping the markets.

Khulani sighed. "I suppose you are right." He was frustrated. Here they were in Nabta and still he could not find the Druids and unless they came across one by chance somewhere in the city. They would have to wait until the sunset ritual that evening. That was hours away still.

After a few hours browsing and purchasing what they needed for the next several days, the two returned to their camp. On their way in, Khulani noticed two Imaziyen warriors nearby in some distress. One was a little older than he and Rebiku and the other younger.

Khulani walked over to them, "Brothers, are you well?"

The taller one looked at Khulani. He was clearly upset about something, while the younger one was holding his arm as if to restrain him from leaving.

"Those jackals from Sai stole our travel packs!" he said, angrily pulling away from his friend. "Now we have lost all the sorghum that our tribe would sow before winter, and I have no more sheep or goats to trade for more!"

"Where is this place you call Sai? Can we help you find these men?" Rebiku seemed almost angry himself. He was quick to react emotionally when he thought a wrong had been done to someone.

A confused look distorted the Imaziyen warrior's features before he replied, "You must be new to this land. Sai is the island city that splits the Aur River in the kingdom of Kerma south of TaShemau. I don't know if they are still here. It has been hours, and by now they could be leagues away."

"Why do you think they took your packs if it has been hours and you only now discovered their loss?" Khulani calmly tried to bring down the tension.

"They were camped next to us all week, and we became friends"—the Imaziyen spat on the ground—"and last night they shared our fire and we drank heqet together. But something was in the brew they gave us that made us tired, and we awoke to find our packs missing just before you arrived."

Khulani looked over at the cold fire pit in the abandoned camp. "What are your names, brothers?"

"I am called Iqhunde, the leader of a Hunt Pack in my tribe, and this is my younger brother, Cebo. He has not yet been called to Tazallit lhnna." The Imaziyen appeared to relax a little.

Khulani introduced himself and Rebiku and then said, "I do not believe you will find the men from Sai, as you called them, Iqhunde. It looks as if they have gone from here many hours ago. Even if you over take them, they will have the advantage of numbers, and the sorghum is not worth the lives of you and your brother."

Iqhunde shook his head in disgust. "It is true what you say, we have no choice but to return to our tribe in shame."

Reaching into a small pack at his side, Khulani produced two long sticks of silver, "Take these and buy your sorghum. I will not allow my brothers to be shamed if I can help."

Iqhunde's eyes widened in surprise. "I am grateful for your generosity, brother." He took one silver stick from Khulani. "One will buy all the sorghum we need, and I will owe you a debt not just for the silver, but also for my honor."

Clasping hands to forearms, the Imaziyen said their goodbyes, and Khulani watched them walk back toward the city to buy their sorghum before the market closed. Returning to their own camp, Rebiku reclined on his mat while Khulani organized his pack with the supplies they purchased. Feeling watched, he looked over to see Rebiku smiling in a knowing way.

"What is it, brother?" Khulani asked.

"You are a good man. I think you will be a good Druid too."

Khulani smiled back. "Let us rest until this evening and maybe we will finally find these Druids we have journeyed so far to meet."

Chapter 14

The Stone Circle

At the top of a hill less than a league outside the city, Khulani beheld a sight that he would never forget. Several massive stones were set into the ground, each standing more than twice the height of the tallest Imaziyen. They formed a wide circle at the top of the slope. Many smaller stones of various sizes seemed to grow out of the ground inside and outside the circle of the larger stones in no particular pattern as far as he could tell. High above his head, small globes of light orbited several of the largest stones at varying speeds and color. A figure wearing a dark hooded robe placed a stationary globe of soft blue light into shallow depressions carved into the stones facing the inside of the circle. The blue light illuminated the interior of the open circle and a cluster of six hooded figures conversing within. Khulani assumed that these were the Druids.

He was a little surprised that they were all light skinned or tanned. Not one of them shared the ebony skin that was natural to the Nabta people. In fact, he had seen no light-skinned people at all since they departed on the ship from Thipsu so many weeks ago. Khulani wondered if there were any dark-skinned Druids or if he might become the first one.

He glanced around at the gathering crowd. Already, about a hundred residents of the city and a few foreigners had arrived early to observe the nightly ritual, and many more were making their way up the hill. Khulani and Rebiku stood outside the edge of the stone circle with everyone else. They arrived early on the chance that Khulani would be able to speak with the Druids before the ritual began. He watched the Druids closely and calculated the chance that he would break some rule or protocol if he approached them inside the circle. Almost as if they read his mind, the six Druids in the center of the stone ring abruptly turned and looked in his direction. Unbelievably, one of the Druids gestured for him to join them.

Khulani walked forward, followed by Rebiku. Immediately the Druid held up his hand and shook his head. Khulani hesitated and then turned to his friend. "Rebiku, wait for me here. I will return in a moment."

Reluctantly Rebiku returned to stand with the watching crowd. They were clearly astonished that one among them was selected to enter the circle, and Khulani surmised that this must be something that almost never occurred. He turned back and walked the rest of the way to the Druids.

To his relief, the nearest Druid smiled warmly. "We have been expecting you."

Another spoke, "You may watch the ceremony with your friend, and when it is over you will return with us to our enclave within the forest."

"How long will I be there?" Khulani asked.

The Druids laughed quietly as if he had told them an obvious joke, then the first Druid said, "You are standing at the start of a path that you will travel the rest of your life. Tell your friend to go home. Now go. We are about to begin."

Khulani felt numb. What was he getting into? They had just arrived and now they expected him to tell Rebiku to go home?

"What did they say?" Rebiku asked when Khulani rejoined him.

"That I will be here awhile. They are taking me to their enclave right after the ceremony."

"Then I will wait for you in the camp. When do you think you will return?"

Khulani put his hand on Rebiku's shoulder. "My brother, I don't know when I will be back. It may not be for a long time."

"I will wait!" Rebiku said fiercely.

"You cannot. What if it was months, or years?"

Rebiku was adamant. "It does not matter. I promised your father and the Amgar that I would look after you."

Khulani shook his head. "No. You must return and tell them everything that has happened. That is your duty now."

"But—"

"Rebiku, please," Khulani interrupted. "They must know everything that has happened and that you have brought me here safely. You cannot waste your life waiting for me."

Rebiku stared hard but kept his silence, and Khulani turned away to watch the ritual. He couldn't look at his friend's face knowing how upset he must have been.

The sun was nearly set, and the Druids had taken their places around the interior of the stone circle. They began a slow rhythmic chant that was soon taken up by the crowd of onlookers that had more than tripled in size since they first arrived. The chanting continued with the sun's final descent to the horizon. From his vantage point, the sun was exactly opposite of where he stood, and as it sank slowly in the sky, it followed the exact curvature of one of the large stones in the circle. Just as the fiery globe reached the distant curve of the planet, the stone pillar aligned with the sunset started to hum rhythmically. There were globes of light orbiting the pillar near its peak, and they gradually increased their velocity and changed their color to match that of the setting sun. The spectacle continued until the sun dipped below the horizon, and as the last glimmer of rays disappeared, the globes rapidly spun off from the pillar and disappeared into the night sky. The pillar fell silent.

The crowd, completely silent until then, erupted in cheers as the ceremony came to an end. Quietly all the Druids collected the light globes from the pillars and formed a line exiting the stone circle, except one. The lone Druid walked to were Khulani was standing and motioned to the line. "It is time."

Khulani looked at his friend. All he could see in his friend's eyes was pain and anger. As much as it pained him, he could not allow Rebiku to wait for him forever. He had to return to his life with their tribe, lead a Hunt Pack, find a woman, and have children. Khulani grabbed Rebiku's hand, and something passed between them, although he didn't know what it was, and then he was being gently pulled away by the Druid.

Khulani turned away and didn't look back. There were no words, or maybe there were too many and not enough time. His entire life since he was a small child, the sun had never set on a day that he did not see Rebiku, and now he did not know when he would see his best friend again, if ever. He felt cheated in some way. He knew he would be tested by the Druids and trained by them to control his gift. But he assumed Rebiku would be with him or at least have the time for proper farewells. This was so sudden . . .

Khulani walked in line with the Druids in the darkness of the forest for a long while. He heard the occasional croak of a tree frog, the lone hoot of an owl, and the constant chirping and buzzing of insects. Having little experience with forests, Khulani found it all a bit disconcerting. The Ibhr Rrbi had its share of animal calls at night, but it was quiet compared to this place.

Well into the forest, he had no idea how long they walked. He was jolted from his half daze by the unexpected sight of beautiful young women, completely unclad, standing near or sitting in large oak trees. He had no idea why they were there, and he dared not ask. No one had spoken since they left the stone ring. The light globes the Druids carried illuminated the women, standing so still, silent and watching like the deer Khulani often hunted on the Ibhr Rrbi.

Soon after, the forest became very thick, and the sky was no longer visible. So thick, in fact, that the branches seemed to grow together to form a canopy that not even rain could penetrate. Looking closer, Khulani could see that dwellings and passages leading inward were formed by the thick trees and brush. He guessed that he must be entering the enclave.

The line of Druids filed into a large chamber formed by branches spiraling high above. It had an opening to the sky venting smoke from a sizable, well-tended fire in the center of the room. Here, other Druids lingered and talked among themselves, cooked, or tended to other duties.

The Druids in the line Khulani followed dispersed in different directions except for two. They led Khulani to a side chamber. The smell of the room was incense, clean and inviting, unlike in the taverns of TaMehu and TaShemau, which tended to be overwhelming or distracting. In the center of the room, an old man sat in solitude wearing the same brown robes decorated with beads and feathers as everyone else. He looked up when they walked in, revealing an aged face adorned with faded blue tattoos.

One of the Druids accompanying Khulani stepped forward. "You are in the presence of Cynwrig, Elder Druid of the Nabta enclave. Keep silent and listen."

The Elder Druid beckoned Khulani to sit next to him. Then he placed his hands on Khulani's temples and said, "Be still and relax." Khulani could see the old Druid's lips moving in some sort of chant, and he could feel a kind of probing inside his mind, as if the Druid were inside his head. This went on for several moments before the Elder Druid drew a sudden intake of breath and released him.

He watched Khulani closely. "You are the first of our kind to come from the Imaziyen people. I do not pretend to understand why this has happened, but you have been brought to us for a reason, and you must stay among us for a while to fully understand your gift and train in the way of the Druids."

The Elder paused and seemed to study him intently again before he spoke. "Most Druids' abilities are discovered at an early age. You are not a child and will need to learn much in a compressed amount of time. This is necessary because your power over nature will continue to grow, and you must learn how to control it quickly before it drives your sanity into something similar to a wild animal's."

The elder paused again. "Finally, my visions tell me that you are destined for something significant that could change the world. Take care with your life before you meet that destiny."

Without another word, the two Druids that accompanied Khulani removed him from the elder's chamber and escorted him through the labyrinth of forested passageways deep in the enclave to what would be his room for the foreseeable future. It was a tiny room with no door, just an opening, with walls and ceiling formed by branches and vines and a mat for sleeping in the corner.

Khulani had so many questions he tried to ask the Druids with him. How long would he be here? When could he go back home? What would happen in his life that may change the world? The Druids would only respond, "Be patient, the answers will come."

Left alone in the dimly lit room, Khulani considered how patient he wanted to be. Maybe he could go back home and learn to live with his gift. His mother had done it. But would the Druids allow it? For that matter, would his own people allow it? No one had ever known about his mother's gift except his father. It was impossible. Everyone in his tribe knew he had the gift and was sent to the Druids. If he did return home now, he would only bring shame to himself and to his father. Even Rebiku would be compelled to shun him. He really had no choice—he would have to endure whatever the Druids had planned for him for however long it took.

The figure of a Druid darkened the entry to his room. "I am Munatas, and I will be your master while you are a neophyte."

"I am Khulani, and I will faithfully serve—" His words were cut short when something wrapped around his neck and pulled him up to his tippy-toes from above. Barely able to breathe, he reached up to grab at whatever was strangling him. It felt like a knobby vine. He strained to look up. The vine had come from the ceiling. More vines fell on his shoulders, and in seconds his hands and arms were wrapped up as well. He swayed on the end of the vines, desperately trying to calm himself enough to breathe.

"Listen to me!" Munatas's voice boomed. "You are no longer Khulani! You are no longer a warrior! You will be known only as Imaziyen until you pass my final test!"

Khulani could not speak. He just stared back at Munatas. Would he be killed the first night he was here?

Munatas leaned close to Khulani's ear and whispered, "Do you understand?"

Khulani was barely able to nod. He could see Munatas's tattooed face clearly and was surprised that the Druid's skin was black like his own. He was the only black Druid Khulani had ever seen.

"Good. Do as I say—exactly as I say—and we can avoid this sort of interaction in the future." Munatas dropped a tightly folded, brown hooded robe and a blanket on Khulani's mat. "I will return for you in the morning. I suggest you get your rest. You will need it."

As soon as Munatas left the room, the vines loosened and dropped him to the floor. Khulani fell to his hands and knees, coughing and sputtering, trying to catch his breath. All the while he promised himself that he would kill the man if he ever tried that again—Druid or no.

~~~

Khulani dreamed that he was drowning in the cold waters of Aur River before he abruptly bolted awake. The outline of two Druids stood over him in the darkness. One was holding an empty, dripping bucket in his hands. Khulani was soaked and cold.

"Now that you are awake and washed, grab your old clothes and follow me." Khulani recognized the voice as Munatas's. The other Druid he did not know.

Slowly rising to his feet, Khulani collected his carefully folded trousers and lion-hide cape and followed the Druids out the door. He couldn't tell if it was day or night from the absence of light in his room, but once he was in the hallway, a few rays of dim illumination managed to filter through the tight canopy of branches above. It was morning, and his wet state combined with the chill in the air made him shiver. A few more turns in the hallway, and they arrived in the large main room where the cooking took place. Pots steamed and bubbled over at the edge of the firepit where they hung, attended by young men in robes like his and faces yet to receive a tattoo. Khulani could smell something like a beef stew that made his stomach grumble, and he realized that he had not eaten since the previous afternoon.

"Throw your old clothes in the pit." Munatas pointed at the fire.

"My cape is the only possession I prize, besides my spear. I cannot burn it."

Munatas glared at down at him. He was no taller than Khulani, but his commanding presence made him seem to tower over him. "Who are you?"

"I am Khu . . ." He quickly stopped himself. "I am Imaziyen."

"Imaziyen is what you are, not who you are," Munatas's gaze was intense and determined. "Imaziyen have no possessions that they prize, and we have yet to decide who you are. Burn them."

Khulani hesitated. His cape was the one thing that meant something to him. Since the time that the lion sacrificed its life so that Khulani might have warmth, a pillow to lay his head on, or a mat for him to sleep upon, it was a cherished part of his identity. Now the Druids were telling him that he was no longer an individual. He was a nameless, faceless Imaziyen and nothing more. It angered him that they would disrespect him this way.

"I will not burn my cape!" Khulani's voice echoed throughout the room. A few looked up from their tasks and just as quickly returned to them. "I still have a father and friends who know me as Khulani. They will always know me as Khulani! Not even you can take that away from me!"

Munatas was nodding thoughtfully. He did not seem upset or irritated by Khulani's outburst. "Very well, Imaziyen, you may keep your cape. You are not a slave here, but let me be perfectly clear. You will leave this place as either a changed man who has become a Druid, an Imaziyen who is capable of living with his gift, or a man who is a danger to himself and others, in which case we will kill you. In the end, it is up to you."

Khulani understood then. It was about his commitment to become a Druid and his dedication to learning everything they had to teach him. The experience would change him, and if he prevailed, who he became would only be a dim reflection of who he was today. With final resolve, he walked over to the fire pit and threw his cape and the rest of his clothing into it. He watched it all burn with a mix of emotions. The heat from the fire felt good on his face and dried his robes, and it was hard to feel remorse for what he had done.

"You show promise, Imaziyen." Munatas walked up to stand next to him. "Wisdom cannot be taught. It can only be gained through experience and the capacity to think objectively."

Khulani shrugged. "I may have failed your test, Munatas, but I am ready to learn now."

Munatas placed a hand on Khulani's shoulder. "You did not fail."

~~~

"Have they come to you yet?"

"Who?"

"The women."

Khulani had no idea what his new friend, Aedan, was talking about. "The only women I have seen are Druids, and none of them have required a task from me yet."

Aedan laughed, his bright red lips contrasting starkly against his pale skin. Khulani had never seen a man with a complexion the pallor of snow, like he had seen only on the peaks of the Uari Ssamal mountain range, and short white hair to match. "They are not Druids!" Aedan whispered.

"Then who?" Khulani was intrigued now.

Aedan kept his voice low. He was a neophyte like Khulani, and neither of them wanted to be caught gossiping while they were washing cups and bowls. "Do you remember the women in the forest when you first arrived here?"

Khulani nodded. "I do. They were beautiful, and I believed them to be a dream or delusion."

"They are not a dream! They are real!" Aedan had been a neophyte for a year longer than Khulani and was a welcome source of friendship not long after they met. He was also a great source of information that made Khulani's life far less difficult than it otherwise might have been. He secretly suspected that it was a common practice for the Druids to put experienced neophytes together with new ones to reduce the anxiety and stress of the new arrivals. As far as he was concerned, it was working.

"Why would those women come here?"

"They are Dryads, Imaziyen!" Aedan said it as if that should mean something to him. It didn't. "They come to the enclave often to breed with the men."

To say Khulani was stunned was an understatement. "To . . . breed?"

Aedan laughed again. "I know, its sounds strange at first, but it is the only way they can reproduce. You see, they are unable to birth a male issue, and they need the seed of a human man to assist with that part."

"Why do they choose the Druids for that task?"

"They are magical creatures unable to travel far from their trees. The Druids are also magical and believe in the balance of nature just as they do. It's a natural pairing, and believe me, my friend, it is no task."

Khulani couldn't believe what he was hearing. "What happens to the children that they birth? Are those the women Druids I see around the enclave?"

Aedan raised his eyebrows high upon his forehead. "I have not considered that, but I don't think so. From what I have been told, the Dryads are very hard to get with child, and when they do, the one who fathered the child usually never knows. After the child is born, the seed of an oak is planted with the placenta, and the tree that grows from it becomes the one that the newborn Dryad is related to the rest of her life."

"But I am not a Druid yet, Aedan. Why would a Dryad come to me?"

"They can sense magic, and they seem to prefer the younger men. Once Master Munatas allows them to seek you out, they will come to you so often that you will have to learn to place a barrier over the entrance to your room to keep them out!"

The Dryads reminded Khulani a lot of the Amazigh women he and Rebiku were seduced by in the Uari Ljanub mountains. Before he found out about the Dryads, he thought the Amazigh were a unique tribe of women who had broken with the tradition of dominance by their male counterparts. Among the Imaziyen women were respected, especially when they were shamans or one of the rare few who became warriors. Otherwise they were responsible for domestic tasks of the village and child rearing, and they would seldom be permitted to involve themselves in decisions affecting the entire tribe. The irony of the extreme examples was not lost on Khulani, and he wondered what a society would be like if both men and women could participate equally.

Finished with the washing, Khulani left Aedan to return to his room to meditate and practice concentration exercises. When he arrived, Munatas was waiting for him.

And he was holding Khulani's spear.

Khulani bowed. "How did you get that?"

"Your friend, Rebiku, is a stubborn one. He gave this to a Druid a few weeks ago at the lunar ritual. He said to tell you that he is still waiting."

"A few weeks ago?"

"Yes, I waited until now to return it to you because I did not want it to be a distraction."

Khulani was a little agitated by the fact that Rebiku did not leave for home immediately. "Why have you brought the spear to me now? Shall I burn it?"

Munatas handed him the spear. "That is up to you, but I hope not. Your skill with that spear is as much a part of you as the gift of nature you carry inside of you."

Khulani stared at the shaft of the spear. It felt good in his hands, and he longed to practice with it again. "You don't believe it will be a distraction now?"

"Your focus has become acute, and your concentration is far better than what I would have expected. I think you can handle it." Munatas left Khulani alone with the spear and his memories.

In the months since he had arrived at the enclave, he learned how to read and write. He decided to put pen to paper and send Rebiku a letter, even if the Druid who delivered it had to read it to him.

To my Hunt Pack Second and lifetime friend,

It is with profound sadness that these words are delivered to you rather than from my own mouth. It seems that I will be staying a long while among the Druids in Nabta. The elder has confirmed that my gift is of the same likeness as their own and something else that he has not revealed to me yet.

I need you to return to our tribe and families and tell them that you have delivered me safely to my destination and that everyone should be glad of what you have done. No truer friend could have withstood our journey with the grace that you have.

Tell my father I will make him proud. Tell our Amgar that I will bring honor to our tribe. Tell our Hunt Pack that they are as well as ever under your leadership. And remind yourself that I am your friend and that I will find you once again when the Druids are done with me. Take Wind Dancer as your own and ride him often. He needs the exercise.

Go well with the spirits, Tafukt, and Ayur.
Khulani

"He begged me to read it several times over before I left him." Gorry was the young Druid who Master Munatas assigned to take the message to Rebiku in Nabta. He had been scheduled to spend a couple of weeks in the city anyway teaching the shamans about charting the stars and only just returned.

"Did he say if he would be leaving?" Khulani studied the Druid carefully. He knew that Gorry was not the talkative sort and would likely not think to volunteer the details of the conversation.

"He was very reluctant at first, and he kept asking me to bring him to the enclave to speak to you."

"So, he was not leaving?"

"No, he finally decided that he would go."

"Thank you, Gorry."

The Druid grunted and left Khulani's room.

Khulani felt relief flood through him. At least he wouldn't have to worry about Rebiku waiting alone in Nabta for his eventual return. By now his friend was probably at least halfway home depending on the route that he took. He envied that Rebiku would be home soon.

~~~

Khulani lay on his mat, staring at his spear propped up in a corner of the room. He could barely see its long outline in the dim light. His mind was on Rebiku. He wished he knew which way his friend was returning home. If he returned the same way they had come together, would he once again meet the friends they had made along the way? Khulani missed Rebiku and looked forward to the day they would meet again. He fell asleep thinking about the adventures they shared together in their lifetime.

A pulling sensation brought Khulani awake. Not physically awake, he could still feel his body sleeping fitfully, but his consciousness was fully aware of something happening to him. The pulling continued. It was persistent and felt much like pulling a spider's web off his face that he had accidentally walked into. Except that this was all over his body. Then there was a distinct 'pop' and the pulling stopped. He was floating now and could clearly see his sleeping body beneath him. It was an odd sensation to be detached from his corporal state and he was surprised that he felt no fear.

His body faded away along with the room where he slept and the Enclave he now called his home and he was flying over the Ibhr Rrbi at incredible speed. There was no wind or sensation of heat or cold. It was as if he passed through the scenery with no effect on anything at all. And then everything stopped and he found himself seeing through the eyes of another . . .

Rebiku rode through the endless green grasslands of the Ibhr Rrbi. He was riding Wind Dancer—no, the image shifted and the time of day changed—he was riding his own mount. Time passed fast and then it slowed down. The sun rose, sailed across the sky and set. Rebiku slept in the open under the stars and rode always when there was daylight. He always seemed to be in a hurry. The days were longer than the nights this time of year, and he covered a lot of distance. Then the cycle repeated. It was the monotony of solitary travel through an environment that changed very little, and Khulani witnessed it over and over.

Rebiku was anxious and worried, and Khulani knew it was because of him. He was gradually feeling what his friend felt, seeing what he saw and know his thoughts. At night was the worst. Rebiku stared up at the sky and worried about Khulani and about what Boa and the rest of the tribe would say. Would they say that he abandoned his friend? Would he be shamed and stripped of his spear? It was an extreme line of thought, but Rebiku's emotions always got the better of him. Other times he thought about Binah, the Amazigh woman who was his companion in the mountains so long ago. He wondered why she gave him the strange gold charm. He wondered why he had kept it. He gazed at it every night and strained his mind for any new memories he might glean from that foggy night. It had a symbol written on it—a ribbed diamond with an X in the center and a sharp-angled line connected to each side—the symbol of fertility. What an odd thing. When she gave it to him she told him that it was important for him to keep it with him until they met again one day. He was surprised that Khulani had not received one from Asha. Maybe it was a personal gift and not a custom of their people. There was something special about Binah, and even though he knew her for only one night, he felt like he needed to see her again. Perhaps he would go find her after he returned to his village. Except that winter was approaching and the mountain trails would be impassable. Maybe next spring. Already the air was becoming considerably cooler, and Rebiku was glad to have found heavier clothing prior to leaving the city of the Nabta people. He never did find out what they called it in their tongue.

Time passed quickly again, and there were mountains and rocky formations in the distance to the west. He must not be far from the Imaziyen city of Tasili n Ajjer. No, he would not stop there. His path was taking him away from the rocks and farther north along the grasslands.

Khulani could see clearly through Rebiku's eyes, feel the wind on his face, and understand his thoughts. It was a peculiar thing to be a passenger inside his friend's head. Even while he knew it was just a dream, everything was so vivid and real . . .

Something was stirring in the direction of the mountains that got his attention. In the distance, a group of mounted men were riding hard toward the north in a roughly parallel course to his own. They looked like they might be Imaziyen, but he could not be sure. Behind them, nearly on their heels, was a smaller group of what might have been men, except that they looked much larger and they were not mounted, yet somehow they kept up with those they pursued. In just the span of a few seconds, both groups disappeared behind a rise and out of sight.

Rebiku spurred his mount forward, intent on catching up to the strange procession. They were moving so fast that he thought he might lose them, but when he crested the rise behind which they had disappeared, he had to stop and catch his breath. A dozen Imaziyen with spears pointed outward in a defensive position clustered next to their dead and dying mounts. They had run their horses until they could run no more, and now they were forced to face their pursuers.

Six giant humanoids, twice the size and height of his brothers, carried clubs so large that they could easily have been from the trunks of trees. They circled and feinted with their clubs while shouting insults and predictions about how they planned to strip the meager meat from the humans' bones.

Instinctually, Rebiku planted his heels in his mount and charged down the hill to help his countrymen. He knew they were not a part of his tribe, but that did not matter. The Imaziyen below were mounting a respectable defense after a long chase that exhausted and killed their mounts. They planted their spears against the onrush of the giant men and drew their curved long knives, expecting close combat.

Khulani felt Rebiku's fear and his own rising.

The giant men appeared to bear the pain of spears in their guts and thighs, brushing them aside as if they were merely an annoyance.

By the time Rebiku was close enough to strike, four of the Imaziyen and one Giant were lifeless on the green-turned-crimson grass of the plains. Without regard for himself, Rebiku charged into the back of one of the Giants and impaled the massive creature on his spear. The shaft went deep into its tough flesh, producing convulsions that pulled Rebiku off his mount and sent him roughly to the ground. Khulani saw the images blur and felt the instinctual self-righting as Rebiku rolled to his feet with his long knife in hand. He did not need to look at the impaled Giant to know that it was dead. Instead, he focused on his next target.

In Khulani's tribe, there were few who could best Rebiku in hand-to-hand combat. He was well-known as a master with spear or blade. Even the older veterans respected his natural abilities and set him the task, even as a boy, of training the younger boys in their first lessons in the art of combat and self-defense. Khulani knew at this moment how much he had underappreciated his friend's raw skill. Rebiku never shied from a fight when he knew one couldn't be avoided, and now he was fighting for his life and the lives of those he rushed in to aid.

His charge had eliminated one of their adversaries, leaving four giant men to deal with. No easy task. Fortunately, the Imaziyen were putting up a good fight, and the distracted Giants had not yet noticed Rebiku's arrival from behind. He had the advantage.

Striking into the lower back of the nearest one, Rebiku tore out the Giant's kidneys, sending him into a writhing ball of pain. Massive as the Giant was, Rebiku skipped over him and on to the next. There were three left, and Rebiku sliced at the ribs and spine of one of them. The Giant managed to turn to face him, and for the first time he realized that the creature had only a single eye in the center of its head instead of two.

He paused in startled disbelief, giving the injured Giant a precious few seconds to react. The Giant swung his massive club quicker than expected, impacting Rebiku in the chest. The force of the blow broke a few ribs. Khulani could feel the cracking inside Rebiku's chest cavity and the brief shock of pain. His body was flung to the side by the blow, and the Giant followed closely behind, out of step and falling off-balance.

Rebiku stopped his backward motion and spun to face the Giant. The thing was too close, but it wasn't the club that had Rebiku worried. The Giant was falling on him, and he had no time to sidestep. Dropping to a crouch, the pain from his chest nearly made him lose his senses, and blood exploded from his mouth in a red spray. Khulani was horrified: Rebiku was going to break the Giant's fall.

Khulani would never forget the emotion he felt next from Rebiku—joy. Rebiku felt joy at the certainty that he would take this Giant's life even if it cost him his own. The Giant's body came crashing down on Rebiku, pinning him to the ground, its colossal weight too much for his broken ribs, collapsing his lungs. But the Giant would never get up—Rebiku's long knife was solidly lodged in its heart.

Khulani's friend felt no pain. In fact, there was no feeling at all. The light around him began to dim, and as his consciousness was dragged into eternal darkness, Rebiku's final thoughts were of him and Khulani hunting together in the lush grasslands of the Ibhr Rrbi.

Then Khulani was suddenly above the scene. Was he still with Rebiku? The last two Giants were running away, and the surviving Imaziyen pulled Rebiku's body out from under the massive corpse to kneel around him sadly.

Khulani awoke in the cold black of night with the stark certainty that his friend was dead.

Chapter 15

Return to Nekhen

"It has been ten days, Khulani. The time for mourning is over." Munatas was standing at the entrance to the small branch-enrobed room, blocking the little light that could find its way in.

Khulani sat on his mat, legs crossed, palms over his knees in meditation. He opened his eyes. "I am no longer mourning. I am angry."

"What is the source of your anger?"

"I am angry at myself for sending Rebiku away, and I am angry at the monsters that killed him."

"The anger with yourself will pass once you realize that you had no way of knowing what could happen. Rebiku could have departed when you told him to and he might have survived his journey home. It was his choice to wait, and when he made the decision to finally go, his fate was sealed." Munatas's voice was sympathetic, but firm. Khulani had not thought of it that way. Even still, he could not blame his friend, and he didn't believe in fate. Things just happened that were unforeseeable and unexpected. Was a rabbit fated to be killed by a fox the moment it made the decision to leave its burrow? He learned growing up on the Ibhr Rrbi the fragile nature of life.

"What are the giant one-eyed creatures that I dreamed killed my friend?"

"The Druids call them Kaiko, One-eyed, but most in the Western Kingdoms know them as Cyclops."

The words *Western Kingdoms* and *Cyclops* were foreign terms to Khulani. "Are these Cyclops from the Western Kingdoms, then?"

Munatas walked over to help Khulani to his feet. "Come with me, Imaziyen. It is time you learned about the world you live in."

Khulani followed Munatas through hallways he had never tread before, passing rooms filled with unusual lights, floating objects, and wonders he could not comprehend. Like the rest of the enclave, the walls and ceiling were created with stone and living branches with open entryways and no doors.

After several twists and turns, they walked down a long corridor that ended in an open, multileveled room filled with shelves holding thousands upon thousands of books and scrolls. Several Druids wandered along the bookcases lining the walls or sat at tables in the center of the room reading. The few who looked up at their entrance paid them little attention.

"What is this place?" Khulani asked.

Munatas opened his arms wide as if to embrace the room. "We call it a library. Soon, you will be spending many hours of the day in this chamber learning the wisdom of Druids and wise men from times past."

Munatas guided him to a large table near the east wall of the room. Several tall baskets sat next to it holding dozens of long rolled-up parchments. The Druid began to pull out one after another, briefly opening each one before returning it to the basket. Finally, he chose one and unrolled it on the table, pinning each corner with a weight to keep it flat.

Khulani noticed colorful images on the parchment arranged in jagged and smooth patterns. There were dots on a few of the patterns and strange writing next to each one. "This is a map, or drawing, of the landmasses and bodies of water in a portion of our world. Imagine you are a bird that can fly very high. This is an idea of how the earth would appear."

Khulani was amazed at what he saw. "What do the patterns mean?"

"The blue-colored patterns are water." Munatas pointed to places on the map. "Here is the Great Sea, and here is the River Aur that you traveled down to come here." He pointed to many other patterns indicating mountains, grasslands, forests, and lakes.

"This dot nestled deep in the mountains you call the Uari Ssamal is your holy city, Tazallit lhnna." Munatas moved his finger down the map slowly. "This is part of the Ibhr Rrbi where your tribe is, and all of this is also part of the Ibhr Rrbi. It is quite vast. And way down here is the city of the Nabta people and the forest where you are now."

Khulani was beginning to understand. "What is the scale of distance on this . . . map?"

Munatas pointed to a line near the bottom of the map separated into sections and put his little finger on it. "This is called a scale. They are different for every map. The length of my finger represents about three hundred leagues."

Khulani knew what a league was on the ground and learned a little about how to calculate distance on water from Musa. Three hundred leagues was a significant distance, and many of those scales would fit end to end on this map. "This is the world?"

Munatas laughed. "No, just a small portion of it." He rolled up the map and lay out another one. "The scale of this one is larger." He placed his little finger next to the scale again. "See? Three hundred leagues extends a little over half the length of my finger."

Khulani recognized the same patterns of mountains and the Great Sea. They were just smaller.

"Up here is where the Western Kingdoms are located. This area includes Lyonesse, Eriu, Ys, and the cities of the Tuatha De." Munatas pointed near the top of the map. "You will learn about these lands soon enough. Above them is the land called Fomoire, where the Cyclops are from."

"What is this over here?" Khulani was pointing to an enormous landmass surrounded by water on the extreme western side of the map.

"That is the Emerald Isle, where the Atlanteans come from." Munatas pointed to a dot on the southeast coastline of the island. "The City of Atlantis is here. Your people know them as the Enlightened Ones."

"I met one when Rebiku and I were in Inbu-Hedj. Of course, I have heard stories about them my whole life. They are extraordinary."

Munatas smiled broadly. "They are a forward-thinking people dedicated to the peaceful progress of all civilizations. You will see them among us from time to time, sharing their wisdom and knowledge. Although I have never been to their home myself, I have read much about them. And so will you." He gestured to the bookshelves around them. "I'm sure you will be as impressed with them as the rest of us."

Khulani skimmed over the map further. "Show me where my friend died," he said quietly.

Munatas paused and then pointed to a dot on the map. "The writing next to this dot means Tasili n Ajjer, the Imaziyen city. My best guess is that your friend died somewhere east of there."

Doing a few quick calculations in his head, Khulani couldn't believe what he discovered. "The Cyclops were over one thousand leagues from their home. How is that possible?"

"Elder Cynwrig believes your vision, your dream, was real. As do I. We don't know why the Cyclops are there nor for how long. We also believe that the Imaziyen were not aware of their presence, which means that they only recently arrived or their settlement is far off and they found your brothers, and your friend, by unfortunate accident."

Khulani looked Munatas squarely in the eye. "Then I must return home and gather our Hunt Packs to find these Cyclops and avenge Rebiku."

Munatas's gaze did not waver and neither did his serious tone. "You may do that, Imaziyen. We will not stop you. But not until after you have completed your training. Then, you may avenge your friend if you still believe it is what you must do."

"And if I go now?"

"You will be lost to us."

Khulani could not let his anger make him forget the sacrifice Rebiku made so that he could be here. "Then you have given the Cyclops the gift of living until I am finished here."

A mysterious, knowing smile briefly touched Munatas's lips. "We shall see."

~~~

SY5486

Ten Years Later

Khulani was standing in the tall grass with Aedan and two other neophytes, staring through the darkness at the flickering lights from the TaShemau city of Nekhen. Behind them stood a dozen Druids, including Munatas, all watching. Khulani gripped his spear tightly and push the butt into the ground a little more to keep it steady in the strong wind that blew from the east that evening. The last time he was in Nekhen, Rebiku was with him. And although it was ten years since his friend's death, he still thought about him every day.

This was the city with the zoo that held the reptilian. He heard they were going to rebuild it. Khulani still kept the ring the creature had given him and wondered if he would ever be able to fulfill the obligation thrust upon him by the creature. It was an obligation that he was reluctant to undertake. As far as he knew, the reptilians were a world away and likely to kill him on sight. Perhaps he would bring it up with Munatas when they returned to the enclave.

Khulani didn't know why they were here—he doubted it had anything to do with the zoo. That's how all the training missions were with the Druids. He and the other neophytes would learn new skills and abilities, meditate on them, master them, and then go out on a supervised mission. Tonight, they were going to be challenged in some way that would require them to use the environment.

Most missions were fairly simplistic and boring, Khulani laughed to himself. The last one the Druids had them parting earth to make furrows in the ground and redirecting the flow of water to irrigate a field to be planted. The farmers were certainly pleased not to have to do the work themselves. Some of the neophytes, like Aedan, did not accompany them on all the missions since they had already mastered the skills being tested. Tonight was different for some reason. Aedan was with them, and there were more Druids than usual present. It all made him a little nervous.

"It's time." Master Munatas was calm and assured as always. Khulani wished he had that confidence. "Assume your flight form with night vision."

Khulani was sure that meant owl. He let his mind slip into calm focus and visualized the form of an owl. He sensed Aedan and the Druids almost instantly shift. It took him and the other neophytes a little longer. The most difficult part was *feeling* like he was an owl, not just looking like one.

When he first learned to shapeshift, he was sure it was an impossible task that he would never master. How could one feel like an owl, or any animal for that matter? His gift allowed him to know what animals were feeling when they were near, but not what it was like to be one.

And then it came to him one night when he was working with a mouse. He discovered that he could see through its eyes, hear what it heard, and eventually feel what it was feeling. That's when it clicked for him, and from then on he studied many different animals whose form he wanted to assume.

Khulani lurched into the sky, joining the fifteen other owls heading in the direction of Nekhen. They had a plan. Munatas would take him and Aedan to the southern district of the city while the other Druids and neophytes split up into small teams to search the other districts. For what they were searching, Khulani had no idea. The Druids would only tell them to keep their eyes open for anything unusual and that they would know when they found it. Khulani wanted to roll his eyes at that. Why the Druids had to always be so enigmatic about everything, he surely did not know.

The night was clear, if windy, and the crimson glow from the crystal pyramid shone brightly over the city they approached. That's where the Atlanteans would be. He learned to think of them that way rather than as the Enlightened Ones now that he had trained under a few of them. Not that they were not enlightened; they certainly seemed to be. It was just that for him to continue to think of them in that way was ignorant and unfamiliar. They came to the enclave every few months to share their vast knowledge of the cosmos with the Druids, and he got to know a few of them very well. If asked, they would tell him about their city, their culture, and other cultures he knew nothing about.

It was from the Atlanteans that Khulani learned one of the mysteries of the Druids. Most people assumed that the Druids' knowledge of the solstices, lunar cycles, and other celestial bodies came from their deities Eriu and Sunna, but the truth was that it came from the Atlanteans. It was through their expertise and knowledge that the Druids erected the great stone circle where they practiced their rituals. And there were many such circles, some much larger and more complex, in many places around the world.

Nearly over Nekhen, Khulani followed Munatas and Aedan when they broke off from the rest of the group and began a slow glide down toward the southern edge of the city. The owl was Khulani's favorite bird form. The large rounded wings with a broad surface area allowed for silent and almost effortless flight. Its great, sharp talons combined with acute night vision and extraordinary hearing made it the perfect nocturnal predator.

He shadowed Munatas and Aedan high above the streets and avenues, tracking their lines and curves until they reached the edge of the district, and then they followed another in the opposite direction. It was still and quiet this time of night, with not a soul on the streets. Not even those who slept outside. Khulani found this odd. Last time he was in Nekhen, there were taverns open all night, and it was not unusual for those who could not afford an inn to sleep outside in a cart or on a roof. Something had happened in Nekhen. Since he was only a neophyte, he was not allowed to receive much news from the outside. The Druids considered it a distraction to their learning.

Master Munatas precipitously broke downward at a steep angle toward a dark cul-de-sac. Khulani and Aedan followed. When they reached street level, Munatas smoothly transformed and settled his human feet on the ground. Khulani tried the same move and wound up rolling a few paces, bruised but unharmed, except for his ego.

"You will need to work on that," Munatas chuckled.

Aedan helped him to his feet, and they joined Munatas standing in the center of the street.

"It will be coming soon," Munatas observed. "Did you hear it?"

Both Khulani and Aedan shook their heads. Khulani heard many sounds while in flight, from the skittering of rats to muffled voices inside houses, but what the "it" was, he had no idea.

"A terror with the power of a god."

Khulani was startled by the soft voice behind him and he spun around quickly, spear leveled. It was a woman. An Atlantean woman wearing a long, flowing white gown.

"This is Master Ycae of the White Hall." Munatas honored her with the usual bow. Khulani and Aedan followed suit.

Like all Atlanteans, Master Ycae was beautiful even in her advanced age. Her trailing white gown matched her equally white long hair that flowed dramatically behind her in the wind rushing into the cul-de-sac. She nodded to Khulani and Aedan before addressing Munatas, "Are the others in place?"

"Yes, Master Ycae," Munatas nodded. "They are joining your brethren at the locations you provided even as we speak."

"Good." She looked over at Khulani and Aedan with a smile that reached up to her kind eyes. "What about these children you have brought with you? Do they know what to do?"

Munatas smiled as well, although his gaze was hard on them. "We shall see."

Master Ycea snapped her head forward and looked into the dark street beyond where they stood. "Prepare yourselves, gentlemen. It is here."

Khulani turned to face the open end of the cul-de-sac. He could see nothing in the darkness, but he could sense something coming closer. Whatever it was, it knew they were there and gave the impression that it was tasting their fear in the air. At least, *Khulani* was afraid.

It came slowly closer, and he realized there were others that came with it. Khulani thought he could hear a faint dragging sound, as if it were pulling itself along the ground, and the slow patter of sandaled feet. Then it was close enough that he knew it was an animal . . . of sorts. He could feel the cold, dispassionate need to kill from it—not driven by rage or hunger—and nothing else. Khulani could not even determine what type of animal it was. He waited with the others, spear clutched tightly in his hands.

From somewhere in the city came the concussion of an explosion followed by faint screams. From another direction, closer than the last, he was startled by the crackle of lightning. He stared ahead, waiting for what he knew was coming and was surprised to see a lone man wearing a white shendyt and nemes step from the darkness. He appeared to be a priest.

"Bear witness to the earthly incarnation of our lord, Apep! Your sacrifice will be your salvation in the land of the dead!" From the darkness, a massive head with fangs as long as Khulani's spear shot over the priest and toward Munatas. It smashed into an invisible barrier of air, which deflected it toward one of the low two-story buildings forming the cul-de-sac. A brief scream rent the air when its uncoiling body crushed the priest in its fluid advance. Behind it came several more priests carrying clubs and daggers, running with the eager intent to use them.

The massive snake was only stunned a moment before it began to coil again for another strike. Khulani was the closest to it, and he knew it would try for him next. In desperation he reached into the ground below the pavers with his mind and found roots from weeds pushing up between them. He pressed his will upon them, and in seconds they erupted in a protective ring around him that formed a dome over his head. He felt the pressure of the strike and relief that it held. The snake recoiled, having been rewarded with a mouthful of thorns and thistles.

The protective thicket fell to the ground and Khulani glanced around quickly—Master Ycae was casting a spell, Munatas had somehow conjured plantlike elementals to combat the onrushing priests, Aedan was calling down bolts of lightning that appeared to only agitate the snake further, and above them the sky was a mad swirl of clouds around the eye of a black vortex. The snake raced around the exterior of the cul-de-sac and coiled to strike the Atlantean from behind. Seemingly unconcerned, Master Ycae continued her cast.

Watching in disbelief, Khulani screamed for her to move. Did she not hear him? There was no time to pull up another barrier to protect her. He threw his spear. It left his hand at the same time the snake released the tension to strike its prey. Less than a span above her head, the spear bit deep into the fleshy part of the snake's maw, arresting its attack and sending it flailing its head back and forth to remove the impediment. Master Ycae never even flinched.

Taking advantage of the beast's preoccupation, Khulani turned to face the remaining priests. Several where dead or dying, and at least a score more were pulverizing the last few elementals with their clubs.

Munatas waved his arms, causing the earth to erupt in front of him, sending several priest flying through the air to crumple unmoving where they landed. Khulani couldn't do that, but he could do something else. He sent out a call.

Behind him Aedan cried out. Spinning around, he saw his friend pinned to the wall by the violently thrashing body of the snake. There was no way to release him. Khulani had to do something. Thinking quick, he ran as fast as he could toward the head of the snake. It would be an impossible feat, but he had to try. There was no planning, and he had to time it perfectly—he jumped. To his absolute surprise, he caught the shaft of the spear and yanked it from the flesh of the snake.

Khulani rolled to his feet to face the serpent. It was coiled and angry hovering just above him. In another part of his mind, he knew his call had been answered, and he commanded his new legion to attack the priests closing in on Munatas. To his brief satisfaction, he heard their screams as hundreds of rats charged from every hole and gutter in a wave of death by a thousand bites.

The snake did not strike. Khulani did not understand. It hovered above him, staring down at him with the eternal depth of dead eyes, but it did not strike. Khulani chanced a glance to where Aedan was pinned earlier. The other neophyte managed to crawl away once the snake stopped flailing, but he was badly battered and beaten.

"Finish it." Master Ycae calmly told him.

"What?" Khulani spared another glance for the Atlantean.

"I can't hold it forever," she scolded him. "Finish it off so I can send its body to rot somewhere in the middle of the Ibhr Rrbi. Its priest will never find the body so far away."

"What would that matter?" he asked.

"They are a death cult and might have the knowledge to resurrect it. Now finish it!"

There was only one good way to kill a snake, he thought. Khulani carefully gauged the distance and jumped. With one thrust, his spear entered the base of its jaw, traveled through its soft palate and into its brain. Seconds after he landed, the snake head hit the ground next to him, and with a few twitches of its body, it was dead.

"If you value that spear, take it quickly and move away!" Master Ycae called to him.

Without hesitation, he pulled his spear from the snake and moved to stand with Master Munatas and Aedan at the opposite side of the cul-de-sac. All the priests were dead, and only a few rats remained to scavenge at their remains.

Master Ycae spoke a few words that Khulani could not understand, and a narrow funnel of fast-moving wind stretched down toward the body of the snake. Seconds later, the serpent was sucked into the vortex and disappeared. Soon the sky was clear again of all but the stars.

Khulani knelt next to Aedan and laid hands upon his shoulders. He forced his will upon his friend to heal the broken bones and internal damage. Warmth flooded through him and into his friend. It was like controlling the currents of a fast-moving river. Sometimes he could imagine actually seeing the flows of magic. A little more effort, and he was done.

Aedan struggled to his feet and stood on his own.

"How do you feel?" Munatas asked.

"Exhausted, but not unwell." He looked at Khulani. "How did you do that?"

Khulani shrugged. "Just as we do anything with magic—I captured the will to do so."

That was the difference between those who used magic and the Druids. Rather than controlling the flows of magic energy provided by a crystal, like the Atlanteans and human wizards, the Druids acquired their power from the energy of nature and their strength of will. He did not understand it fully yet, but he was learning quickly, and healing came the easiest to him.

Munatas looked deep into his eyes, almost as if he were trying to see into the depths of his soul. "It appears that we not only have a rare warrior-Druid, but a talented healer as well. What do you say to that?"

Khulani wished he could see into his own soul for the answers as well. "I am the son of my father and my mother. I am Imaziyen."

Chapter 16

Final Tests

"Why can I not draw upon the Orichalcum Crystals for power as the Atlanteans and human wizards do?"

Ycae was levitating twelve orbs of light in the air while illuminating the currents of magic that flowed from her to the orbs. "We have a harmonic symbiosis with the Crystals that is part of who we are. From the time Atlanteans have been on this world there has been the Orichalcum, and vice versa. Never has there been one without the other. As far as the humans, it was a surprise to us that they could be trained to use the power of the Crystals. The Dwarf wizards also have this ability."

Master Munatas was standing next to Khulani, helping him to match his flows of magic to those of Ycae, attempting to take over control of the floating orbs. "As you know, the power of the Druids is derived from nature, and although the sources of magic are different, they can work together in extraordinary ways."

"How do you draw power from the Crystals, Master Ycae? Is it the same way that I do from nature?"

"Nature magic is based on your connection to the energy in living things around you and your strength of will to draw from it." With her free hand she created an image in the air of sparkling dust that looked like a Druid conjuring with magic from his environment. "For those of us who take power from the Crystals, it is a matter of opening ourselves to their energy and channeling it into the form that we desire."

Khulani carefully took over control of the orbs from Ycae. He was pleased that he maintained their positions even after Ycae withdrew her magic. "Are there any other sources of magic?"

"There is one other for certain," Ycae replied. "That of faith."

"Is that the source of magic for the Imaziyen shamans?" Khulani began to slowly manipulate the color and positions of the globes in the air simultaneously.

"That is correct, very perceptive." Ycae smiled. "It is also the source for priests and holy men of every culture that we have encountered. Including our own."

Khulani was surprised at that statement. "Wouldn't that imply that every deity from every belief system would have to actually exist to transfer power to their faithful?"

"The power of faith is a mystery even to us." Ycae held up her slender hands in a gesture of uncertainty. "It is quite a debate among the spiritual leaders and one of the best-kept secrets from society at large."

Khulani had a burning question that he had been wanting to ask for some time now. Maybe now was the right time. "I have been struggling to reconcile my Imaziyen beliefs with those of the Druids. Our sun god is Tafukt and our moon goddess is Ayur. Similarly, Eriu is the goddess of the moon and Sunna the deity of the sun for the Druids. Since I have been in the enclave and learned to read, my studies have revealed that there are many deities for the sun and moon worshipped by different peoples all around the world. And I wonder, are there so many gods, or maybe just a few known by different names?"

"You have a penchant for asking the most difficult of philosophical questions, Imaziyen," Master Munatas laughed. "If you ever find the answers, I pray you will let us know."

"Do not allow your neophyte to become one of your hermit philosophers living in some obscure cave, Munatas," Ycae chuckled. "This one might have more to offer one day."

Munatas grunted, but made no comment.

Khulani had the orbs spiraling from the floor to the ceiling and back down again. He deftly altered their individual speed and color in the course of their circuit.

"You are mastering control of the flows of magic well, Imaziyen." Munatas made a quick hand motion, and suddenly the orbs fell to the ground.

"What happened?" Khulani exclaimed.

"It is one thing to master control of your own magic and quite another to protect against another's." Munatas raised the orbs from the floor, floating them in the air once more. "Take them from me if you can."

Khulani instantly brought his will to bear. It was much easier now than it used to be.

In the months following the mission against the priests of Apep in Nekhen, Khulani's skills had improved substantially. He was learning the secret ways of the Druids and becoming one with nature. Munatas initially allowed him to participate in the sunrise and sunset rituals, and later on the more important ceremonies associated with the summer and winter solstices. For the Druids, there was much emphasis on the Sky Hunter constellation in the southern sky and in particular the three stars that made up his belt. There were many other stars that held significance, depending on the ritual involved, especially a bright star below the hunter that the Nabta priests identified as the light of creation carried by their own goddess.

Khulani learned how to use the stone circle outside of Nabta to predict these occasions as well as when the best time for planting and harvesting would take place. The Nabta priests, devoted to their fertility goddess represented by the Sacred Cow, were heavily involved with these rituals. The Atlanteans, whom the Nabta revered as the Star People, would also attend.

Khulani found it curious at first that the Nabta people associated the Atlanteans with the stars until he saw, for the first time, one of their great sky ships arrive at the Druids' enclave. It would descend out of the sky from a great height and always at night, lending the impression that it had come from the stars. Then it would hover in a clearing near the stone circle to allow the Atlanteans to disembark. The vessel resembled a much larger scale of the sailing ships that he had seen from afar when he and Rebiku were at sea for the first time years earlier. Once Khulani understood how to use the calendar of the stone circle, he realized the ship would arrive on a regular schedule, every thirty days, without fail.

"Imaziɣen, we are sending you to join our mission in the Nabta city. There you will learn to develop your skills as a healer," Master Munatas told him.

Khulani was elated. He had not been out of the enclave for many years, except for the rituals at the stone circle and the occasional mission. To be around new faces and the bustle of the city would be a welcome change from the enclosed spaces of the forest. Best of all, he would be within sight of the Ibhr Rrbi and might even get the chance wade through its tall grass from time to time.

~~~

SY5490

Four Years Later

Khulani sat quietly on the floor in his room, deep in meditation. He visualized the joyous freedom and serenity of flying over the endless grasslands of his home. He was riding currents of air in his owl flight form, barely twitching a muscle as he slowly manipulated his speed and elevation. The act of flight freed his mind from earthly constraints and allowed him to access the higher powers within himself for a better understanding of the lessons that the Druids passed along. According to Master Munatas, neophytes rarely had the ability to access their higher consciousness until several decades into their training. For Khulani, it came naturally, similar to his ability to "feel" animals and creatures around him and even communicate with them now at a very basic level.

This year would mark a decade and a half of training in the Druid enclave. Over the years he learned many things about his abilities, the world, and himself. He watched friends come and go and witnessed the passing of Elder Cynwrig just a year earlier. It was shocking to find out that the old Druid had lived nearly to the age of one hundred and fifty. No surprise to anyone, Master Munatas was chosen as the next elder to succeed him. But the thing that hurt Khulani the most was the loss of his best friend, Aedan. Before his death, Elder Cynwrig determined that Aedan's training was at an end and sent him north to Eriu. After more than a decade of friendship, it was almost like losing Rebiku all over again, except that there was hope that he and Aedan might see each other again one day. The previous year was a year of loss in many ways indeed.

Within his calm dome of tranquility, there was a light tug on his awareness, an alarm bell of sorts letting him know that someone was approaching the doorless entrance to his small hutch.

"Hello, Faelan," Khulani said, greeting the startled neophyte when he entered. Khulani had not moved, and his eyes were still closed, yet he could feel the heightened apprehension of the young man.

"Greetings, Honored Imaziyen," the neophyte stuttered nervously. "Please forgive my interruption, but Elder Munatas has sent me to summon you to meet with him."

Khulani opened his eyes briefly. "I will be along."

Faelan bowed. "Of course, Honored One, I will tell them you are coming."

"Don't worry, Faelan. I already have."

The neophyte swallowed with an audible gulp, bowed once more, and departed as quickly as his feet would carry him. Khulani chuckled to himself. Faelan was a recent neophyte said to have much promise as a researcher and lore master. The boy was from Eriu, and Faelan wasn't his real name. The name *Faelan* meant *Little Wolf* in his native language. Master Munatas gave him the name because of the tenacious manner in which he pursued knowledge.

Khulani made his way along the branch-and-vine-lined corridors. Often, he would cross paths with a neophyte who would bow and utter "Honored One" when he passed. He still wasn't used to the title. It was the title granted to a neophyte when they were in the last stage of training and expected to be recognized as a Druid soon. Khulani reflected on how difficult and lonely many of his days in the enclave had been. Even with the frequent social occasions with Aedan and the occasional pleasure of a Dryad, his training was a solitary endeavor with internal focus. The last few years were the best. The missions became more challenging and numerous, and his time among the Nabta people developing his talents as a healer was rewarding.

So far, he passed every test, completed every challenge, and bested every adversary as he grew in the power of nature and understanding of the Druids' way of life. Now he had been summoned by Elder Munatas, and if his intuition was correct, the Druid would be offering him his final test.

Outside of Elder Munatas's chamber stood two neophytes. One stepped forward at Khulani's approach and politely asked him to follow. The neophyte led him to a large room that he knew only as the Council of Elders chamber. Khulani was surprised. In the fifteen years since he joined the enclave, on only two occasions could he recall elders from Eriu meeting in this place. Perhaps Elder Munatas planned to utilize the chamber for more than formal occasions.

The neophyte stopped outside and gestured for Khulani to enter. Inside, the room was filled with the haze of incense. It smelled like the forest after a summer rain—fresh and earthy. Ahead of him, in the center of the room, stood five small bowls elevated on stands. The bowl in the center was a little larger than the others. Beyond the bowls, he could see four figures sitting on the floor. Khulani could not identify them in their hooded robes, but he knew they were watching him closely to see what he would do. One of them had to be Elder Munatas. Who were the others?

He expected to be summoned and charged with a final test. What he didn't expect was that the test had already begun. Khulani approached the first of the elevated bowls on his left. Inside there was a small mound of soil. He considered its meaning. Often, he found that the tests could be answered in many different ways. There was no absolute wrong or right. He would be judged on the results.

Khulani placed his hands over the bowl and reached for his will. "From Mother Earth I bring life," he sang. Removing his hands from the bowl, a small green sprout slowly grew into a short oak sapling.

He moved to the next bowl. Here he found a smooth river rock. Placing his hands over the bowl, he sang, "From the stone I call forth the tears of Eriu." There was a sharp crack, and from the broken river rock came a small trickle of water.

Skipping the center bowl, he moved to the third. This one held a lock of blond hair. Once again, he sang, "I call forth flame from the golden hair of Sunna." A spark ignited the hair, and it burned with a bright yellow glow.

In the last bowl, Khulani found a tiny feather. "May the breath of the goddess stir to make wind," he sang. The feather whipped around the bowl, caught up in a tiny vortex.

Now came the hard part. Khulani moved to the center bowl. He had no idea what to do beyond what his instinct suggested, and that was to combine the elements into one. Slowly he willed power into bowls simultaneously and then redirected the flows of magic from each individual bowl into the larger bowl in the center of the chamber. He could sense the elemental magic of earth, water, fire, and air combining equally, producing a bright white column of light that reached the high canopy of branches that formed the ceiling. Alternate flashes of colors—green, blue, red, and yellow—illuminated the haze in the room in a pattern of light that rotated within the column, emitting a vibrating hum that rose in pitch with the speed of the lights spinning inside. Khulani didn't stop. He kept adding power, and the light grew brighter. A moment later, the column of light seemed to pull the power from him, using what it needed, and he no longer had to focus to feed it. The light was in control, and he was its instrument of power. It drank deeply.

Khulani was worried. Could he stop this? It was pulling more energy through him than he had ever channeled, with no sign of letting up. If he didn't regain control, it could destroy him and everyone in this room. Delicately, he tried to slow the flow of magic through him. When he did, the light pulled for more. Khulani considered cutting the flows altogether, but the backlash could be just as dangerous. He would have to take back control through sheer will, and he understood in that moment that this had to be the essence of the test.

Physically bracing himself, Khulani wove flows of constraint around the rivers of magic streaming from the small bowls into the larger one. He would have to be precise and apply the restrictions equally and at the same time. This was a battle of control and balance, and he could afford no misstep. Time seemed to slow, and he no longer heard the sound of the hum from the column of light. He could see the threads of magic that formed each element and began the slow process of unravelling each one.

Khulani worked as fast as he dared, removing the strands of power before they could take root again in the whole. Time slipped by, or so it seemed, until the last threads of magic were released simultaneously, leaving only the white light in the center bowl. Why was it still there? The blur that had been his surroundings for what seemed like hours came into focus. The hooded figures still sat where they were before, and the haze in the room was no less thick.

"Impressive," one commented.

"Why were we not informed of this one before, Munatas?" another spoke.

"One of this skill should have been known to us," a third commented.

"Elder Cynwrig thought it best to wait until we were sure." That was Elder Munatas. "Now we are." There was no apology in his voice. New as he was as an elder, Khulani was impressed that he was not intimidated by his peers.

They sat as if waiting for something more.

Khulani took a hesitant step forward. He couldn't get any closer with the bowl holding the column of light blocking his way. Were they expecting something else from him?

"What are you waiting for, Khulani? Take the damn stone!" Elder Munatas snapped.

Khulani was struck by his words. Master-now-Elder Munatas had never once used his name since the day he came to the enclave. He used it now. And what was that about a stone? What stone?

He peered carefully into the blinding column of light. There *was* something there, hovering at shoulder level, easy for him to reach if he dared. If Elder Munatas commanded it, then he would dare.

Khulani did not hesitate. If the light burned his arm to ashes, then so be it. He reached in and took hold of the object inside. It was smooth and circular, with a hole in it center. The light did not burn—he felt nothing from it at all. He pulled the object out of the light, and the sight of it made him gasp.

It was a Druid stone.

All the colors he had seen before in the light swirled slowly in the stone like clouds, and there was a cord attached to it that smelled of fresh oak. The light in the room suddenly dimmed. He looked up to find the column of light was gone, and so were all the bowls with their stands. All that remained were the shadowy figures of the elder Druids and the haze of incense.

Khulani bowed deeply.

"You are in the presence of Elder Maedoc, Elder Ninian and Elder Seisyll." Elder Munatas gestured to each one in turn. "They have come from Eriu to meet you."

"Come closer, Honored One, and sit." Elder Maedoc beckoned.

"Yes, Revered Elder," Khulani replied and sat down a pace in front of them.

Elder Munatas leaned forward. "We have one final mission that will also serve as your final test before you earn that stone in your hand."

Khulani nodded silently. He gripped the Druid stone, feeling its smooth surface in his palm. It felt as familiar to him as his spear.

"You must travel to Mount Etna in the Sicans lands and retrieve the Seeds of the Dryad, which were stolen two years ago by a Kaiko who goes by the name of Kumida. And you will go alone."

"A Kaiko? Cyclops? Is he the one that killed my friend Rebiku?" Khulani felt a spark of rage and tried hard not to show it.

"He is not the same. This one has recently fled Fomoire for reasons that are not important to you." A flash of recognition crossed Elder Munatas's features, and Khulani knew his emotions had betrayed him. "You will leave at first light and proceed to Etna. Once you have recovered the Seeds, you will take them to the enclave north of Kenno in Eriu."

"I will hasten to retrieve the Seeds and return them to the enclave in Eriu, Elder Munatas," Khulani confirmed, "and then I will return here as quickly as possible."

Munatas shook his head. "No Khulani, after you return with the Seeds to Eriu, the elders there will assign your next task. You will not be returning here. Your training in Nabta is at an end."

Khulani couldn't believe it. He knew nothing of Eriu except for what he had read in the library. Nabta felt like . . . home now. On the bright side, perhaps he would find Aedan sooner than he ever imagined. "I understand, Elder Munatas."

"Do you have any questions?"

Khulani was curious about these Seeds he would risk his life to retrieve. "Please enlighten me as to the Seeds of the Dryad, I am not familiar with what they are."

Elder Seisyll spoke up, "Each Dryad has within her a magical seed. When she dies, her body is returned to the earth, and from her death sprouts new life in the form of a Great Oak or Aspen. To the Dryads, the Seed is sacred. They value it in the same manner as we value our souls. The seeds also have strong magical properties, and it is rumored that anyone possessing a Seed will benefit from a kind of protection against disease and illness. This Kaiko, Kumida, may have as many as three or four of the Seeds in his possession. The Giants are well aware of the legend of the Seeds and certainly would understand their usefulness."

Elder Maedoc removed his hood and fixed Khulani with cold, gray eyes. His face bore blue tattoos and a pierced white eyebrow under a shock of thinning white hair. He looked as ancient and wrinkled as the tallest oak. "We are the protectors of the Dryads, and when we fail them, we must do everything in our power to safeguard their legacy. The Seeds are their legacy. Do not fail us Khulani."

~~~

"You have done well in your time here. Frankly, better than I expected, at least in the beginning." A rare smile broadened Elder Munatas's face.

"I have you to thank for that." Khulani stood in his small room facing his master. It suddenly seemed smaller than ever.

"I was simply your guide."

Khulani held up the Druid stone that he created earlier in the Council chamber. "What do I do with this?"

"Put it on and never take it off again." Elder Munatas was still smiling, but there was no jest in his voice. Khulani had never seen a Druid without the stone, even when they bathed. "It will enhance many of your strengths in unexpected ways. For some, peeking through the center hole brings visions of the future, others can see through illusions. For me, it strengthens my control over elements of earth. It is different for everyone."

"I may wear it even if I have not been consecrated as a Druid?"

"You may." Elder Munatas nodded. "An Honored One is only a step away from being consecrated as a Druid; however, do not think that the journey ends there."

"Do you think I am ready, Elder Munatas?"

The elder hesitated before he spoke. "Let me ask you this. Do you still desire revenge on the Kaiko that killed your friend?"

Khulani was not expecting that question. For years he stoked the fire of anger and vengeance in his heart, until a time came when there was nothing left for him to fuel. "I loved my tribal brother, and I will never forget him. Do I desire revenge? In my mind I still do, but no longer in my heart. At least not before I know the true circumstances of the encounter."

"Spoken like a true Druid. You are ready."

"Thank you, Elder Munatas, I will always remember your wisdom and instruction." He took the Druid stone and slowly hung it around his neck.

Turning away, Elder Munatas paused. "One word of advice. When you travel in animal form, stay out of sight of people if you can. No matter what your form, there are those who would fling an arrow at you simply for the sport of it."

Khulani watched his master leave and wondered if he would see him again. Their relationship was never warm, more like cordial. Elder Munatas was a hard taskmaster and often relentless in his expectations. Khulani certainly wasn't the easiest student to train either. He was sometimes stubborn and sensitive to others disrespecting him. It was part of his culture. Humility was never his strong suit, and that was one of the first things he had to learn before anything else. Those were very difficult months. In the end, it was worth it, and he respected Master Munatas for never giving up and for forcing him to learn the hard lessons. In many ways, he had been like a father.

Khulani picked up his pack and grabbed his spear, then he left the tiny room without a backward glance. He had seen enough of it. His mind was on his mission to Etna, and he was determined not to fail.

Chapter 17

Strange Encounter

The Sicans, as I knew their people in the early years of their civilization, were not considered an ancient society. Their culture was more contemporary, shaped by the natural merger between the Capsians and the people of Hellas, and the peculiarity was clear in their physical appearance and the fusion of their ethos. Overall, I think it made them quite unique!

—Wodanaz the Wanderer

Soaring freedom. There was nothing to compare with it, and Khulani felt sympathy for those that would never feel its touch. Almost effortlessly, he rode the rising columns of air with his broad wings and tail feathers on nearly a perfect plane. He could glide for long distances before exerting energy to pump his wings for just a few deep beats before he soared again. From his lofty elevation, he could spy the movement of rabbits, rats, and small birds, but he wasn't hunting today. The form of the golden eagle was amply sufficient for high-altitude, long-distance flight, and with over six hundred leagues to his destination, efficiency was a necessity.

A few leagues north of Nabta, he planned a flight path that would take him generally northwest for the next five days. Maybe less if he had the energy to fly at night in owl form. He was on the southern edge of the Ibhr Rrbi with the expanse of it to the north and west as far as his sharp eyes could see. It was comforting to be over the grasslands again. It still felt familiar despite a decade and a half of scarcely having the chance to experience its beauty.

Briefly he thought to stray a little farther west and visit his father. He feared the changes that he would find there and the acute void of Rebiku's absence. It was a tempting idea, but Khulani discarded it quickly. Once he had the Seeds, then he could afford to make the detour.

At night Khulani followed the stars, and by day he navigated by landmarks and the position of the sun. Before leaving the enclave, he studied the star charts and terrain maps carefully and copied a few to reference along the way. His first instinct was to fly straight to the southern coast of the Great Sea, assume the form of a fish, and head straight toward the eastern coast of the Sicans. When he discussed his plan with Elder Munatas, he was vigorously advised to avoid water forms until he was more familiar with the dangers that swam unseen under the waves. Considering that Khulani knew almost nothing about the sea, he was inclined to agree.

The leagues rolled by quickly, and despite the occasional downpour, his flight toward the coast was uninterrupted. One of the best things about his current flight form was that the golden eagle only required food every few days, and with Khulani's ability to sense animals combined with the eagle's exceptional sight, finding a meal was an easy task. Going hungry would not be his greatest challenge on this journey.

Five nights later he was standing in the foothills outside the Capsian city of Thipsu. It was the city from which he and Rebiku had embarked on their first sea voyage that would take them to Thunis and beyond so many years ago. Khulani felt a pang in his chest from the memory of his friend and how young and naive they were at the time. Suppressing the unhappy feelings, he lay down on the soft grass to get a little rest before walking into the city the next morning.

~~~

"The dockmaster directed me to your ship. He said you might be stopping in the Sicans city of Kronio on your way to Rasna." Khulani stood on the deck of the Capsian trade vessel called the *RrwaH* addressing the Captain Aderfi.

The captain, a middle-aged man with dark ebony skin and a halo of black kinky hair swept back by the wind, looked him up and down nervously. "Are you a Druid?" he asked hesitantly. "I never heard of a black Druid before."

Khulani smiled warmly. He needed the captain to relax. "There are a few of us, so I have found out, but not many. I am Imaziyen."

"Imaziyen!" the captain exclaimed. "An honorable people. I have never known one to leave the Ibhr Rrbi."

"So it appears that I am quite unique, then." Khulani was wearing the simple brown hooded robes the Druids provided to him rather than the lion-hide cape he burned so many years before. Although he had yet to begin tattooing himself, there were several clusters of feathers and beads attached to his clothing with leather thongs that identified him as a Druid. "What about Kronio then?"

Captain Aderfi's face flushed with embarrassment. "Ah, yes, we plan to stop there before we sail on to Rasna."

"That is good news. May I book passage with you?" Khulani pulled the small purse from the folds in his robes. He still had the gold and silver strips the Amgar of his tribe gave him years before.

"Of course you can!" The captain appeared pleased to have a Druid on his ship. "And I will not take payment. It would be an honor for you to travel with us on the short voyage to Kronio."

Khulani wanted to laugh, but he kept it inside. He had not intended to represent himself as anything other than what he was, but to constantly explain that he was *nearly* Druid would have been complex and confusing. Elder Munatas suggested he let people think what they wished since it didn't matter anyway. Besides, the captain probably thought having a Druid onboard might come in handy if they happened to cross paths with the murderous Lukka or a creature of the deep. "Thank you, Captain. I will do my best to stay out of the way of your crew.

The *RrwaH* departed Thipsu an hour later. The captain expected that they would arrive in Kronio by the next afternoon with calm seas. Unfortunately, they would have no such luck, and on the crossing over the channel to Kronio, they were met with heavy storms out of the southeast during the night.

"Pull the sail and turn to the wind!" Captain Aderfi yelled above the beat of wind and rain. "Keep the line, or we'll have the deck awash!"

Khulani was fearful for himself, but he was far more fearful for the twelve sailors and the captain. He had never experienced a storm on the sea, and the way the small craft was tossing about in the choppy waves, he was sure it would capsize any moment. Considering his options, he found himself impotent against the raw power of nature at this scale. Elder Munatas told him once that there were Druids who were capable of manipulating the weather, but Khulani was not one of them. All he could do was hold on.

In the distance, flashes of lightning briefly illuminated swirling clouds and sheets of rain. They were out of sight of land, and there were no other vessels of any size that he could see. If the ship went under, Khulani could transform into a shad, the only fish he was familiar with, and hope he wasn't eaten by something larger before the storm was over. Sadly, there would be nothing he could do for the crew.

The small ship began to roll back and forth at a steeper and steeper angle. "Watch that dead roll!" the captain shouted.

The sailor who piloted the ship held the tiller like a fat pig he was trying to wrestle control over while the rest of the crew tied a rope that was bound to the mast around their waists in case they were tossed overboard. Khulani thought that was a good idea and quickly located a rope on the rolling wet deck that he hoped was attached to something solid. He tied the rope around himself and held tight to the anchor block on the bow of the ship.

Up and down the *RrwaH* crashed over the waves. From his vantage point, Khulani realized that the captain had deliberately turned the ship into the storm to gain the best control and stability over his vessel. Still, it rolled violently from side to side, sending waves of foaming seawater across the deck, soaking him through and through. It was all the crew could do to bail what was left behind and keep the ship from foundering. If Khulani hadn't been so frightened, he might have felt sick, and he bailed with the crew as best he could.

It went on and on, for how long he could not be sure, until the lightning passed, the rain stopped, and the waves smoothed again. Battered and exhausted, Khulani untied himself and staggered on shaky legs to the stern of the ship. The captain sat alone at the tiller. "Is everyone OK? I can heal anyone injured."

The captain, bleary-eyed and exhausted, looked up at him in the darkness. "Everyone is fine, except my navigator. We lost him over the side before I could tie him down."

Khulani sat down heavily next to him. "May the sea spirits guide him to the stars."

The captain nodded sadly. "And I have no idea where or how far the storm has blown us."

Khulani looked up at the sky. The clouds had cleared enough that he could see a few of the stars he recognized. "We are a few leagues north of where we started." He pointed toward the east. "The Sicans coast is that way."

"In that case, we better get the hold bailed and the sail back up. We're going to arrive in Kronio several hours later than we planned." The captain climbed to his feet and called a sailor over to man the tiller, and then he went about the ship shouting orders to the crew.

Khulani returned to his usual spot on the bow and watched the first light of day crack the horizon. He marveled at the beauty of the sea and its ability to inspire terror on a whim. They lost a life that night, and he was sure it would not be the last sacrifice demanded by this fickle spirit.

~~~

It was nearly dusk, and Khulani was relieved to be back on dry land again after the harrowing experience at sea the night before. He stood outside the port of Kronio, which was separated to the east of the main city by almost a league. Not far from the docks, torches illuminated a large open market crowded with locals browsing an impressive array of raw and cooked seafood offered by local fishermen and exotic goods displayed by merchants from many lands. The sounds assaulted Khulani's ears. He didn't think he would ever get used to the deafening cacophony created by the haggling and hawking.

The native Sicans were a lighter-skinned, tan people who dressed in chitons and peplos much like their neighbors in Hellas to the east. Khulani doubted he could tell the difference if the two peoples were standing together. They mingled affably with people from TaMehu and the Capsians who, he had learned in the enclave's library, were their closest trading partners. He observed the carts of goods the Sicans merchants sent to the port or sold in the market. Obsidian, lemons, olives, grapes, and olive oil as well as a nut called *pistachio* were among the most typical goods proffered for export. A sailor shared a few of the pistachios while onboard the *RrwaH* before the storm. They were delicious, and Khulani considered purchasing a bag when he returned.

He glanced around. There were people everywhere. Often, a stranger would touch his robes, show a sign of respect, or utter "Knowing One" in greeting. He was surprised at how well-known and respected the Druids were here and he contemplated changing into local clothing to avoid so much attention. Mostly he wanted to transform into his owl flight form and be on his way. He could follow the winding road east from the port and into the hills to Kronio, and it would take far less time to fly than to walk. He was sure about that.

Moving off the road, Khulani walked a few paces into the grass and reached for his will. Seconds later he was flapping his broad wings to gain altitude. There were a few gasps of surprise from those nearest to him, but no one cried out in alarm. They would have a good story to tell their children one day, he thought with an internal grin.

From high overhead, Khulani watched people and carts traversing the road between Kronio and the port. The entire way was lit on both sides by torches, giving him the impression that the port was busy regardless of the time of day or night. His sharp eyes followed the incline of the road as it wound through the increasing elevations of the hills and terminated at the gates of the high walls that surrounded Kronio. The city had a commanding view of the port and the surrounding approaches by land and sea. In the unfortunate event that raiders from the Lukka lands or pirates of Tartessos invaded, the Sicans might not be able to protect their port, but they would be safe and secure behind their city walls until the marauders departed.

As he approached, Khulani's night vision detected an oddity in the high hill that supported Kronio. Several hundred small cave openings, some sealed and others open, dotted the gradient from bottom to top on the western and southern slopes. No light shone from any of them, indicating that they were probably not inhabited. It was a curiosity that he had not read about in the enclave's scrolls that described the Sicans' culture.

Khulani flew high over the encircling stone wall. Kronio was a city of narrow alleys and crowded homes constructed with combinations of stone, mud brick and wood. Almost all of them had flat roofs where the residents would sleep in the hottest months. Separating the clusters of housing were several small markets. Each appeared to be dedicated to a category of goods. The owl's eyes were sharp enough to see that one market sold fish and seafood, another had vegetables and fruits, and a third with spices and olive oils. There were dozens of them throughout the city. Slowly he circled above it all. He thought it was likely that the rooms for rent would be near the markets, preferably not the fish market, and he glided into a deserted alley to transform.

Khulani landed near the city center where the largest of the markets was located and found an inn right away.

"Welcome, Knowing One," the innkeeper greeted Khulani. The Sicans' term for the Druids as "Knowing One" was based on their belief that the Druids could see the future and might also offer protections in the form of blessings to ward off evil spirits. Khulani noticed a triskele that dangled from a leather cord around the innkeeper's neck. He had seen similar symbols carved into walls and pottery and assumed it was a symbol of their deity.

"Greetings to you." Khulani smiled in return.

"It is very unusual to have the honor of a Druid in my establishment. If there is any way I can be of service, please don't hesitate to summon me."

"I thank you for your hospitality. All that I require is a good meal and a clean room for the night."

"Of course!" replied the innkeeper. "It would be my pleasure."

Khulani removed his coin purse which, like it had with the Capsian captain, caused a panic to come over the innkeeper. "No, no, please. Put that away. I will not accept payment from a Knowing One. It would disrespect my inn and bring a curse upon it!"

Khulani laughed softly, "You know that's not actually true."

"Maybe not." The innkeeper smiled. "But if I took your coin, everyone in the city would know within the hour, and my business would be shunned. Perhaps you could just offer a small blessing before you depart?"

"I would be pleased to do so," Khulani agreed.

Khulani sat on a mat in the corner and ate a meal of round, crusty bread with olive oil and beans he was unfamiliar with. He was thankful that he was able to finish without being interrupted by patrons seeking blessings or a hint of their future. Not that he would have minded conversation, but now that he walked among people in the garb and accessory of a Druid, most were either enamored or intimidated by him. He was never one to enjoy much attention, and now he seemed to draw every eye.

~~~

The light of a new day fell early on the hilltop city of Kronio, and Khulani was up with it. To his surprise, the innkeeper was already in the kitchen, and he happily prepared a warm porridge with pistachios and sweet grapes.

"What are those caves on the steep slopes below the city?" Khulani inquired while he ate. The addition of pistachios to the porridge was startling and delicious.

The innkeeper lowered his voice in quiet reverence, "Those are the burial chambers of generations of families from our city and the surrounding territory. The city rulers and wealthiest patrons are entombed near the top, whereas the more common citizens are near the bottom."

Khulani was only a little surprised by that. "They are in full view of anyone. Don't you worry about grave robbers?"

"Grave robbers?" the innkeeper laughed. "Forgive me, Knowing One, but what would anyone want with old bones? Other than a few everyday mementos, we do not inter our dead with much of value."

Khulani thought maybe the Praas of TaMehu and TaShemau could look to the Sicans on that account. So much of their resources and wealth were literally wrapped up with their royalty. He finished his porridge and patted his full belly. "Your porridge on its own is worth the blessing I will bestow upon your inn."

"Thank you, Knowing One." The innkeeper bowed, trying to hide the blush that reddened his cheeks.

Khulani stepped to the center of the room and commenced with a low chant. He had only cast blessings in practice before now and always under the supervision of Master Munatas. He hoped he got this right and didn't produce an infestation of rats or insects. He gathered his will, and the magic poured through him. Unlike other conjurations, a blessing was a slow build that required him to carefully frame the desired blessing in his mind. When he was ready, he released the spell, causing the room to light up in a soft yellow glow. Only the innkeeper was witness to Khulani's incantation.

"You have Eriu's blessing for prosperity, good innkeeper." The blessing was technically for good fortune, but Khulani thought that was basically the same for an inn. He smiled at the innkeeper, who stood motionless near the front door, staring around the room at the fading radiance. Clearly, the man had never witnessed an act of magic in his entire life, and Khulani doubted that the dumbfounded innkeeper noticed when he quietly exited the inn.

The street was just beginning to come alive with workers and tradesmen. Those few who were near reacted in surprise when Khulani transformed into his golden eagle flight form and lifted through the morning haze and into the bright sky above.

He flew at high altitude over the increasingly rugged, mountainous terrain ranging from heavily forested valleys to sparsely forested peaks. Occasionally, his acute eyesight spied the movement of an array of wildlife, including foxes, squirrels, weasels, hare, hedgehogs, porcupine, and a few wild cats. There were many varieties of birds as well, from owls and falcons to partridges and the frequent golden eagle like himself. So far nothing particularly threatening that he had to concern himself with.

The route he followed was a road heading roughly east and northward. The innkeeper told him that the nearest city to the east was the Sicans largest city, called Kamikos, and days beyond that he would find the fiery mountain of Etna. In the first two days of travel, he observed many villages of various sizes and oftentimes heavy merchant traffic that bottlenecked through them. He was glad he could sail above it all with the freedom to go any direction he chose without regard to whether or not a road led there.

From what he knew about the Sicans, their two main cities, Kronio and Kamikos, were independent city-states that formed a loose confederation of trade and protection. Their economies were based on agricultural trade with Hellas and the Capsians, both of whom they shared many cultural ties to as well.

On the afternoon of the fourth day since he left Kronio, the high plateau dominated by the city of Kamikos came into view. It was a vast city, easily three times the size of Kronio, with higher walls and a steeper elevation. Just like Kronio, Khulani could see hundreds of small cavern entrances dotting the nearly sheer slopes below the city. The masses of people who moved in and around it was astonishing to his eye. He was sure there were far more people here than any other city he had visited. Of course, from above he could see them all at once rather than the few at a time he would see if he were on the ground.

Even with the crowds, the city was beautiful. There was a large market at its center adjacent to a structure that appeared to be a palace. Bright white columns supported buildings with as many as three levels, and lifelike statuary dotted the lush gardens of colorful blooms within its walls. There were several domes that appeared to be covered with copper and gold that symbolically reflected the wealth and magnificence of the city for all to see.

If the palace was exceptional, what Khulani saw next was extraordinary. A statue of a woman as tall as any tower and dressed in a long peplos marked the entrance to the temple district. Remarkably, the gigantic statue held one fist thrust toward the sky holding a red glowing crystal like the one he had seen at the apex of pyramids in TaShemau and TaMehu. It didn't take much of a leap for him to guess that it had something to do with the Atlanteans.

Khulani wanted to stop and explore the city further, but he resisted the urge. He had come here for a reason, and he was determined not to be distracted from his mission until it was complete. If he survived, he would come back this way again with the luxury of time to explore as much as he pleased.

He flew roughly northeast. There were no roads leading to where he was going, but he needn't follow one anyway. From his altitude, he could just see through the haze of the atmosphere and over the curve of the horizon. There, a dark plume of smoke gave away the location of the active volcano, Mount Etna. When Elder Munatas first explained to him what a volcano was, he thought it was hardly a good location for the Cyclops to settle. Until the elder explained that Kumida had deliberately brought his tribe all the way from Fomoire in the belief that Etna was the home of their strange god, Arges. Khulani anticipated that he could cross the distance in two days.

On the evening of the second night, he cruised in owl form above the patchwork of steep forests and rocks, heading almost due east. He searched the slopes below him for the sight and sounds of nocturnal stirrings that could be his next meal. At night he felt safest in the air since there were few predators that had the sight for it. On this night, however, something else flew, and it was like nothing he had ever seen. Not even in a dream could he have conjured such a creature. He was so focused on the ground for prey that he didn't see it until it was nearly on top of him. It was his sensitive hearing that saved him. The great beast was larger than the largest mammoth on the Ibhr Rrbi, with the body of a snake covered in golden scales, the head and legs of a lion, and huge leathery wings that beat the air fluidly and alerted him to its presence. Searching for a meal, he was sure he was about to become one himself and he dove straight for the cover of the forest.

He landed heavily on the thick limb of a tall oak and searched the sky through the branches for pursuit. There was none. High above, the creature gracefully flew on. Almost directly above him, Khulani could sense that it was a highly intelligent creature with a strong aura of magic. It turned its head and peered down precisely where he was perched when it passed and for just a second, Khulani was aware of its consciousness reaching out to him, probing, and then it was gone.

He sat in the oak for a long time, worried that the creature might return. Whatever it was, it was astonishing, and he hoped never to cross its path again. Finally, he spied a hare rush from the brush below him and he had his meal. Khulani decided to rest the remaining hours of the night in the oak and start off again in the morning. The next day, he expected, would be the day he faced Kumida, and by the end of it he would either have the Seeds of the Dryads or have no more worries on this earth.

Chapter 18

Kumida

SY5490

Rocky volcanic structures, ancient lava flows, and steaming caverns were Khulani's first impression of the land around Mount Etna. The air was densely warm, with smoke and steam evacuating from cracks in the ground at the mount's base, making it difficult to approach further without straining to breathe. Natural life-forms were scant to none in the vicinity, making him doubt that even the Cyclops could survive in this infernal acreage. He flew wider around the southern edge of the volcano, searching for signs of their settlement.

He got his first hint with the sight of several narrow plumes of smoke rising lazily from what he could only assume were cook fires. They were at least half a league farther south and farther away from Etna than he would have expected. Perhaps the Cyclops found no pleasure with the extreme heat and odious scent of sulfur produced by Etna's constant belch.

Khulani gained altitude with a few powerful beats of the golden eagle's broad wings. He wanted to observe his quarry for a while without being noticed. Considering the size and violent nature of the Cyclops he would be facing, he hoped to get a look at Kumida and glean some small detail that he could take advantage of before the confrontation. Notwithstanding that any plan he devised would almost certainly hinge on the necessity of surprise.

Not far from the camp, he first saw one, and then another of the one-eyed giants wandering about the landscape, scavenging roots and small animals where they could find them. There were no signs of crops or agriculture and when he came upon the settlement itself. Khulani was surprised to find that it was more or less a roughly permanent campsite with a loose arrangement of huts, lean-tos and shallow fire pits arranged around the dark opening of a cave. The ground was rocky and barren of vegetation to the perimeter of their habitation, which was surrounded by a sparse forest. There were bones scattered all around and left to lie where they had been discarded after the flesh from them was consumed, and fresh guts were piled in random spots with no regard for sanitation. It was a revolting scene to behold. Even at the height where he slowly circled, Khulani could easily identify the pungent scent of death. The whole settlement was a sad display of nature defiled, and he was infuriated by it.

It was still early morning, and not many of the Cyclops had roused themselves from their crude shelters. Khulani decided not to wait. His rage would exhaust him if he didn't act soon.

The time would be now.

With so many still asleep, they would be far less prepared for him and would react slowly, giving him the time to put the rest of his plan into effect. He couldn't delude himself: it really wasn't a plan as much as an instinct about how to deal with them, specifically Kumida.

He folded his wings and dove.

Khulani spread his wings to slow his decent seconds before he met the ground, but it wasn't the claws of the golden eagle that he stood upon when he landed. To the young Cyclops that happened to be wandering near the entrance of the cave, it must have seemed as though he just appeared out of thin air.

"Tell Kumida death has come for him," he told the creature.

Clearly unsettled by Khulani's sudden appearance, the Cyclops ran inside the cave after a startled grunt. A moment later, a loud bellow erupted from the darkness, and then silence. At first, Khulani worried he might have to go into the dark cavern to confront Kumida, and then an enormous form strode out, ducking under the entrance to the cave. If he thought the other Cyclops were large, nearly twice his own height, Kumida was massive and at least half again as tall as the others. The

Cyclops that Khulani sent into the cave emerged behind Kumida with a nasty welt upon his face. A reward for the abrupt awakening, no doubt.

Kumida walked to within five paces of Khulani and peered down at him. "What is this?" He half turned back to the injured Cyclops. "This is why you woke me? Why isn't this human roasting in a pit right now?"

The Giant's rumbling bellows awakened the entire tribe—there must have been at least twenty-five of them—and they slowly crowded in around him.

Khulani stood calmly with his hood up. He wanted to maintain an air of mystery until he was ready to strike. "Are you Kumida?"

The Giant shifted in surprise and uncertainty. "I am Kumida. How do you know my name?" The Cyclops's voice was deep and rough like gravel when he spoke.

Khulani glanced up. Kumida wore no shirt, and only a piece of dirty fabric covered his genitals. He had coarse black hair carpeting his chest, and it nearly concealed a long necklace decorated with beads and painted bones. Human bones. "Then I have found you."

"So, you have found me. Now tell me why you are here before I rip you to pieces and suck the marrow from your bones."

A nervous laugh rippled through the throng of gathered Cyclops.

Khulani did not lose his composure. "I have arrived on behalf of the Druids to avenge the grove of Dryads you and your raiding party captured, raped, and murdered in Eriu."

Kumida stared at him in disbelief and then laughed uproariously. "That was a few years ago. Nobody cares about a few dead tree-whores. What will you do, little man? There is not a human that exists who can match my strength and power. Look around you. Even if you did strike me down, do you believe you would leave here alive?"

Khulani was prepared for this. With a wave of his hand, a wind barrier surrounded the space around himself and Kumida. "Now it is just the two of us."

"What are you? Sorcerer? Wizard? Priest? I have eaten my share of all. Your magic will not work on me the same way that it will on others!" With alarming speed, Kumida swung his club the size of a great oak trunk with the intent to crush in Khulani's skull or remove it altogether.

Standing firm, Khulani knew that Cyclops were resistant to most forms of magic cast upon them. The legend, according to Elder Munatas, was that an enterprising Tuatha De had added this exceptional quality in an effort to make the Cyclops the perfect combat soldier. After the Breaking it would cause them all manner of fits to banish them to Fomoire. Apparently, they finally overcame the Giants through guile and trickery, and Khulani studied precisely how in as much detail as was available. The Cyclops may be resistant to many spells that were cast directly at them, but they were just as affected as anyone to the indirect effects of certain incantations.

Side-stepping the first assault, Khulani created another wind barrier directly in front of him. Kumida brought his club down again and connected with the invisible barrier. The energy of the strike rebounded back through the club and into Kumida's arms, jarring him so violently that he fell backward onto the ground.

Immediately the earth dropped beneath the Giant, leaving him sprawled ungracefully in a pit on his back. He struggled to rise, and the earth around him sprouted thick roots and vines that entangled his limbs and torso, preventing the raging Giant from regaining his feet.

With calm certainty, Khulani walked over to the immobile Cyclops and slowly drew his long knife from the sheath at his belt. Kumida, perhaps realizing what was about to happen, screamed desperately for his followers to seize Khulani and kill him. Two dozen large bodies surged forward, but the wall of wind effectively rebuffed their repeated attempts to overcome it.

"You want the Seeds?" Kumida cried urgently. "Take them! They are in a pouch on my necklace!"

Khulani bent and jerked the pouch off the leather cord. Inside, he counted four small incandescent oval shapes with swirling patterns that matched his Druid's stone. "These will meet only half of the retribution required by the elders, I'm afraid."

Kumida's face darkened. "What is the other half?"

"Your heart."

Kumida struggled against the vines that held him. Even his formidable strength could not break them. "I will give you the heart of another! As many hearts as you require as long as one is not my own!"

The wind barrier did not prevent the sight and sound of what was happening within from escaping, and suddenly the efforts of the Cyclops to reach them ceased. Instead, they stood back and quietly watched, betrayal in their eyes, while Kumida struggled in vain.

Khulani stood back and glared down at Kumida. "You want to save yourself?"

"Yes!" the Cyclops pleaded.

"Then tell me about the Cyclops in the Ibhr Rrbi."

A look of desperate confusion raged across Kumida's face and then he smiled. "They must be the other survivors from my tribe. They went their own way after we were forced to leave Fomoire. Their leader is a coward named Steropes. I did not know until today where they ended up."

Khulani bent back down to stare hard into Kumida's eyes. "It was one of their number that killed my brother. Even your life is not enough to pay for his loss."

"Wait!" the Cyclops begged. "You promised to release me if I told you what you wanted!"

"I lied."

Kumida's screams reached a shrill pitch before Khulani silenced his cries forever.

Standing from his bloody work, Khulani carefully wrapped the still heart in strips of linen. It was as large as a sweet melon and just as heavy. The elders wanted it unspoiled, so before he placed it in the leather pack he carried specifically for its safe transport, he cast a spell of preservation on it.

Carefully packing away his prize, he felt a sudden cold chill of fear streak through his body. Something else was inside the wind barrier. His head snapped up, and his eyes immediately focused on a dark shadowy void, blacker than the space between the stars, rise from the dead Cyclops body. Khulani was stunned by the pure concentration of evil that it seemed to radiate, sending more sharp shivers of fear through his body. The spectacle was so shocking that he nearly dropped the heart.

His mind racing, he grabbed desperately for his will to conjure some method of protection, although he didn't know what that would be. What defense could he raise against this vile evil? What could it do to him? Before he could risk an action, the black void simply disappeared. Khulani sank to his knees and stared at the place where it had hovered above the body. Did the elders know this would happen and neglect to tell him? Could it be a similar evil to the one the Druids captured after the long-tooth died? He resolved to ask them when he arrived in Eriu. *If* he ever arrived in Eriu. At the moment, he just wanted to leave this terrible place as quickly as possible.

The silence was palpable, and when he looked around, he was astounded to find that there was not a single Cyclops in sight. He had no idea where they went, and he didn't care. He was just relieved not to have to deal with them.

He looked down at the small pouch in his bloody palm that held the Seeds of the Dryads and wondered at the irony of such an image. So many lives were lost because of Seeds that were meant to bring the gift of life. Khulani would return them to the elders that they might someday grow into the giant oaks that Dryads would one day call home, never knowing the twists of fate that brought their homes to them.

With his actions that day, the Druids' promise to the Dryads was fulfilled, and the dead were avenged. He dropped the protective ring of wind that still surrounded him, transformed once again into the golden eagle, and immediately took flight. He glanced one last time at the abandoned settlement with Kumida's lifeless corpse half buried where he left it. Soon, nature would take its revenge and wildlife would find sustenance from his passing. Khulani felt no remorse whatsoever.

~~~

"Your father is dead, Khulani." The Amgar was matter-of-fact, as if it was not a recent event.

"When?"

The Amgar placed a hand on Khulani's shoulder. "He died naturally three years ago. His body was entombed with all honors in a Tumuli that sits near the others on the Ibhr Rrbi."

Khulani was devastated. When he arrived at his village that morning, he was sure to receive a welcome homecoming only to be told that his father no longer lived. He wanted to go back to the day he and Rebiku left their village for the Tazallit lhnna, not knowing that when he returned the two people he loved most in the world would be gone. Would he have made different decisions? Maybe not, but at the very least he would have made sure the time he spent with them was sweeter.

"And there is something else." The Amgar sounded reluctant to even bring it up. "It's about Rebiku."

"I already know."

The Amgar nodded silently. If he wondered how Khulani knew, he didn't ask.

"Thank you for honoring my father when I could not be here to do so." Khulani nodded respectfully to the Amgar and turned to walk down the dirt lane toward the hut he once shared with his father.

The Amgar reached out and held him by the shoulder. "There is one other thing."

"Yes, Amgar." Khulani turned to face him.

"A woman arrived in the village last year. She was an Amazigh from the Uari Ljanub. Her name was Asha, and she was looking for you."

Khulani's heart was racing. Why had she come? "What did she want?"

Sadness filled the Amgar's eyes. "She had a child with her. A boy, thirteen at the time, and he wore a gold charm that matched the one returned by the Imaziyen that brought back Rebiku's body. She said the boy was the child of Rebiku."

Khulani felt as though he had taken a blow to the chest. He struggled to breathe, and his eyes welled with tears. "Did she say that she was the mother?"

"No," the Amgar appeared taken aback by the question. "She said the boy's mother was an Amazigh named Binah, but she had died of illness when the child was very little."

Poor Rebiku. He had a child that he would never know! "Where is the boy now?"

"The Amazigh Asha stayed a month and then left the child with Rebiku's parents. He is with them now. Is the story true, Khulani? Is the boy a child from Rebiku?"

Khulani felt pain in his heart that threatened to make it stop. It was a tragic end for his friend and the child born by the dalliance of one night so long ago. "It is true." He barely got the words out before he sobbed like a child in the arms of the Amgar of his tribe.

~~~

Khulani entered the dim hut and stood staring around the main room. It seemed so much smaller than he remembered. The basket where he and his father always kept the wooden bowls they ate from was where he expected it to be, and even the mats on the floor were in their usual place. Except for the cold hearth, which was always warm in the mornings, his home would have appeared as if his father had only stepped out for a moment.

Khulani tread the rest of the way inside and sat down on his mat. He thought about the evenings he spent in this room with his father learning how to sharpen his long knife or mending his hartebeest-hide riding pants. His mother had just died, and the activities they shared helped to bring them closer. It was a painful time. As Khulani grew from a small child to a teenage boy, the mentoring and wisdom from his father propelled him to a leadership position with his first Hunt Pack. Of course, his gift was a great help as well, but without his father's guidance, he might have been just a strange boy attuned to the feelings and emotions of animals.

It was in this room that Khulani learned about politics, compromise, the importance of carefully studying one's adversary and exploiting their weaknesses. It was also where he learned the importance of compassion and the sanctity of life. His father knew about and understood his gift. It was the same with his mother, a secret they shared so that she would not be sent away to the Druids like he was. But with Khulani it was different, and his father encouraged him to explore his unusual abilities. Everything Khulani knew about the savannas, leading a pack, and honor as a warrior, he had learned from his father. He could have asked for no better mentor in life.

The flap to the hut was pulled to the side, and to his astonishment, in walked Elder Maedoc. "I expected that I might find you here."

Khulani immediately jumped up and bowed. "I am surprised to see you, Elder Maedoc. I thought to see you next in Eriu."

"In truth, I am on my way to Eriu now." The old Druid sat on the mat where his father used to sit. "I spent a few extra weeks with Elder Munatas, and then I thought to stop here in case you did as well."

Khulani thought that was quite a stretch to just happen to show up in his village at the same time, but he kept that to himself. This Elder Maedoc was a clever one. "Our chance meeting is very fortuitous, then." He pulled the strap of the bag that held Kumida's heart over his neck and shoulder and placed a small pouch on top of it. "Here are the heart of the Giant and the Seeds of the Dryads."

"You have accomplished more than anyone could ask or expect in the few years you have been with us, Khulani," Elder Maedoc commented. "That business with the Cyclops was quite impressive. There were many long-standing Druids who would not have survived that encounter. You did well to understand your enemy prior to confronting him. It appears you have a mind for strategy."

"Thank you, Revered Elder," Khulani replied. Then he thought to ask, "How could you know?"

Elder Maedoc smiled and gave him a wink. "You don't really think we would send you off alone to face a threat as dangerous as Kumida, did you? You did well enough on your own, there is no question about that, but we always had a couple of birds keeping an eye on you."

"Then you know about the black void?" Khulani asked.

The look on Elder Maedoc's face was one of concern. "I have not heard an account of one. Tell me about it."

"Elder, something happened when Kumida died. A force or presence left his body. It acted as if it was reluctant to leave. I could feel the evil inside, and it covered me like a blanket of ice. Could this have been his soul? Did Kumida possess the capacity to carry so much evil in him?"

Elder Maedoc was silent for a few moments. "It was not his soul. The soul is a very subtle thing. Whatever you saw, or felt, must have been residing inside of him. Perhaps even controlling him. There are stories in the ancient texts that discuss this very thing—demons loose in the world that had to be rounded up and stored away since they were impossible to kill in this world."

"Fifteen years ago in my village, the Druids Grian and Buadhach saved my life from a long-tooth, and they captured the dark essence that escaped from it. Was that the same thing?" Khulani knew there had to be a connection.

"I have heard something about that," Elder Maedoc confessed. "But I am unaware of the details."

Somehow Khulani knew the Elder was lying. Why would he lie? "Should something be done if they are loose again?"

Elder Maedoc's expression turned grave. "If they are free again, then of course something must be done, but we are speculating. I will send a report to the Arch-Druid, Caomh the Enlightened. He may ask you to tell him more. Although, I am sure that he and the Conclave will have the resources to look into this further if they choose to."

"Of course, Elder."

The elder's took on a more subtle, relaxed tone. "I understand that a woman brought a child to your village and claims he is the son of your friend Rebiku."

"It is true." The reminder of the child brought emotions welling up inside of him again. "I believe it is the truth."

"Khulani, you carry too many burdens." The Druid's features softened as he spoke. "You have endured the deaths of your friend Rebiku and your father, the trials of becoming a Druid, and the stress of missions that you cannot fail. It is too much for anyone."

"I will endure, Elder, I am strong." Khulani worried that the Elder thought he might be too weak to handle the challenges he might face.

"No, no," Elder Maedoc pat Khualni's knee. "I don't mean that. You are one of the strongest I have known both physically and emotionally. I think it is time to relieve some of the pressure you have been under."

"What are you saying, Elder?" Khulani held his breath.

"I have another mission for you." The Elder showed his teeth when he smiled. "Next spring, when the weather is good to travel north. You should stay here for the winter and get to know Rebiku's son. I know that would mean a lot to you."

"My life is the Druids now, and you are my master. I go as you say, Revered Elder."

"Yes, yes. Well, the King of Ys has a daughter who has been acting . . . strange, lately. Her name is Ahes. I want you to go to Ys, spend some time observing her conduct, and then report to me at the Kenno enclave by the summer solstice."

Khulani was excited about the prospect of going to the fabled city of Ys. It was one of the places he read about in the enclave's library at Nabta. There were many accounts of its beauty and grandeur, although sadly not a single drawing. "That is a mission I would relish."

Elder Maedoc picked up the pack holding Kumida's heart and the pouch of Seeds. "Consider it a reward for your exemplary work."

The old Druid disappeared through the hartebeest-hide flap that covered the door. Khulani spirits were lifted by the thought of spending the winter getting to know Rebiku's child and then going to Ys next spring. He lit the hearth and lay back on the mat to stare up at the woven reed ceiling of the hut. There was a small hole from neglect that he could see through to the white clouds floating in the sky. His father would be proud that Khulani still dared to dream.

Cast of Characters

Arch-Druid Caomh the Enlightened: Leader of the Druids devoted to the goddess Eriu.

Bochus: Imaziyen Hunt Master who first encountered the long-tooth.

Buadhach: Eriu Druid.

Captain Aderfi: Captain of the Capsian merchant vessel the *RrwaH* (Breeze).

Captain Hepzefa: Captain of the TaMehu river trader the *Mew-Hanej* (Water Reed).

Captain Khuy: Captain of the TaShemau river trader.

Captain Uetu: Captain of the TaMehu merchant ship the *Rom* (Fish).

Cynwrig: Elder Druid of the Nabta enclave.

Deezigre of House Osris: The Atlantean High Priest of Pontus responsible for the Orichalcum Crystals located in the Crystal Pyramid of Iunu at the Necropolis of Inbu-Hedj.

Elder Boa: Father of Khulani and elder of the tribe.

Elder Maedoc: Elder Druid from the enclave outside of the Eriu city of Kenno. He became Khulani's master after Elder Munatas.

Fergus and Finn: Eriu Druids.

Frinya: Healing shaman and close friend to Khulani's mother.

Grian: Elder Eriu Druid.

Intef: Proprietor of an inn at Thunis. He is also the cousin of Captain Uetu.

Khulani: Young Imaziyen warrior born with a special gift.

Kumida: Leader of the Cyclops that settled near Mount Etna.

Master Munatas: Master of the neophytes at the enclave near Nabta.

Master Ycea: Master of the White Hall in the Imperial Order of Wizards in the City of Atlantis.

Musa: Captain's Second on the TaMehu merchant ship the *Rom*.

Praa Khamet: The current ruler of TaMehu.

Rebiku: Young Imaziyen warrior and best friend of Khulani.

Steropes: Leader of the Cyclops that settled near Tasili n Ajjer.

Tafrara: Elder High Shaman with a talent for healing.

Glossary

Amazigh: An Imaziyen tribe that dwells in the Uari Ssamal mountains. Their leaders, warriors, and shamans are "without husbands," and the men take a subjugate role in their society.

Amgar: Chief of an Imaziyen tribe.

Apep: Serpent god with a cult of followers who believe in human sacrifice. Worshipped in TaShemau and TaMehu.

Atum: Patron deity of the city of Inbu-Hedj.

Aur: River with an unknown source that runs north through Kerma, TaShemau, and TaMehu before dispersing into a wide delta that dumps into the Great Sea.

Ayur: Imaziyen goddess of the moon.

Grand Shaman Badru and Chief Amgar Dia: Honorary titles of the High Shaman and Amgar selected each year to preside over the Naming Ceremony at Tazallit lhnna.

Heqet: An alcoholic drink from TaMehu

Hewetkaptah: Temple dedicated to Ptah.

Ibhr Rrbi: Sea of Grass, where the Imaziyen live.

Imaziyen: Ancient tribes in modern-day North Africa that preceded the Berber.

Istsa snake: A common venomous snake that inhabits the grassland and rocky places in the Ibhr Rrbi.

Kaiko: One-eye or Cyclops.

Kalasiris: A long dress wrapped around the body and over the shoulders from a single piece of fabric. Typically made from linen.

Long-tooth: An unusually large saber-toothed mountain lion possessed by a Chaos Demon.

Nemes: Traditional and common headdress worn by the people of TaMehu, TaShemau, and Kerma. The most notable feature is the cloth that covers the back and sides of the ears and neck.

Neophyte: Acolyte of the Druids.

Per-aat: Temple dedicated to Atum.

Praa of TaMehu: Ruler of the kingdom of TaMehu. Translates to *Pharaoh*.

Ptah—Creation god, patron of sculptors, painters, builders, carpenters, and other craftsmen. Patron deity of the city of Inbu-Hedj in TaMehu.

Punt: A mysterious land of wonder inhabited by Little People. They trade in exotic goods, mainly with the Praa of TaShemau.

Sacred Cynocephalus: Sacred when given as a gift to the Praa, the Cynocephalus are a strange race of short humanoids with a baboon-like head.

Shendyt: A common kilt-like garment that wraps around the waist and extends to the knees. It is traditionally worn by the people of TaMehu, TaShemau, and Kerma.

Shenti: A kilt-like garment typically made of linen and fastened at the waste by a girdle.

Tafukt: Imaziyen god of the sun.

TaMehu: The kingdom that predated Upper Egypt in the time of Atlantis.

TaShemau: The kingdom that predated Lower Egypt in the time of Atlantis.

Tasili n Ajjer: The only permanent settlement of the Imaziyen, although the residents rarely come into contact with the Imaziyen of the Ibhr Rrbi.

Tazallit lhnna: The City of Peace where the Imaziyen gather every year to recognize new warriors and shamans, as well as to discuss trade and resolve disputes among themselves.

Uari Ljanub: Southern mountain range that parallels the Uari Ssamal. The Shad River originates within its peaks.

Uari Ssamal: Northern mountain range along the coast of the Great Sea. The Tazallit lhnna is located in one of its valley's.

Utjenet: "Gods land." Also containing the Pleasure Gardens of Atum. A place known to the people of Punt where wondrous and exotic luxuries can be found.

About the Author

Born in Homestead, Florida, Ravek Hunter grew up in the United States and Belgium. He earned a bachelor's degree in marketing from Florida International University and went on to become a sporting goods executive. He currently serves as a consultant in the same industry and occasionally assists his wife of fifteen years at her floral design company. The proud father of two boys, Ravek counts reading, exercising, and family travel among his leisure hobbies.

Over the past thirty-five years, Ravek's passion has been researching ancient civilizations, with a focus on the origin stories behind their mythology. His writing style attempts to immerse the reader in the story by bringing to life historically accurate and rich details of the culture that frames the narrative during the time period in which the novel is set.

Inspired by classic fantasy authors like Robert Jordan, Terry Goodkind, and R. A. Salvatore, Ravek writes to entertain and provoke his readers, who, he hopes, share his fondness for mythology.

Connect with Ravek Hunter

Thank you for choosing this work of blood, sweat and tears by *Ravek Hunter*! If you enjoyed reading this novel, please consider posting a review, telling me what you think on one of the social media platforms listed below or reach out via my direct email:

Friend me on Facebook:

https://www.facebook.com/Ravek-Hunter-Literary-LLC-238417183579740/

Follow me on Twitter:

https://twitter.com/RavekHunter

Subscribe to my blog:

https://www.goodreads.com/author/show/17885196.Ravek_Hunter

Visit my website:

https://www.WorldsofAtlantis.com

Email: Ravekhunter@gmail.com